WHEN THE ROSE
SPEAKS ITS NAME

Shield & Crescent Press, an imprint of Black & Green Games
Published 2024

ISBN-13: 978-0-9978204-2-3 (paperback)
ISBN-13: 978-0-9978204-3-0 (hardback)

Title: When the Rose Speaks Its Name: A Sherlock Holmes Anthology / edited by
Alexandra Fox, EC Boss, S.J. Lock, Rita Smith, and SM Lawson
A charity anthology showcasing queer Holmes and Watson inspired by the original
Arthur Conan Doyle canon. Short stories, microfiction and poetry by thirty
international authors, exploring intimate connections between these two iconic
characters.

Cover courtesy of Anke Eissmann (Khorazir)

WHEN THE ROSE SPEAKS ITS NAME

A SHERLOCK HOLMES ANTHOLOGY

EDITED BY

ALEXANDRA FOX   EC BOSS   S.J. LOCK   RITA SMITH   SM LAWSON

SHIELD AND CRESCENT PRESS

'If we could fly out of that window hand in hand, hover over this great city, gently remove the roofs, and peep in at the queer things which are going on, the strange coincidences, the plannings, the cross-purposes, the wonderful chains of events, working through generations, and leading to the most outrè results, it would make all fiction with its conventionalities and foreseen conclusions most stale and unprofitable.'

— SIR ARTHUR CONAN DOYLE, *A Case of Identity*

'What's in a name? That which we call a rose
By any other word would smell as sweet.'

— WILLIAM SHAKESPEARE, *Romeo and Juliet*

'What a lovely thing a rose is! ...this rose is an extra. Its smell and
its color are an embellishment of life, not a condition of it. It is only
goodness which gives extras, and so I say again that we have much
to hope from the flowers.'

— SIR ARTHUR CONAN DOYLE, *The Naval Treaty*

What the rose whispers
before blooming
I vow to you.
I give you my heart,
a safe house.

— ESSEX HEMPHILL, 'American Marriage'

CONTENTS

ILLUSTRATIONS

WHEN THE ROSE

Sherlock Holmes

John Watson

Mary Watson

SPEAKS PLAYERS

Irene Adler

DI Lestrade

PREFACE

You hold in your hands an anthology of original writings and illustrations inspired by and based on the stories and novels about Sherlock Holmes by Arthur Conan Doyle. In each of these stories, the author is looking at this iconic character through a queer lens.

An international group of authors have volunteered their efforts to celebrate the great detective and his relationship with his companion John Watson. In the process, they are raising money for the UK-based charitable organisation akt, which supports LGBTQ+ youth experiencing homelessness or living in hostile environments.

Many short stories, poems, and microfiction pieces debut in this collection. We share with you the 221B: microfiction of 221 words, ending with a word that starts with the letter 'b'—a literary form in miniature. The majority of the stories appearing here have never before been published. A selection of pieces has been lovingly reprinted. All are labours of love.

Most pieces are set in Victorian England, while the rest bring the familiar characters into another historical period, including the present day. Each author explores their own interpretation. Original illustrations for the stories unite the myriad versions with a unique 'cast' of players seen throughout the book and in our illustrated *dramatis personæ*.

This anthology was inspired by a significant date in Sherlockian history: after over a century and many legal wrangles, the final Sherlock Holmes stories by Sir Arthur Conan Doyle entered the public domain on 1 January 2023. The 58 short stories and four novels written between 1887 and 1927 received (near) instant acclaim and have enjoyed international interest, attention, and imitation in the century and a quarter since then.

Since their publication, there has been speculation about the nature of the relationship between Holmes and Watson. Their camaraderie, intimacy, and mutual admiration have inspired the romantic imaginations of countless fans who have seen them as potential lovers. However, homophobic laws made gay relationships and queer identities criminal during Doyle's time. Champions of gay rights suffered legal consequences and, in some cases—as with the celebrated author and playwright Oscar Wilde—died from the fallout of writing openly about queer love. Having all the stories in the public domain removes any remaining obstacles to exploring the love between Holmes and Watson with a queer eye; we now join an already vibrant community of creators who have opened this space.

Thank you for helping us bring Sherlock Holmes and John Watson out of the closet. Embracing Arthur Conan Doyle's invitation to William Gillette that he 'may marry him, murder him or do anything you like to him,' we have chosen to bring to light a love that might have been. Presented here in a rosy glow of newness, through trying times, and on to a homely domesticity, is a love that we hope everyone, regardless of identity, may peacefully enjoy.

THE CURTAIN
RISES

ON STAGE PLEASE

SM LAWSON

Miri stepped back and looked over the props table with pride—each item was laid out neatly, clearly labelled, with masking tape lines creating borders for each object. She knew everything was there, but she checked her list again just in case. Tonight was the dress rehearsal, and despite the tradition that the dress rehearsal had to go badly for the opening night to go well, she didn't want her part to be the one that went badly.

'Miri, be a dear, this button's loose?'

The costumes were older and had a tendency to fray, so Miri already had a needle threaded and ready; it was a matter of a moment to fix Bernard's costume, a Victorian-era replica tweed suit. 'You look smashing, Bernie,' she said.

'It itches,' Bernard said, wiggling. He ran a finger over his upper lip. 'The moustache itches too.'

'That'll be the spirit gum. Your skin will get used to it.'

'Shan't,' Bernard said with a grin. His moustache flexed. 'Ah shit.'

Miri looked at her watch. 'You've five minutes before the places call, you have time to fix it. Can't have Doctor Watson's facial hair flying across the stage, can you?'

'Attention, cast? Cast and crew, may I have your attention?'

'Oh hell, now an announcement?' Bernard said, pressing hard over the moustache to flatten it.

It was Matt, the director, standing downstage centre, looking harried and faking calm. Actor heads began to pop out from backstage to listen. 'Friends, I just wanted to say how proud I am of everyone for their hard work this week during tech, despite all the difficulties.'

'Oh God, not now,' Emma, dressed for Mrs Hudson, groaned.

'I don't need to remind you how important this production is—to be performing *Sherlock Holmes and the Cursed Judge* on the eve of the one hundred fiftieth anniversary of the publication of the first story by Sir Arthur Conan Doyle. It is a great honour to be telling this part of the story ...'

'Oh God, wrap it up so we can finish sometime this century,' Bernard whispered.

'... to be part of this great tradition of storytelling, of the greatest character in English literary history.'

'Hear, hear,' said Sidney, waving his deerstalker in the air. Bernard rolled his eyes and Miri rolled hers back.

'So have a great dress, everyone, and I'll give notes afterwards. Thank you!'

'Merde,' Bernard said to Miri as he departed for stage left and his first entrance. Sidney puffed up to Miri's side.

'My pipe, please?'

Miri sighed. Sidney was the author of the play, the actor playing Holmes, and a self-styled expert on Sherlock Holmes. This meant that he felt he didn't have to think independently outside of anything but playing the role. The pipe was on the table in front of him, clearly labelled 'Holmes/pipe'; it had been since the first rehearsal, and yet he asked her for it every day. She handed it to him, and he nodded his thanks as he went onstage.

She looked at her watch and saw the time: one minute to eight. She turned on her headset. 'Places, please,' she said. 'On stage please. Places, please.'

Everything went quiet. This was the moment that Miri loved, the one that kept her working in theatre despite the insane hours, the low pay, and the hard work: the hush of everyone ready and poised to make magic.

'House to half. House out. Lights one, go. Sound one, go.'

The lights came up on the Victorian set, and Sidney, as Holmes, was already on, lounging on a divan, 'smoking.' (Not real smoke, it made Sidney cough.) Miri watched as Bernard, off set, knocked on the door.

'Come in, Watson, for I perceive it is you by the tenor of your knock.'

Bernard opened the door and walked from the darkness of backstage into the light of the set. ''Pon my word, Holmes, your deductions truly amaze me, despite the years of our acquaintance.'

'I furthermore deduce that you have been visiting one of your patients in Bethnal Green by the splatter of mud on your trouser hem. Tell me, how is his recovery from pneumonia?'

'Great Scott, Holmes! How could you possibly know?'

'It is due to my superior intellect and powers of observation, greater than any man who drew a policeman's salary!'

'Ha!'

Miri's head whipped around at the laugh she had heard, trying to recognise the voice or see the offender who had interrupted the rehearsal. There was a brief murmur backstage as everyone else tried to do the same, to no avail.

'Quiet backstage,' Matt said sternly.

After a micropause, Sidney continued. 'Come now, Watson, I have just received a telegram from the Met. It seems that my assistance is required for another case which has baffled the Yard.'

'Excellent! Might I assist you, Holmes?'

'But of course, Doctor Watson; I should appreciate the company. I am glad of your documentation of my cases.'

'Nonsense!'

Miri glared at a group of actors huddled backstage; but they looked back at her, not looking glibly innocent when she knew they were otherwise, but rather with confusion.

'Watson, this case is a fascinating one, though far beneath my capabilities. However, for this instance, I believe we should call upon Irene Adler, the only woman I respect, for her assistance.'

'Lies! Slander! Libel!'

'Right, stop,' Matt shouted. The heads of the actors backstage peeked around every corner of the set; Miri stepped to the wings, wanting to identify the culprit who was daring to disrupt the important rehearsal. 'Who's interrupting? This is quite unprofessional. Who is it?'

'It is I,' said the same voice.

Two men stepped forward onto the stage, both dressed in Victorian garb and utterly unknown to the company.

From her position in the wings, Miri could see both in front of the set and the back of it, those behind and those up front. She was therefore probably the only person to see that the men stepped out from the wall of the set itself, and that they were not backstage prior to their appearance. It was as if they had walked directly out of the wall.

'Who the hell are you?' said Matt.

The taller of the two men, thin but somehow powerful under his woollen clothing, bowed slightly and elegantly. 'Sherlock Holmes, at your service.' The man's eyes glinted with intelligence and mischief as he gestured gracefully to the shorter, moustachioed man beside him. 'And my partner, Doctor John Watson.'

Sidney turned to Matt, outrage written across his face. 'You've replaced me?' he sputtered. 'How dare you!'

'I don't know these loonies,' Matt said. 'Someone call security.'

Fred, who played Detective Dimmock, muscular under his greatcoat, stepped forward. 'Come on, guys, off you go. We don't want trouble.'

Fred reached to pull at the arm of 'Watson', but his hand passed through the man as though he was smoke. There was a collective gasp from the company.

'My dear sir, have patience,' ghost-Watson said. 'We are neither real nor substantial, as you see. We have come through for a few moments, only a very little while, to speak our truth.'

Pale, Fred staggered back and sat abruptly into a chair. 'I don't understand,' he said.

'Use your eyes, gentlemen! And ladies, of course,' Holmes said, spotting Miri and Emma in the wings and bowing slightly. He was smiling, as though amused. 'When you have eliminated the impossible, whatever remains'—he waved his hand as though shooing a fly— 'and so forth. I don't need to repeat the rest to you, I'm sure.'

'Whatever remains, however improbable, must be the truth,' Sidney said, stunned.

'Ah! It is you I wish to speak with most,' Holmes said, turning to Sidney. Sidney paled in response. 'You are the author of this play, I presume?'

'Y-Yes,' Sidney croaked.

'Upon which of my esteemed partner's stories have you based this so-called dramatic piece?'

'Um,' Sidney said. Holmes tilted his head towards Watson, without taking his eyes off Sidney. 'It's, um, a pastiche. An amalgam.'

'And what justification can you give for maligning our characters as you are?'

'What?' Sidney said. Miri could see the blood rushing back into his face. Sidney never could stand to be countered, not in rehearsal, not in performance, and, apparently, not by a ghost either. 'My portrayal of Sherlock Holmes is based upon years of study of the stories and peripheral research. It is accurate!'

'That is why we are here,' Holmes said. 'Because the truth is some-what ... different.'

'What do you mean?' Bernard said. 'What's wrong with it?'

Sidney huffed at the suggestion that his work was wrong, but Holmes continued as though he hadn't heard. 'First, to suggest that I would boast of my intellect publicly, and particularly to Watson, portrays me as the worst kind of braggart. Yes, I am intelligent; however, my ego was not entirely wrapped up in others knowing that.

'Second, Irene Adler, "the only woman I respected"—pah! Nonsense. An intelligent woman to be sure, but certainly not the only one in London, and definitely not the only one worthy of respect.

'Third, and most important to myself,' Holmes said, turning to Sidney with a glare, 'how dare you portray my partner, Doctor John Watson, as a bumbling fool?'

'He's a foil,' Sidney said. He was clearly rising to his argument; Miri had seen him do this in rehearsal after rehearsal, as well as in the bar afterwards. 'He represents the reader with his lack of intelligence, and—'

'Lack of intelligence?' Holmes roared.

'Comparative lack of intelligence,' Sidney said, retreating somewhat.

Holmes's ghostly face went red, somehow, and he had opened his mouth to retort when Watson laid a calming hand on his arm. Holmes checked himself, took a deep breath, and continued in a more regulated tone. 'I ask you to remember, sir, that Doctor Watson is just that—a doctor, requiring many years of study, even in our "unenlightened" times. He was considered a good enough doctor to be a medic in Her Majesty's army, to have earned several service awards, and also to have served in one of the best hospitals in England. His intelligence is not to be disputed.'

'I simply mean that compared to yours ...'

Watson patted Holmes's arm again. Miri noticed that his hand had stayed on Holmes's arm throughout the discussion.

'Do you think I would choose someone stupid as a companion? Do you not understand how wearying that would be?'

'Yes, but as a narrative tool ...'

'Doctor Watson is not a narrative tool! He is my partner!'

'How dare you portray my partner, Doctor John Watson, as a bumbling fool?'

'In many of the stories, he …' Sidney stopped, seeing Watson's hand for the first time. 'Partner?'

'Yes.' Holmes took Watson's hand into his own. 'Partner. My equal. Companion. In every sense.'

'But, but, but', Sidney spluttered. His worldview was being challenged, and Miri could tell he didn't like it at all. 'Holmes and Watson are one of the greatest examples of friendship in literature!'

'Yes, friendship, absolutely. But also love. They are not diametrically opposed; they can exist in the same space.'

'Hear, hear,' Bernard said, and Watson smiled as though holding back laughter. He nodded at Bernard, tipping his hat.

'Love? Nonsense,' said Sidney.

Holmes let go of Watson's hand and strode forward. 'Yes, love. I thought you said, mere moments ago, that you had read all the stories. Haven't you? How can you read those stories and doubt? The evidence is there, to be seen by all who have eyes. Of course we love each other!'

'But in the era that the stories were written ...'

'There is no denying that there were archaic laws at the time, and so our dear author, Sir Arthur, could not be forthright. But the evidence is there. In addition, are we not here before you, testifying our truth to you?'

Sidney was quiet for once, standing in mute astonishment. It was quite a sight: two men, dressed nearly alike, but one real and substantial, and the other ... well, Miri could still see the armchair right through him.

'Do you not see?' Holmes said, softly, patiently. 'Do you not see that there are other ways to view things than just the one? The truth of the tale does not rest in the way the words lie on the page, nor even in the academic analysis, as painful as that is for me to say.' He laid his hand flat on his chest. 'It lies in the way the story settles into your heart.'

There was a moment of silence—not of shock, but of a group of living humans reassessing everything they knew.

Holmes smiled and patted Sidney on the shoulder, causing him to startle at the lack of corresponding sensation. 'Don't worry, young man,' he said. 'You have been taught one perspective all your life; I cannot expect you to align your thoughts to this perspective imme-diately. But know this: we were able to come forward from the shadows of fiction tonight, in order to share our truth. Are you willing to learn?'

Sidney was still for a long moment, then nodded slowly.

'Then I am willing to teach,' Holmes said.

Holmes sat next to Sidney, and the rest of the cast, still stunned, gathered in close to listen.

'You'd never think he was poetic, would you?' Watson said.

Miri jumped; she hadn't realised that the ghost of Doctor Watson was standing next to her, both of them observing Holmes and the others.

'No', she said. 'But ... yes, a bit. There were some parts in the books where I thought there might be something more.'

'Ah,' Watson said, as though she had said something incredibly profound. He looked her over, his eyes darting to her black clothing, the props table behind her, the prompt script on the table. Miri saw the intelligence there that wasn't present in Bernard's performance of Watson, or any other Watson she had seen in the movies. 'You are the stage manager, I believe?'

'I am, yeah.'

Watson nodded and smiled at her warmly. 'I think we're very alike, you and I.'

'Really?' She blinked in confusion. 'I don't understand.'

'Yes. As I understand the role of the stage manager, at any rate. We both hide in the shadows, watching others perform in the light. We prepare what is needed'—Watson gestured at the props table—'for others to shine, to be able to do their best. We ask for none of the adulation for ourselves, but all for others. Am I correct?'

Miri's back straightened with a pride that she had never felt before. 'Yes. Yes.'

'We are both storytellers, my dear.'

He nodded at her, and Miri felt the shock of connection, of an unlikely but fast friendship. Then Watson turned to the stage.

'Come now, Sherlock, my dear. You have lectured these poor artists enough.'

Holmes barked a laugh and stood. 'You are right, as always. Our time grows short.'

Matt straightened out of a hastily formed, whispering huddle of the cast and turned to Holmes and Watson. 'As we explained to you, we cannot change the script at this point, with opening night tomorrow, but Sidney will write an introduction which will be read to the audience, reflecting the things we've learned tonight. Is that satisfactory?'

Holmes glanced at Watson, who nodded. 'It is. Thank you.'

'Thank you,' said Sidney, and there was genuine gratitude in his voice, at a level Miri had never heard from him, acting or not.

Holmes took Watson's arm, and Miri could see that their profiles were growing fainter, more transparent. 'Are you ready, dear heart?' Holmes said.

'Always, if you are at my side,' Watson replied.

'For eternity,' Holmes said with a smile, and they walked upstage and through the wall, and were gone.

There was a long moment of complete silence.

Miri thought about what Watson had told her and cleared her throat. 'All right everyone,' she said. 'Beginners, please. Reset for top of Act One.'

Everyone nodded and moved into place.

'Right. House to dark. On stage please.'

ACT I: SPRING

REIGATE REDACTIONS
RITA SMITH

Redaction *(rɪ ˈ dak shun)* **noun** *the editing of text by obscuring or removing sensitive information in preparation for publication or release*

'Do you think I ought to take a wife?' Watson asked.

All had been peaceful until that moment. The heavy brocade curtains were pulled back to let in the fragile afternoon sunlight of early spring. The flatmates, the world's only consulting detective and his Boswell, a former army doctor, were ensconced in their armchairs, enjoying the pot of tea and plate of biscuits provided by the landlady. Holmes, despite protestations of having no appetite, had eaten four biscuits, but only as a vehicle for transporting tea to mouth.

Holmes hadn't choked on a biscuit when Watson posed the unexpected question, but spitting tea down the front of his second-best dressing gown had been a near thing.

'A wife? What for?'

'Do you think I ought to take a wife?'

'Not an actual wife, of course,' answered the doctor. 'More of a literary device. My readership in *The Strand* is growing and we ought to think of the consequences.'

'Consequences? Consequences from people with time enough to read rag pile serialisations?' Reining in his rage, Holmes added 'Albeit serialisations in one of the better rags. Please enlighten me as to these *consequences*, Watson.'

'When one repeatedly hears himself described as a *confirmed bachelor* keeping company with the eccentric detective Sherlock Holmes,' Watson began.

He saw at once that he had taken the wrong tack—Holmes's face grew pink before turning deathly white. The detective carefully and deliberately placed his cup and saucer on the side table and strode to the window. He took up his violin and began to pluck the strings and adjust the tuning.

'Heaven forfend that you should *keep company* with an *eccentric*,' Holmes replied through a locked jaw. 'Do as you like.'

And before Watson could plead his case, Holmes tucked the violin under his chin and began to play a particularly violent Sarasate cadenza.

THEREFORE, when Sherlock Holmes left for the Continent to investigate the connection between the Netherland–Sumatra Company and Baron Maupertuis, he travelled alone. If Dr Watson had known that his flatmate was probing the inner circle of an international cocaine-smuggling operation, working with Interpol to set up stings in Amsterdam and Paris, he might have flown to Holmes's side long before receiving word from Lyons that the detective was lying ill in the Hotel Dulong.

After six years, Watson was accustomed to his partner's temperament. Through trial and error, he'd learned that a mutable combination of patience, acquiescence, and obstinance was required during Holmes's fits of temper. In this case, during the spring of 1967, Watson chose to meet the lack of communication with his own obstinate silence. *Two can play at this game*, he'd thought over a lonely pint the day after Holmes's departure. He busied himself with revising his latest piece for *The Strand* and opening his surgery schedule to new patients. Anything to keep from noticing that Baker Street was silent and dull; while he was not driven mad by hearing the same six notes repeated *ad nauseam* whilst Holmes composed, neither was he awakened by cheerful violin *divertimenti*. And who could have predicted how quickly the fumes of shag tobacco dissipated without daily replenishment, besides the chemist-detective himself? Mrs Hudson, of course, was delighted to dust daily without fear of admonishment, but Watson rather missed the tiny particles of human detritus that usually covered the stacks of books and papers. Leaning on a soldier's discipline, the doctor managed to remain stoic as Holmes's absence grew from days to weeks. Still, choosing to believe that his partner was sulking about what Watson referred to as 'the unfortunate wife question', he took the most economical rather than the most efficient means of travelling to Lyons when summoned.

As he travelled across France, Watson read every article he could find about the Maupertuis case in the *International Herald Tribune*. Governments from Jakarta to Paris and Singapore to Amsterdam were grateful for the victory over the insidious crime ring. Officials on three continents sang the praises of the brilliant British detective. As always, his heart was full of pride at Holmes's accomplishments. That part of his stories was true: he delighted in his friend's abilities and wondered daily that the man had chosen a simple military doctor as his companion.

In Lyons, Watson found Holmes lying motionless and sweat-soaked in a ravaged room. Clothing and paper littered every possible surface; fortunately, the housekeeping staff had emptied the ashtrays and removed the plates of uneaten food. After opening the curtains, the doctor wasted no time in examining his patient. He was relieved to find no new needle marks in his lover's alabaster skin. What he did find was a man laid low by fatigue, malnutrition, and a black fog of depression.

'You must learn to take care of yourself, old man,' said Watson, shutting his medical bag with a snap. 'You can't continue to push yourself beyond your limits. When did you last eat?'

Receiving no answer from the lump in the bed, he settled himself at the spindly Louis XV-style desk with a menu and his French dictionary.

'Bonjour,' he said into the telephone. 'S'il vous plaît un déjeuner pour chambre ... deux vingt, erm, huit. Je voudrais commander un bouillon de bœuf, pain et thé. Et peut-être some, erm, quelques petit gâteaux?'

Holmes moaned and pulled a pillow over his head.

'Problem?'

'Pourquoi faut-il que tu massacres la langue?' was the muffled reply.

'Oh, I don't know, because you will insist on butchering your health? Look, I know my French is rubbish; if I'd known that I would fall in love with an international celebrity I might have played less rugby and studied more French. Of course, I can shout abuse in Swahili ...'

'Are you?'

'Able to swear in Swahili? You know—'

'In love with me?'

Watson lay down on the bed next to Holmes. He brushed the over-long and unwashed hair from Holmes's forehead before placing a gentle kiss there. 'You know I am. I shouldn't have said what I said about a wife. And I shouldn't have let you go off by yourself. I'm an idiot.'

'Yes. You are.'

As are you, my love, thought Watson.

It wasn't easy, but within three days Watson had Holmes fit enough to make the journey to London and their rooms on Baker Street. The detective's mood and pallor still concerned him, but he hoped that the familiar setting would soon set things to rights.

He was enjoying a second cup of coffee and nibbling on the last piece of toast when Holmes exited their bedroom with his cashmere dressing gown insouciantly thrown over silk pyjamas in a rather audacious paisley print. This was a distinct change from the thin cotton boxer shorts and vest Sherlock had worn since their home-coming two days before. It meant something; exactly what, Watson couldn't yet decipher. He studied the detective swooping about the room.

'You've been scheming, Watson.'

'Have I?'

'Your open address book is to the right of the telephone, you've been rereading that missive masquerading as Christmas greetings despite the fact that it is April, and, most telling, you reek of self-satis-faction.'

Watson smiled. Improvement at last! 'Well done, as always, although perhaps scheming is a strong word. Do you remember Colonel Hayter—we served together in Kenya? He's always on about visiting him in Surrey and I thought the country air would do you good. Just what the doctor ordered, so to speak.'

'The country? A house-party in the country? Surely you realise that would be more deleterious than restorative? Making conversation with this Colonel and his wife and a table full of dreary guests? No thank you, Watson.'

Only after Watson explained that Colonel Hayter had never married and that they would be completely free from social conventions at Hayter's bachelor establishment did Holmes reluctantly consent.

Watson drove them to Reigate in a hired Cortina the next morning. Holmes grumbled half-heartedly throughout the journey but managed to shake the Colonel's hand when they arrived. Hayter, an affable gentleman with greying hair and a hearty laugh, had a good ten years on Watson.

'Harold Hayter. Pleasure to finally make your acquaintance, Mr Holmes.'

'You seem comfortable in your retirement, sir,' noted Watson.

The colonel laughed. 'No sirs here, Watson. And yes, I am rather enjoying my life as a country squire, keeping up with the village gossip and mucking about with the dogs.'

On cue, two springer spaniels with liver-coloured spots trotted into the sitting room. They sniffed at the visitors and accepted affectionate pats from Hayter before setting off towards the front door at full speed.

'That'll be Dickie,' smiled Hayter.

A few minutes later a slender gentleman entered the room with the dogs at his heels.

'Duke! Lady! Be still!' commanded Hayter. Instantly the dogs lay on the hearth rug, although their tails beat a steady tattoo on the floor. 'Allow me to introduce Brigadier Richard Andrews, my, erm—'

The slender gentleman held out a hand. 'Partner. Dickie Andrews, the pleasure is mine. And Dr John Watson, at long last!'

It wasn't until Andrews was settled on an ottoman near the hearth that Watson noticed that the left sleeve of his jacket and shirt were neatly hemmed just below his elbow. Hayter held out an open cigarette case to him and Andrews leant forward with a cigarette between his lips when Hayter proffered a lighter.

'Korea,' said Andrews, answering the unspoken question. He blew smoke towards the ceiling. 'Landed in Normandy and made it through Italy with nary a scratch, but two months in Korea and I managed to get on the wrong end of a mine.'

'So you're retired as well, Brigadier,' mused Holmes.

'Dickie, please, or Andrews if you must,' insisted Andrews.

Hayter added, 'Dickie refuses to retire. He lectures at Sandhurst during the week, only comes home on the weekend.'

Watson saw Holmes's knowing grin. *Berk,* he thought. He'd deduced as much and was only drawing the brigadier out. Then Watson smiled inwardly; a weekend in the country, this country, was exactly what the doctor ordered.

Over dinner, the conversation turned to current events. Labour seemed to be gaining traction in Parliament and both the Prime Minister and the Home Secretary were in favour of liberal reforms.

'The Wolfenden Report's been languishing for ten years,' argued Holmes, 'do you really think anything will come of this new bill?'

'I really do,' answered Andrews. 'It won't be enough, of course, but it will be a start. As long as the coppers'll arrest every bloke who minces or ogles a bona basket...'

'Dickie!'

'Really, Hal, don't be naff. Holmes and Watson know what we're about.'

Holmes hummed in agreement.

'It's not as if we're going cottaging every night; what a man does in his own home is sacred privacy. And that's the Archbishop of Canterbury, Hal. If he hasn't got a handle on the rightness or wrongness of our trade, who does?'

Watson noticed that despite blushing, Hayter was working to remain composed. 'Shall we retire to the library for whisky and a smoke?' he asked.

The four men made themselves comfortable in the library. Both Holmes and Hayter were pipe smokers and Holmes was pleased to offer his host some shag tobacco. Andrews kicked his shoes off and reclined on the settee, placing his feet in Hayter's lap. He blew smoke rings over the colonel's head.

Watson sipped his whisky before changing the subject to Baron Maupertuis. 'Even I haven't heard the whole story yet; how did you bring down the Netherlands-Sumatra Company, Sherlock?'

Holmes was pleased to describe in detail the many tricks he'd used to gain the baron's confidence and lead Interpol to the heart of the operation. 'It was less a matter of discovering what happened than proving that it had happened—indeed was happening,' he concluded.

The detective's pipe was cold and his skin sallow with darkening rings under his eyes. Watson rose to stretch.

'What a wonderful start to the weekend, Hayter,' he said. 'I trust you'll be with us tomorrow, Andrews? It's just that I'm quite fagged; time for bed, I think.'

'Yes, yes, of course. It is rather late,' replied their host. 'We've put you in the guest room at the end of the hall. There's just the one bed, but it is a gargantuan old thing. I trust that will suffice?'

'That will do quite nicely, I'm sure,' answered Holmes, rising to stand beside Watson.

'Dickie will show you up—I'm going to check the doors. There was a bit of trouble Monday, a break-in at old Acton's place. No great damage done, but the culprits are still at large.'

Andrews said, 'Hal, you never mentioned—'

At the same time Holmes exclaimed, 'Were there any features of interest?'

Watson interjected 'I'm sure the details can wait until morning,' as he took Holmes by the arm and steered him to the door.

At breakfast the next morning, Hayter held court with the story of the burglary whilst Holmes peppered him with questions.

'Acton's library was quite tossed over', the colonel said, 'but the thieves took the oddest assortment: a copy of Pope's *Homer*, two candlesticks, an ivory letter weight, an oak barometer, and a ball of twine!'

'Sounds like they took whatever they could grab,' Watson commented.

'Even your county police ought to make something of that,' said Holmes; 'why, it is obvious that –'

Watson held up a warning finger. 'No! You are here for a rest, remember? A little light deducing perhaps, but you mustn't overexert yourself.'

Dickie Andrews let out a snort that he tried to hide with a rather ungentlemanly slurp of his tea. Hayter shot him a look that only encouraged more contagious laughter until the entire table was laughing gaily.

Thus, the men were caught short when Hayter's butler rushed in, flustered and upset.

'Have you heard the news, sir?' he gasped. 'At the Cunningham's sir!'

'Another break-in?' asked the colonel, his cup in mid-air.

'No sir, murder!'

The last remaining titters ceased. The four men were quite still.

'Who was it? The J.P. or his son?'

'Neither, sir. William, the chauffeur. Shot through the heart. They say William came upon the thief as he was breaking in and tried to stop him.'

'When?' Andrews asked.

'Last night, sir, about twelve.'

After dismissing his butler with solemn thanks, Hayter turned to his companions. 'This is no good,' he said. 'Old Cunningham's a decent enough fellow and William's been in his service for years. Learnt his way around an engine in the war. Not only drove for the J.P. but kept his cars in running order.'

'Do you reckon it's the same person who broke into Acton's?' asked Andrews.

'How curious!' said Holmes. 'One would expect a practised gang of burglars to vary the scene of their operations and not to crack two cribs in the same district within a few days.'

'It must be someone local, don't you agree, Dickie?' said Hayter.

'The Actons and the Cunninghams are certainly the biggest targets in Reigate,' Andrews mused. 'But that damned lawsuit has sucked them both dry, I imagine. Old Acton has some claim on half Cunningham's estate, and the lawyers have been at it for years.'

'If the culprit is local, there shouldn't be much difficulty in running him down,' said Holmes with a yawn. 'It's all right, John, I don't intend to meddle.'

Just then the butler announced Inspector Forrester, a keen-faced young fellow in search of the famous detective, known to be stopping for the weekend. The inspector explained that the perpetrator had been seen by both Cunninghams, father and son.

'He was off like a deer after killing poor William Kirwan. But Mr Cunningham saw him from the bedroom window, and Mr Alec Cunningham saw him from the back passage. It was quarter to twelve when the ruckus started. Mr Cunningham had just got into bed, and Alec was smoking a pipe in his dressing-gown. They both heard William calling for help and Alec ran down to see what was going on. The back door was open, and as he came to the foot of the stairs, he saw two men wrestling outside. One of them fired a shot, the other dropped, and the murderer rushed across the garden and over the hedge. Mr Cunningham, looking out of his bedroom, saw the fellow only as far as the road. Alec stopped to see if he could help the dying man and so the villain got away. All we have is a vague description and a scrap of paper.'

'Paper?' asked Holmes.

'Yes, sir. It must have been torn from a larger sheet. Of course we will have it analysed, but we are just a country outpost and will need to send it on to a larger precinct.'

'And what was written on this scrap of paper?' asked Holmes. 'Surely you've copied it into your little notebook there.'

'Yes, of course, sir. It reads as if it were an appointment—*at quarter to twelve learn what may be.*'

'This William, the chauffeur, he lived in at Cunningham's?' asked Holmes.

'No, sir,' answered Inspector Forrester, 'He lives at the lodge with his mother, but with this Acton business he must have thought to have a walk around before retiring for the night. Then he comes upon the robber who shoots him to make his escape.'

The four men followed the inspector to the Cunningham estate, an easy walk across the fields. Hayter and Andrews seemed rather excited to see the famous detective at work, but Watson fretted in silence.

Holmes slid his arm into the crook of Watson's. 'John, your weekend in the country is a distinct success,' he said. 'I am having a charming morning!'

At the Cunningham's, Forrester led them 'round to the kitchen door. He nodded to the constable seated at the table and made to lead his companions further into the house.

'What is this?' demanded the elderly gentleman standing at the bottom of the kitchen stair. 'Haven't you finished *investigating* yet? Surely you've disturbed us enough today!'

'Afraid not, Mr Cunningham,' answered the unflappable Forrester. 'This is the famous detective Sherlock Holmes, visiting from London. He has graciously agreed to assist our constabulary.'

'Father? What is going on?'

A younger version of the elderly Mr Cunningham appeared in the kitchen.

'The invasion continues,' replied his father.

Forrester took control of the situation. 'Mr Holmes, I'm sure, has some questions for you and I want to ask—'

Suddenly Holmes's eyes rolled upwards and he began to shake. With a groan he fell face down on the kitchen floor.

'Sherlock!' Watson shouted in alarm.

He was at his friend's side in an instant. With Hayter's help, he was able to move Holmes into a chair. He sat worrying his lip with his teeth as he held Holmes's wrist, ostensibly taking his pulse but actually clinging to him. Watson's relief was palpable when Holmes finally roused himself.

'I am sorry, gentlemen. Watson here will tell you that I've recently been quite ill and am susceptible to these little spells.'

Watson managed to stay quiet despite a strong desire to drag Holmes back to Hayter's house and force him into bed. Of course it would do no good—the fool would only find a way to return and complete the investigation. Much wiser to stay by his side in case he fainted again.

'Now if you gentlemen would humour me a little longer, I would like to see the view from the bedroom windows—whence you observed the attack on your chauffeur.'

With that, Holmes was upright and climbing the stairs. At the landing he stopped and turned to the senior Cunningham. 'Is this your son's room?' he asked as he pushed open a door. 'I understand from Inspector Forrester that Alec Cunningham was in his dressing room at the time of the attack. It's just through here?'

'Yes, yes', answered Cunningham *père* as Holmes crossed the room to peer into the dressing chamber. 'Are we quite finished here?'

Holmes exited the bedroom and turned on the landing. 'And this room, I presume, is yours? May we?'

Neither Cunningham was happy with this intrusion, but they led the little company into the other room.

The elder Cunningham's chamber was plainly furnished with an ancient carpet, an iron bed, and a wardrobe that might have been new before the repeal of the Corn Laws. Watson was quite aware that Holmes had dropped back from the others as they gathered around the windows. The short hairs at the back of Watson's neck prickled; the detective was plotting. The frisson of excitement was intoxicating; this was what he lived for, this electric connection between Holmes and himself. His every nerve was alert and firing, vigilant for the smallest sign that he should spring into action. He could only compare it to those intimate moments when it felt as if they were but one person.

A bowl of oranges and a carafe of water sat on a small table at the foot of the bed. As he passed it, Holmes leant over and knocked it over. The glass smashed to pieces and the fruit rolled across the floor.

'You've done it now, Watson,' sniffed Holmes. 'A pretty mess you've made!'

The game was on! Watson bent to retrieve the fruit, returning the oranges to the bowl as Andrews stepped back to right the little table, both of them taking care not to step on the shards of glass littering the threadbare Persian rug.

'Graceful I am not,' chuckled Watson, leaning into his assigned role. He felt his cheeks grow warm and silently congratulated himself on his authenticity. 'A thousand pardons, sir,' he continued, addressing Cunningham senior.

'Hullo!' cried the inspector, 'where is he?'

Holmes had disappeared.

Watson concentrated on schooling his face. *Clever boy,* he thought. *My darling, beautiful, clever boy!* The fainting spell, the knocking over of the table, all diversions. Holmes was onto the solution. Watson furrowed his brows and hoped he looked befuddled.

'Wait here an instant,' said Alec Cunningham. 'The fellow is a lunatic, in my opinion. Come on, Father, we'll find him!'

'I am inclined to agree with Alec,' the inspector remarked to Watson. 'I didn't realise he'd been ill. Perhaps—'

His words were cut short by a sudden cry, 'Help! Help! Murder!'

Watson bounded from the room, across the landing, and into the first room. The cries grew hoarse and inarticulate. He crossed into the dressing room to find both Cunninghams bent over a prostrate Sherlock Holmes, the younger choking him with both hands, while the elder seemed to be twisting one of his wrists.

In Kenya, Watson had been fortunate to observe cheetahs in the wild; he'd admired their speed. Like those fierce and graceful felines, he snarled and hissed as he lunged at Alec Cunningham. Grasping him by his shirt collar and belt, Watson pulled the young man backwards until he was able to secure him in a chokehold.

Alec Cunningham struggled for only a moment before submitting with a grumbled, 'Enough.'

Watson released him but positioned himself between Alec Cunningham and Holmes.

At the same time, the inspector easily pulled the father off of Holmes, who staggered to his feet, pale and wheezing.

'Arrest these men, Inspector,' he gasped.

'On what charge?'

'They murdered their chauffeur, William Kirwan.'

'Drop it!' growled Dickie Andrews.

Everyone turned to see Alec Cunningham cocking a revolver aimed at Holmes. When the younger Cunningham did not follow orders quickly enough, Andrews struck his arm, sending the gun clattering to the floor. In a flash, the brigadier had the young man pinned against the bedroom wall.

'Damning evidence indeed,' continued Holmes. 'Firstly, upon examination, you will find that gun is the weapon that killed William Kirwin and the fingerprints on it belong to its owner, Alec Cunningham. Secondly, analysis will prove that the scrap of paper found in Kirwin's hand came from this letter just now pulled from the pocket of Alec Cunningham's dressing gown.'

That gentleman screamed, 'You had no right!'

Holmes wheeled on him, all signs of infirmity gone. 'No right! It is you and your father who had no right to take a man's life! Inspector, you will find that Kirwin followed his employers the night they broke into Acton's library, not to steal a random assortment of items, but to find documents vital to winning the lawsuit. When Kirwin attempted to blackmail them with what he knew, they laid a trap for him and killed him.'

～

'Stop staring at me, John,' Holmes grumbled. 'I'm *fine*.'

They were lying together in the sturdy four-poster in Hayter's guest room. It was well past midnight, and the rest of the house was silent.

John Watson propped himself up on one arm and traced the detective's aquiline nose with a gentle finger. 'Yes,' he agreed, 'very fine indeed.'

Sherlock Holmes rolled onto his side and pressed his back against Watson's chest. Watson pulled the covers over them both and held Holmes close.

'I shall never take a wife,' he vowed, 'real or imagined.'

'I should think not.'

Watson chuckled. 'You are a ridiculous man.' He snuggled further under the covers, freeing an arm to cradle Holmes's head. 'I was stupid and cowardly to think that I need to protect my reputation. And not only because of that report or the new act. I would've killed Alec Cunningham with my bare hands if he'd –'

Holmes patted Watson's hand. 'But he didn't. I was never in any real danger.'

Watson huffed. 'But before that, when you knocked over the table—I could feel you scheming and I was thrilled. You thrill me every day;

whether you are solving a crime or filling the sitting room with chemical fumes or sawing away on your fiddle –' here he nipped at the nape of Holmes's neck to prove that he was only teasing, 'you thrill me as no one else ever has. And so, the world be damned. I shan't pretend to be someone I'm not.'

'Only on paper,' replied Holmes.

'I just said that I wouldn't—'

'I know. But are you going to tell the readers of *The Strand* that you shag me senseless after every case?'

'Of course not!'

'Go to sleep, John.'

'I do love you, you know.'

'As I love you, Watson. As I love you.'

Early the next morning, Watson bundled Holmes and their overnight cases into the Cortina. Despite his protestations, Watson insisted on wrapping Holmes in a muffler and tucking a rug over his long legs.

'I'm not an invalid, John!'

'Never thought you were. Bit of a malingerer, perhaps, but never an invalid,' Watson teased.

Holmes replied by turning his face to the window with a sigh.

'This was to be a rest cure, not a case, you know. If you won't take care of yourself, I must. Won't do for you to catch a chill.'

Holmes said nothing but Watson glanced at him and noted the hint of a smile.

They drove in companionable silence for some time before Holmes said, 'Yes.'

'Yes what?'

'You ought to take a wife, on paper.'

Watson gripped the wheel and focused on the road in order to avoid driving into the ditch. 'I beg your pardon?'

'What we do behind the doors of 221b is no one else's business. What was it the archbishop said? That there exists a "a sacred realm of privacy" into which the law "must not intrude"? I am claiming sacred privacy for our relationship. I will not have your sanity questioned.'

'But what of your sanity, Sherlock?'

Holmes scoffed. 'Thanks to your stories, the general public already believes me to be an eccentric machine, incapable of tender emotions. What could I possibly have to offer you? Certainly not my non-existent heart. Let us keep it that way. Your scribbles provide both income and advertising.'

'I-I-I don't know what to say—'

'There is nothing to say, John. It's decided. You will concoct a wife for yourself and write yourself out of 221b.'

'But—'

'Oh, do keep up! You won't really move out. And as my faithful chronicler and conductor of light, your fictional spouse will be more than understanding of your need to dash away at a moment's notice.'

'Sherlock, I—'

'Yes, darling, I love you, too.'

～

IN JULY, the new Sexual Offences Act passed, 101 to 16, and Watson put the final flourishes on the Reigate narrative.

'What are you calling this one?' Holmes asked.

'I thought *The Reigate Squires* had nice resonance despite being a bit old-fashioned. No one really says *squire* these days—perhaps *The Reigate Puzzles* would be better?'

'Hmmmm,' pondered Holmes. 'Read what you have so far.'

Watson sat up straighter and cleared his throat before reading: 'It was some time before the health of my friend Mr Sherlock Holmes recovered from the strain caused by his immense exertions in the spring of '67.'

'But what of your new wife?' interrupted Holmes.

'Never fear; I plan to incorporate her into my next story—I am considering the Amateur Mendicant Society or the loss of the *Sophy Anderson*, unless you think the Camberwell poisoning case would be of more interest?'

'I trust your judgement completely, John. You know best what the readers desire. Perhaps something even more titillating will present itself in the meantime.' Holmes leant back his chair, blowing smoke rings into the air. 'You are quite right about *Squires*, by the way. Resonant and quaint. Rather like those cunning Cunninghams. Carry on.'*

---

* Despite a 1965 *Daily Mail* poll finding 63% of Britons did not view homosexuality as a crime, the 1967 Sexual Offences Act caused a backlash. Between 1966 and 1974, prosecutions for homosexual offences increased 55%. Men were arrested for simply smiling or winking at each other in the street and accused of 'soliciting or importuning', behaviour still illegal under the auspices of the act.

LET IT BE

N.J. MOWRY

They started to awareness as a warm mug of tea was pressed into their frozen hands.

'Morning.'

'Hmm.' They sniffed at the tea, made exactly the way they preferred it; he already knew so much about them, more than anyone ever had before. Curious.

'What is?'

'Hmm?'

'Curious, you said.'

Sherlock looked up at him and shrugged, then looked back down at the tea in their hands, which were slowly warming up. 'You.'

'Me?'

They sighed and took a sip, then sighed again. 'Perfect.'

'The tea?'

'Not just the tea.' Too cryptic. 'I know we haven't known each other all that long—' they paused as John chuckled at the understatement. 'Yes, fine. Seventy-two hours is a short period of time to make a judgment on the suitability of a companion ... however.'

John took the mug from their hands and set it on the coffee table. 'Five minutes was all it took for me to know.'

Sherlock blinked at the light in those dark blue eyes and found all the words they knew had vanished. They licked their lips and waited for John to say something, anything. Instead, John smiled and offered them his hand. They wondered at how soft and small it was in comparison to their own long, life-battered one. Finally, the words returned. 'You know—'

'Yes. Just let it be.'

INCONVENIENT PROTRUSIONS

BERTIE M.

'Watson. Have you a spare scalpel and some free time?'

Holmes strode into the sitting room as he spoke, appearing with a quickness that would have surprised me had I not long since grown used to it. I marked my book and sat up slowly from where I lay on the settee, so as to see the man more clearly.

'I ... can't imagine what you would need the former for, but I am indeed in possession of the latter. What do you need from me, Holmes?'

Strangely, my friend seemed to ... hesitate, for a moment, before clearing his throat and regaining his bearings.

'I have some inconvenient protrusions that require removal, and I trust no man more to do it than yourself.'

Immediately, a stake of worry was driven through my heart.

Holmes was rarely the best judge of his own health, to the point where I often wonder whether he would still be alive without a live-in medical doctor as his closest companion; I had always done my utmost to take care of it in his stead. But my friend would only let me come so close when it came to physical examinations, and though the man could be prone to dramatic exaggeration (indeed, he was verifiably petulant when plagued with the common cold), it was certainly not impossible that something dire had escaped my notice.

If Holmes believed them removable, then it was quite possible they were merely moles, or cysts, or any manner of harmless growths; but my anxiety at his words was such that I could not shake the fear of finding tumours on him, so malignant from genetics or chemical abuse that there would be nothing I could do. Yet it is the prerogative of a London professional to keep a stiff upper lip, and so I put great effort into manufacturing a sense of calm.

'What seems to be the matter, Holmes—?'

—and quite suddenly, Holmes whipped off his shirt as if to present them to me; but rather than the cancerous tumours that I'd feared, I was instead met with an infinitely more unbelievable sight.

Heat rose swiftly in my cheeks, and I turned away rapidly, shielding my eyes. *'You're a woman?!'*

'Of course not,' was my great friend's irritable reply. 'That is why such protrusions are so inconvenient. They are God's mistake.'

The surety of his words made me doubt the reality of what I'd seen, and I wondered to myself if I was mistaken; if what I'd seen were indeed tumours, or merely fatty deposits of unusual size. Yet when I opened my eyes to look again, my gaze was met by what was unquestionably a pair of breasts.

Immediately, my eyes darted away from them, and Holmes frowned in my direction, apparently confused.

'Your lack of medical professionalism is unlike you, dear Watson. Surely you have seen a great number of chests.'

'Well, yes, but I ...!'

Whatever I might have meant to say afterward dissolved into hopeless stammering, and the continued inability to believe my ears and eyes.

It was true, I supposed, that in all the times we had lived together, I had never seen Holmes undressed. He was never seen around the house without, at minimum, underclothing or his gown, both of which covered the lion's share of his skin, and he bathed at strange hours of the day, so I had never stumbled across him towelling off by mistake. But it was only now that I began to realise it had, perhaps, all been intentional, that I should never see him such; and that the soiled but unbloodied bandages I'd once spied on the floor of his room may have had nothing to do with hiding injury, and everything to do with hiding this secret about himself.

'Himself' ...? Was he truly a man?

It was incongruous, seeing such feminine characteristics on him that I had always known otherwise—he that held some foolish views on the fairer sex, to boot! Had the words been compensation, to keep up this deception? But why deceive me at all? Was he truly so afraid he would lose my respect? But if it *were* deception, then why would he be so insistent, despite the evidence laid bare before me, that he was still a man ...?

But Holmes grew anxious beneath my gaze, though he was clearly attempting to mask it; and the guilt I felt at the alarm in his expression allowed me to ground myself with the knowledge that as much as the *what* might confuse me, the *who* was unmistakable.

He was Holmes, the same Holmes I had always known; and perhaps in time I would figure out the rest.

So I took a breath to compose myself, and asked, 'Will you tell me what's going on, old friend?'

Maybe it was the tone of my voice, or the assertion that our friendship still remained as it had; but the air of unease about him dissipated, and he sat down on the settee beside me, holding his shirt in front of his chest to obscure it.

'It is not a terribly interesting tale, but I shall tell it if you wish.'

I gave a nod, and that was enough to give him the nerve to continue. And so Holmes told me a story I could scarcely believe.

He told me that if you were to ask Mr. and Mrs. Holmes, they would tell you they had two children, but only one son; and that their other child was a bright and moody little girl, who, disgusted with dresses and displeased by the barriers of her sex, had deluded herself into believing she was a man.

He told me it was far more than that—that from the moment he became aware of himself he knew that something about him was dull and unpleasant and fundamentally *wrong;* that it was not something he could place or define until he'd dressed as a boy in a children's play, and understood at once who he was truly meant to be; that he'd developed a fascination with men's clothing, and accoutrements, and their voices and mannerisms and walks, absorbing it all with that keen observational mind until he could replicate it without a thought. His practised hand at disguises, he said, came from necessity—from the need to disguise oneself from the very beginning, and prepare to run away from all he knew.

He told me that he no longer cared whether it was delusion or otherwise, for he should rather die than be once again called 'daughter'; that only Mycroft had remained at his side, and loved a brother as well as he had a sister.

That it was the only way he desired to live.

'The favour that I ask of you', he continued rapidly, as if unable to stop, 'is in your capacity as a surgeon, and in your status as my friend.'

He looked down at his breasts for the first time since they'd been revealed to me, and grimaced, pinching one between his fingers as if it were a particularly pungent bit of refuse. 'I wish them off, and I wish them off immediately.'

What, dear reader, was I meant to say to that?

It was unlike anything I'd ever heard. Beyond the realm of what I'd ever encountered in all my years as a man of medicine. I could not understand Holmes's feelings—nay, I could not even imagine them. So my mind failed to fully comprehend the enormity and permanence of the task which he asked of me, and I was overcome by a great dizziness as I attempted to parse his words.

'... I shall have to think on it, Holmes,' I answered dimly, paralyzed as I was by my own indecision and doubt.

'I understand,' was his quiet reply, and the twinge of melancholy in his words was worse than any wound. 'It is hard to believe. Or perhaps I am simply mad.'

'You misunderstand, Holmes. I believe you. I always have.'

It was not just my faith in him that made me say this, though my faith in him is great—no, it was my sudden recollection of that paragon of military medicine, Dr James Barry, whose grand legacy was forever tainted and confused in the public eye by the posthumous discovery of her true sex. And I found myself wondering, had I lived when Dr Barry lived, if she would have told me a similar story—if, had I been as intimate a friend to Barry as I was to Holmes, I would have been privy to her—or, perhaps, to *his*—greatest secret.

It was not something he could place or define until he'd dressed as a boy in a children's play, and understood at once who he was truly meant to be ...

My companion glanced up at me when I replied, a glimmer of hope in his gaze; and I thought of how little we really knew of the mind and the body and the world, and how much kinder a place it would be if we took more people at their word.

There truly was merit in that favourite phrase of his—the notion of improbable truths.

'Holmes, you're ...' I exhaled deeply, expending my muddled misgivings. '... You're absolutely certain?'

'You are well aware of my single-mindedness, Watson, and scold me for my stubbornness daily. I assure you that this is a subject on which I cannot be moved.'

'Then I swear to you, Holmes,' I said, a hand over my heart, 'that I shall do everything in my power to assist you.'

'You have no more questions?' my friend asked, disbelief and confusion in his eyes.

'Only one,' I replied softly. 'Why did you tell me at all?'

It was curiosity in the plainest sense, not any desire that he hadn't shared the truth; for though certainly my life would have been less complicated without this knowledge, I was nonetheless glad to know it. I only imagined that such a secret would be more easily hidden than revealed, especially from a man like myself—one who lacked his immaculate sense of observation.

My friend perceived, thankfully, that my question held no malice, as was clear from his gaze. But there was still uncertainty in his eyes, and they briefly darted away.

'Because I am tired of hiding things from you, Watson. And I am tired of fearing you wouldn't care for me as I am.'

'Holmes ...'

I laid a hand on his shoulder, gentle as I could.

'... If there is anything in the world that could stop me from caring for you, I have yet to find it.'

He flushed up at that, in the charming way only he could, and I have always sworn that the last of what few barriers we had between us fell for good that day.

Upon my word, I have never ceased to be grateful for it.

PREPARATION for the procedure was the same as any other. I had performed mastectomies before, though not often, and only when there were such cancerous growths as to threaten a woman's life, as the operation had a troublingly high mortality rate. I had faith enough in my surgical skill, or I would not have gone through with Holmes's request at all; but I readily confess my uneasiness at applying such techniques to breast tissue that was perfectly healthy, for if my actions were to cause the death of my dearest friend, then I should never have forgiven myself.

Yet, at every turn of doubt, I remembered the confidence in his decision, and with it, remembered his faith in me.

Holmes was calm, even serene, I would say, as I marked his chest for incisions as carefully as I could manage; for a pen could be sharp, and my friend was far more sensitive than he cared to admit. When I was finished, and moved to draw my hand back, he caught it gently with his own, and held it fast as he looked up into my face.

There was such sparkling hope in his eyes, such unwavering trust; and I knew that what I was doing was right.

'Are you ready, Holmes?' I asked softly, a cloth damp with ether in hand.

'Naturally, my dear Watson,' he said with a smile. 'I place myself in your hands.'

And so, I slipped the fabric over his aquiline nose and watched lashes flutter into medicated sleep; and I bowed my head in prayer for the success of my task.

It must have taken hours, I imagine, but I cannot be sure. Focus gripped me, pulled me beyond the construct of time, until I was nothing but hands and knives and stitches, and fingers minding the pulse upon his throat. When I was done, after an eternity and a moment, I let out a breath I did not recall holding and wrapped him in bandages with a tenderness I was unaware I possessed.

I had done something unthinkable, and I could only hope he was truly happy for it.

Ether is a powerful thing, and it took him quite some time to return to consciousness, so I whiled that time away by pulling up a chair beside the table where he lay, monitoring his vitals, reading a book. I was so exhausted that I wished I could sleep but could hardly risk Holmes's health for the sake of my own. I valiantly fought my own weariness, until, at last, my friend stirred awake.

'Hello, Holmes. Are you feeling all right?'

His eyes opened a crack, and the muscles in his face tensed in a wince that suggested the light was too much for him, mumbling unintelligibly in a drowsy stupor. Chuckling a bit despite myself, I rose to get the blinds, and returned with a cool glass of water.

'I suppose the answer is not immediately yes,' I said with a smile, bringing the cup to his lips.

'Mm,' was his only reply, before downing every drop.

Holmes appeared awake enough by the time he was finished, and I could tell his extremities had regained feeling by the subconscious drumming of his fingers.

'Come, then. Let's sit you up.'

'Is it done?' he whispered, still hoarse despite hydration.

'Why not see for yourself?' I said, unable to smother my pride as I gestured lightly at his torso.

He looked down at himself, tentatively, gazing at the bandages that covered his healing wounds; and the wonder and joy that shone bright in those grey eyes at the sight of it was enough to relieve me of all remaining worry and doubt.

'Now, Holmes, I have to give you a series of ultimatums you are surely not going to like.' I began scribbling vigorously on a pad of paper, for I knew that in the haze of the ether he would most likely forget my words were he paying attention to them in the first place. 'In order for you to recover properly, you are going to need an enormous amount of rest—'

'Absurd,' he interrupted, still entranced by his flattened chest. 'I have never once needed rest.'

I ignored him. 'You will not be able to exert yourself significantly— yes, that means no vaulting over the settee when something excites you—nor will you be able to push anything, pull anything, lift anything, or for any reason raise your arms above your head. And in order to preserve the integrity of your gauze and bindings, you will not be able to shower or bathe, though you will be permitted use of a sponge.'

'Regrettable,' he replied, closing his eyes. 'I pity the clients who must request the services of a greasy-haired wretch.'

'That will not be any issue,' I said with a deep sigh, 'for you will not be taking any cases until you've healed.'

My friend's eyes snapped open as if I'd informed him the Queen had been murdered. *'What?!'*

'I told you you'd be displeased—'

'But how will I rouse myself from the depths of stagnation, Watson?' He gave me a pleading look. 'How shall I not fester and rot, with no manner of exercise?'

'There will hardly be *no* manner of exercise, old boy. After all, you'll have to do arm exercises daily.'

If the utter despair in his eyes was any indication, this was not in fact the answer he wished to hear.

'Then I fear', he lamented, 'that I shall have no other recourse but to die.'

I raised my eyebrows.

'Within days my hearty spirit shall have wilted and departed this earth for good.' Holmes unwisely attempted to rise to his feet. 'Starved for a scrap of interest, it will—'

—and his knees buckled so immediately that had I not been there to catch him, he would surely have hurtled straight to the floor.

'See?' he cried in anguish, as I brought him to sit in his oak desk chair.

'You certainly don't sound very grateful,' I retorted, folding my arms indignantly. 'After all that I went through!'

'I am grateful, Watson,' he replied, soft and sincere. 'So very grateful. I am just also quite bothered.'

'Grateful and bothered, hm?' I sighed and smiled at him. 'Why, that's how I feel here in Baker Street nearly every day.'

He laughed, then winced as the gesture fired pain through his chest.

'Good heavens, I cannot even laugh. This will be a tiresome time indeed.'

'If it is any consolation, dear Holmes,' I replied, absently smoothing his hair, 'I will be beside you for all of it.'

There was little I could do, but my companion seemed calmed by that small reassurance, which in turn served to reassure me.

We sat in silence this way for a moment before he looked up at me once more.

'If I cannot shower or raise my arms above my head, would you be inclined to wash my hair for me?'

I started at the request, for I had never even considered such a thing. Yet, while he had no qualms with it messy, Holmes truly despised it when his hair was unclean.

'I would be,' I answered eventually. 'Though I'm uncertain if it will be in a way that you like.'

'Ah, then I shall be looking forward to that immensely,' my friend replied with a terribly pleased expression. Were I not aware that he was merely under the effects of anaesthesia, his words might have made me blush.

(Perhaps they did anyway. Just a bit.)

'You'll not be showering today, however. The only thing you'll do today is rest.'

'Yes, yes, of course,' he murmured, eyes still dreamy with sedation and glee. And unbelievably, he reached for the syringe at his desk.

'Holmes!' I swatted it from his hands, hardly caring if the needle stung me. 'What on *Earth* do you think you're doing?! You've just had *anaesthetized invasive surgery!*'

'Don't be absurd, my boy,' said my partner, waving me off. 'I was hardly aiming for cocaine.'

'Morphine would be even *worse* in your current state—!'

'No, no, not to worry. This is quite a new concoction of mine.' His eyes glowed in an admittedly infectious manner. 'An experimental isolation of testosterone! Completely untested, of course, but I am nothing if not a willing test subject.'

'Bedrest,' I demanded, firmly grasping his shoulders. 'And don't think you'll change my mind about it. I am in charge of maintaining your health, you know. You'll not win me over.'

I was a fool to say such a thing, and his smile said he knew it; for he had long since won me over in every way that mattered.

'Of course, Watson,' he said, annoyance and affection mixing warm and well in his words. 'I could hardly disobey my doctor, now, could I?'

My doctor.

I wondered if I'd ever get used to him calling me that.

And as I marched him to his bedroom and closed the door behind us (better not to risk leaving him to his own devices, after all), I looked at the singular and extraordinary man before me, and hoped I could live up to his words.

So concludes this little tale.

Initially, this was meant to be a private journal entry—a manner of collecting my thoughts, and a musing upon my dear friend's secret, as well as my own part in keeping it. But with his permission, I have decided that it ought to be published posthumously—long after the pair of us are interred in the earth, and read in a future where, hopefully, such secrets are not so damning, and the eyes of the world are open wider at last. Should my optimistic wishes have been realised, then let this record show that such men as Holmes have always been among us, at last allowed to flourish in the light; and should my dreams have been too far-fetched, then know, dear reader, that even in shadow, compassion remains—a carnation blossoming through the cracks of London pavement.

It is not something that can die, as long as we still live.

'Inconvenient Protrusions' was first published in the *So Far Down Queer Street Journal*, Vol. 3, November 2023. https://downqueerstreet.com/issues/.

RETURN

S.C. FRASER

'Come back to Baker Street,' Holmes asked, his hand extended. 'Please?'

A shiver ran down my spine. His grey eyes gleamed with the promise of more than late-night suppers and violin serenades. And although I had loved Mary deeply, I knew that my life had been wanting without him in it.

'Of course,' I replied, grasping his fingers in mine.

UNTITLED

N.J. MOWRY

As a child in his mother's carefully arranged garden, he spent hours watching flowers, hoping to catch the moment when a blossom unfurled. He always fell asleep in the late morning sun, only to find the flower open and mocking him, it seemed. Years later, he realised he was waiting and observing John in the same way, hoping to sense or capture the moment when John would come to love him.

HEAL THYSELF
RONIT SILVERSEEKER

L ooking back at my time in Afghanistan, particularly on the battlefield of Maiwand, I still find it difficult to pinpoint the action, the specific moment, that shattered my soul. It's easier with the wounds in my leg and shoulder—a bullet tearing through flesh leaves undeniable scars on the body, cannot be ignored or brushed aside as tricks of the mind. Such is not the case with the injuries I had carried with me in my heart back to England.

Another difficulty I found with the condition was the isolation; I could no longer stand the bustle of the streets, and yet upon retreating to my hotel room I yearned for the bliss of silent companionship, the mere presence of another human soul. Perhaps that is what drove me to the club, where I could exhaust my nerves and later simply collapse into bed, even if it meant draining myself of my small army pension, and the challenge of maintaining a good, restful night's sleep—which was also a source of complaint from neighbouring lodgers. It was altogether a pitiful time in my life, culminating in the realisation that I wouldn't be able to keep my room for long, and so that I must find new lodgings, and someone willing to split the rent with me and tolerate my less-than-agreeable state of being. It was my loneliness, but mostly my desperation, that drove me to the Criterion Bar.

During their time in the army many fellows discover their inverted preference of men over women. I had suspected since boyhood that my attachment to my male peers went beyond innocent friendship, and confirmed this in university with a lovely chemist by the name of Robert Sullivan. I had no such relationships as a soldier, as I was separated rather quickly from the 5th Northumberland and attached to the Berkshires shortly before the battle that put a swift end to my service. I was not looking for a relationship when I chose the Criterion as my destination, but I had missed the company and sense of community that came with such places, with folks similar to myself.

I was just settling at the long bar, relishing in the quiet and freedom the place provided, when a voice to my right called, 'Why, if it isn't Watson!' and a hand landed on my shoulder. I am ashamed to admit that my reaction was more characteristic of a feral animal than a man's. Blood rushing in my ears, my teeth gritted, I spun to catch the stranger's hand, digging my nails into his wrist, and preparing for the next attack, determined to strike before he had the chance. Then I caught the look of shock in his eyes and recognised him not as a foe but as Stamford, who had been a dresser under me at Bart's. 'I am— terribly sorry,' I stammered, releasing his arm. 'I've only recently recovered from an illness, you see, and I wasn't expecting ...'

'I might've known,' Stamford took a step back to inspect me, or put a safe distance between us, perhaps both. 'You are as thin as a lath and as brown as a nut! What have you been doing to yourself?'

I relayed to him my adventures in rather impersonal but necessarily sanitised terms, for I had no desire to dwell on my condition after that outburst and concluded with my current attempt to solve the problem of comfortable lodgings at a reasonable price.

'Funny you should say that,' Stamford replied. 'You are the second man today that has used that expression to me.'

At that I perked up. 'And who was the first fellow?'

Thus, I was introduced to Mr Sherlock Holmes, a meeting I have detailed in its entirety elsewhere. Among my readers were my friends from a gentlemen's club I'd joined in 1885, a couple years prior to my debut into published writing, who have teased me over my descriptions of Holmes's delicate hands, delighted smiles, and bursts of laughter, asking whether I had been smitten right there and then, and I always answered truthfully—no, it wasn't love, not yet. Curiosity, perhaps, and a spark of interest, but not love. That would come later. First came learning to share a living space, then the spark of interest grew into a candle in the form of a list entitled *Sherlock Holmes: His Limits*, which my dear Holmes vowed to never let me live down, and then the adventure known to the general public as *A Study in Scarlet*. Then, oh, then came the love.

It was a few days, a week at most, after the Jefferson Hope case that I awoke with a start, hand flying to my mouth to muffle my scream. I sat upright in bed for a few minutes, breathing heavily, before resigning myself to a sleepless night, pulling the dressing gown over my nightshirt and heading downstairs.

I opened the door as quietly as I could so as not to wake my neighbour, but as I did the sound of a violin's sombre melody washed over me. I leaned against the wall and listened to my friend play, the music somewhat comforting. As he finished the piece and started the next, the tension had already left my body, and I closed my eyes to fully immerse myself in this impromptu, private concert. I must have swayed in my growing drowsiness, for in the next moment I stumbled and grunted as pain shot up my bad leg, and the music stopped abruptly. 'Watson?' Holmes called out.

I leaned against the wall and listened to my friend play.

I struggled to get back up, disoriented as I was and with my legs shaking. 'Sorry to interrupt,' I said.

'Nonsense.' He came into view at the bottom of the staircase to my room, and I fancied I could make out his mouth set into a thin line as he set eyes upon my position. 'Are you hurt?' he asked quietly.

'It's not as bad as it seems,' I assured him. At his raised eyebrow I continued, 'I simply wished to come down here and clear my head, but I found your playing to be much more soothing than sitting alone in a dark room.'

He paused for a split-second longer than he should have. 'Would you like to hear me play more often, when war consumes your sleep?' His eyes twinkled at my astonishment, though his expression was purely sympathetic. 'You mustn't take offence, my dear Watson—I can always hear when you dream of war, and the following morning your face bears clear marks of exhaustion, and your wounds ache so that you cannot hide it despite your best efforts.' He offered me his hand. 'Come.'

I chuckled. 'What do you have in mind?'

'Well, the settee is nearly as comfortable as a bed, and I haven't finished my concert.'

Holmes was a blessing, not only as a talented musician but in his unyielding support. I wished to express the enormity of my gratitude and closed my eyes for a moment to search for words, but when I opened them, it was a couple hours past dawn and Holmes was gone. Feeling refreshed for the first time in many weeks, I allowed myself to consider for a moment that if this were Holmes's effect on me from halfway across the room, what it might feel like to fall asleep by his side, with his marvellous fingers running through my hair.

Contrary to what commanding officers may tell you, war doesn't make you heroic. If it had, I would have talked to Holmes sooner. As it was, I kept silent, lavishing in the shared smiles and accidental touches, settling into the domesticity of living together—a coward's paradise, but safer than making unwanted advances and losing him.

Weeks passed in that matter, then months, and I grew comfortable with the yearning in my chest. I was content with Holmes by my side, in concert halls as well as dark alleys. It all changed in such an alley one night in September—we were chasing a burglar, who had made an attempt earlier that evening on our client's life, thus falling into our trap. Lestrade's men lay in wait just around the corner, but the criminal didn't turn; instead, he spun on his heel and threw himself at Holmes, slashing madly with his knife. Holmes caught the burglar's wrist in his hand, swinging him to the ground, whereupon I threw myself down and held the man in place. Holmes gave a mighty whistle and two constables rushed to our side, relieving me and hoisting the criminal up by his arms.

'Nicely done, boys,' Inspector Lestrade put his hands on his hips. 'And thank you for your assistance, Mr Holmes, Dr Watson.'

I expected my friend to merrily remind the inspector of the central piece of the puzzle and suggest we walk home, but Holmes was standing very still, his eyes wide, one arm wrapped around his torso and the other held in front of him, his palm covered in blood. He looked up, his eyes meeting mine.

'Wat—' he managed, before slumping forward.

I leapt forward to catch him before he hit the pavement, and gently lowered him to the ground.

'Keep your eyes on me, Holmes,' I commanded as I began to unbutton his suit, and he blinked twice before focusing on me. 'Inspector, I need my medical bag!' I called without sparing even a glance over my shoulder; the whole world, save for my friend, faded around me.

I made short work of exposing the wound, and to my tremendous relief, discovered that the gash was worse in length than in depth. The chances of a more complicated and deadly injury were slim.

Without bandages in my immediate vicinity, I pressed my handkerchief over the wound, ignoring the blood staining my hands—my shortcomings in the war, my night terrors and doubts, none of it mattered; at that moment I existed for the sole purpose of assisting an injured man, more akin to a machine myself. Soon enough Lestrade returned and handed me my Gladstone bag.

'Hold still, there's a good fellow,' I murmured to Holmes.

'Whyever would I go?' he jested, but his voice was strained. Without warning, I replaced my handkerchief with clean bandages, and he drew a sharp breath, hissing as I secured them in place. 'I don't suppose we could continue this in the comfort of our rooms?'

I considered this, very much of the same mind as Holmes. The bleeding seemed to have nearly stopped, but I had my reservations about a ride back, and walking that distance would be impractical. A carriage would have to do, I decided, and was about to call a hansom. All of a sudden, the world around me reappeared and I found myself surrounded by onlookers, Lestrade and the arrested criminal long gone with one of the constables left to keep the crowd in order.

'Yes, we'd better go,' I choked, the accursed tremble returning to my hands.

When I rose to my feet and wrapped an arm around Holmes I felt as though he was the one supporting me rather than I him. Mercifully it didn't take long to hail a carriage, and the driver was agreeable enough to ensure a slow and careful journey to our home.

The climb up the stairs seemed to drain the last of Holmes's power, for he collapsed as soon as the sitting room came into view, and it took all my power to half-drag him to his bed.

'I am sorry, my dear boy,' I whispered. A strand of hair fell on his forehead, and I couldn't resist smoothing it back despite the tremors in my hands. 'Your wound must be stitched, but I cannot—'

'Doctor,' Holmes said so sharply that I flinched. 'My *dear* doctor,' he continued softly, almost like a caress. 'I trust that no harm will come from waiting another hour or so?'

By this point the bleeding had stopped, and I knew the bandages would provide the necessary pressure and protection. I told him so; my hand found his and squeezed it in reassurance. 'All you have to do is rest.'

'Must you be so cruel, doctor?' he sighed dramatically, and winked. I chuckled and, thinking it best to leave him to his peace in private, had turned to leave the room when his grip around my hand tightened. 'You are, you know,' he murmured as his eyes closed, 'dear to me.'

'As are you,' I replied without thinking. Half a second later it pierced my very heart. 'Oh, Holmes,' I breathed. How long had he known? How many days had I wasted seeing but not observing? I pressed a kiss to his beautiful hand, and he smiled—at me, I knew now—while drifting into sleep.

By the time he awoke almost an hour later I had set my medical supplies before me, Mrs. Hudson had provided a bowl of hot water, and Holmes's hand was in mine once again. His eyes fluttered open, gentle as a summer breeze.

'Watson,' he grinned up at me, brushing the back of my hand with his thumb.

'How are you feeling, dearest?' I asked. A peculiar expression passed over his features for a moment, as though he hadn't expected me to understand nor reciprocate his confession, before morphing into bright joy.

'Far better than I ought to, I suspect. Stings, but not terribly,' he added at my raised eyebrow and the look I gave him. 'Now, I believe you were about to put me back together, so to speak.'

As a doctor I strive to keep my patients relaxed before a procedure, and so it was my duty as well as my greatest privilege to kiss Holmes softly on the lips. 'Yes,' I murmured, running my hand through his hair once more before returning to the task at hand. 'Yes, I believe I shall.'

NEXT TO YOU
SAM GRACIE

Sun and Moon

Untouchable, divine

Inexplicably intertwined

Stars against the night sky

Intimate, distant celestial bodies

Glittering jewellery on velvet

Luxury and brilliance

Deep, rich attracting opposites

Soft, hard – Bright, dark

Black and Gold

An Unusual
Introduction

CS McGuigan

'Returned from Afghanistan, I perceive! I pray that you're recovering well, Miss Watson?'

I looked to the matronly Mrs Stamford, who shook her head. 'I have told her nothing of you.'

Miss Holmes continued.

'Your complexion and appearance are that of a formerly well young lady who has suffered a sudden illness. One that lasted several weeks and caused the loss of considerable weight—you have recently taken in your dress to fit your slighter figure. Enteric fever, I believe?'

I nodded, my shock clearly evident, as Miss Holmes continued her revelations.

'Your dress gives further clues—the embroidery is of the Khamak style, a most intricate design from the Kandahar region. And Mrs Stamford here introducing us—I'm assuming that you know her through her missionary work.'

'Why, yes.' My tongue finally loosened. 'My mother and father are well acquainted with the Stamfords and entrusted me to their care during my recuperation. And you are correct, my father's mission is in Kandahar.'

A slight blush spread across Miss Holmes's handsome features at my confirmation of her deductions, as if a gentleman had paid her a great compliment.

My new acquaintance cut an unusual figure, uncommonly tall, with unruly dark hair that she wore in an unkempt bun.

She offered her hand and I reciprocated, my heart quickening within my breast …

THE NOT-QUITE DATE

SAM GRACIE

J ohn Watson, third year Pre-Med student, was feeling good. It was the break just before Spring Term, he had gone to the Uni bookstore with a gaggle of his rugby mates from Blackheath FC to pick up the books for their courses. He had a decent night's sleep for the first time in what felt like ages and the sun had decided to make a rare late-winter appearance. And now, he was trying to get a date.

There was a small café stand set up inside the bookstore. John was leaning over the counter, trying to get closer to the barista making his tea, and very much enjoying the way she blushed when she smiled at him. There was a burst of laughter from behind him, but John ignored it. The second she placed the tea in his hand, but before he could ask for her number, a couple of rough hands dragged him from the counter.

He protested, loudly, as he was manhandled over to the front of the shop, where a large corkboard displayed local events, people looking for flatmates, and the like. Nothing on this board felt worth getting cockblocked in such a rude manner.

'The fuck am I looking at, then?' He griped, still clutching a cooling to-go cup of tea.

Greg leaned in and poked one flyer in particular with a grin.

'Blind Book Date?' John read aloud, frowning. 'I'll have you know, I had a perfectly good non-blind date, in progress just over there.'

Greg only laughed. 'She's going out with Tomas, mate. She was just trying for tips with you.'

John's face darkened at that. Just his luck, really. Though he tried not to advertise the fact, he'd hit a little dry spell in his love life recently. Med school and rugby practice took up almost his entire life, at present.

'So, what, then? You're trying to set me up with a random book nerd?'

Bill piped up over his left shoulder, pointing to an empty bookcase near a group of empty tables. 'Nah, you bring a book you like and put it on the shelf, there. Then if someone picks up the book—bam—you've got your date.'

'And you already have something to talk about! It's brilliant!'

'If you like the idea so much, why don't you do it?' John grumbles back at Greg, trying to turn away from the whole ordeal. Clearly, his friends thought less of him than he thought if they think he's getting desperate enough to try blind dates.

Greg only rolled his eyes good-naturedly at the question. He'd been in a solid relationship for the last year, and everyone knew it, John was just trying to get a rise out of him.

'I'll do it with you, John!' Russel ducked around Greg's shoulder to smirk up at him. He was a first-year and very eager to be *one of the guys*. Overall, he seemed harmless, if mildly annoying.

'Excellent,' John muttered, hoping he didn't lay the sarcasm on too thick. Russel didn't seem to notice and grinned all the more.

'Brilliant! I better go back to the flat to find a book.' Russel waved and with a tinkling of a bell on the door, he was gone.

What, right now? John's eyes snapped back up to the flyer, and then widened. This wasn't some far off thing he could forget about later and skip. It was starting in just under an hour, and from how he was still being firmly held in place in front of the flyer, John doubted there would be a graceful way to back out now.

Not that it had to be graceful. He could get mad and stomp out, and the idea did appeal somewhat. He felt like he was being deliberately thrust into an uncomfortable situation for the amusement of his traitorous friends. On the other hand, despite all current appearances, his team was some of the most supportive and steady mates he'd ever had. Legitimately, this was a very low risk gamble on everyone's part. Worst case scenario here, John's book was never chosen, and he got a sunny afternoon in a nice bookstore with (now that he's had a chance to taste it) decent tea. His friends got a chance to help without the risk of it going horribly wrong. If his book was chosen by someone ultimately not compatible with John, at least he could enjoy an hour or so to chat about his favourite book with someone else. No harm done there, either.

'Yeah, alright,' John murmured, and the handful of young men gathered around sent up a cheer as if he'd just led their team to victory somehow. He rolled his eyes and pushed at them to let him have some breathing room. They slowly started to disperse, purchasing their books and heading back to their dorm. Only Greg stayed behind.

'All joking aside, you sure you're okay? I won't tell the mates if you decide to bugger off.'

'Nah, I'll stay. Russ will give me away if I don't show, anyhow.'

Greg gave John a supportive slap on the back and made his way out of the bookstore. The event started in about 20 minutes, which didn't give John time to run back to his flat. He contemplated what he would have even brought back if he did have time. One of his crime drama paperbacks? A book of poetry he kept in the back of his tiny bookcase so visitors wouldn't see it? (He had a reputation to uphold, after all.) His secretly favourite book of all time: a science fiction novel written in the late '60s about a race of people who could transfer their consciousness into a willing body using magic that only worked when the moons of the planet aligned just right?

John shuddered, thinking that may be a little bit too personal for meeting a stranger, even if they also enjoyed the book. He started perusing the aisles of the bookstore for what would be a good representation of himself while also not digging deeper into his soul than necessary.

Eventually, indecision and lack of time caught up to him and he ended up setting the Anatomy & Physiology textbook he had purchased earlier onto the shelf. He smirked to himself at the duality of representing himself and the blatant innuendo. Hopefully, if someone does pick up the book, they will have a good sense of humour.

John settled himself into one of the tables set up for the event in the café side of the building, directed by the staff who had set it all up. People set books in the bookcase and took a seat one by one, giving him awkward smiles. Russel returned a bit breathless and put a colourful copy of *The Hobbit* on the bookcase before finding a seat. It struck John as an odd choice to bring a book so obviously catering to young people, but on the other hand, it was also a good way to find people who had similar childhoods. This was turning out to be much more complicated an endeavour than he originally thought.

When all the tables had one person at each, the remaining people who trickled in were directed by the staff to choose a book instead of placing one. John sat, rotating a fresh cup of tea with his fingertips as he watched the process. One woman perused the selection and, looking disappointed, turned and left without choosing. John couldn't help but wonder what book she had been hoping to see. Another participant found the book they had brought along matched another in the bookshelf, and proudly showed everyone as if they had won The Price is Right. They found their way to the table of their book-twin, and they started speaking excitedly in hushed tones like giddy conspirators. It was hard not to smile at how happy the two of them were to find a kindred spirit, and it made something twist in John's chest.

While he was thinking, a pretty blonde giggled at his book but didn't pick it up. Choosing a collection of Walt Whitman poems instead, the young woman took a seat at a table with a hipster looking bloke in corduroys, making John kick himself for not running back to his dorm for Keats.

A tall, dark-haired girl in a baggy sweatshirt timidly pulled *The Hobbit* from the bookcase. John could *feel* Russel perk up from two tables away as the staff directed the girl over.

Perfect. If Russel managed to pull and he doesn't, the lads will never let him live it down. It will be the running joke of the season. John adjusted in his chair to get comfortable sitting alone, regretting all the choices today that have led up to this moment. An anatomy book? What had he been thinking? What idiot would go looking for a date and pick a textbook? John huffed a grumbled sigh into the heel of his own hand, waiting for the night to be over.

SHERLOCK HOLMES WAS HAVING a bad day. The insufferable weak sunlight of late winter that had taunted his foul mood was starting to set, and he was wide awake. This morning, after being awake for four of the last five days, he had fallen asleep in the middle of a delicate experiment. He had opened his eyes this afternoon, sore from the odd sleeping position, and found acid had eaten away a pound-coin sized hole in his desk and part of his shirt sleeve. On top of that, his normally distant, 'very important, far too busy to visit' brother had legitimately shocked Sherlock by calling to his flat out of the blue—the man was practically tethered to Westminster or his beloved Diogenes Club at all times. Mycroft then managed, in his irritatingly pompous way, to imply he was wasting his efforts at university in the same breath as asking if he was 'doing alright'. Whatever that is supposed to mean. Now Sherlock was stomping his way to the bookstore to gather the materials for his next term, just to spite his brother and the doubts that crowded into his mind.

He was so inside his own thoughts and overstimulated by the time he entered the shop, that he paid no attention to the crowd in the café side of the bookstore. He wanted to make quick work of this errand so he could get back to his experiment in peace. As such, Sherlock was deeply confused when he picked up a textbook that looked interesting from the front of the store and started to skim it to see if it was relevant to his pathology course, and a middle-aged woman—clearly on staff with the bookstore—gently ushered him toward a group of tables full of couples. His face darkened as his attitude turned vicious. He hated not knowing what was going on. Indeed, he was winding up to snap hateful deductions about the woman's affair and her ailing cat so she would unhand him, but finally took a better look at his destination.

A dark blond, deeply tanned man sitting alone at the table glanced up at Sherlock with a mixture of hope and confusion that drained all the vinegar from his blood. It was honestly a little endearing. Whatever it was that was happening here, this young man had been alone for most of it and was clearly miserable. Sherlock sat down in the chair across from him out of a sense of overwhelming curiosity. This was absolutely not what he had meant to be doing, but it was certainly so much more interesting than buying textbooks.

The staff member walked away, leaving the pair in awkward silence as Sherlock ran his fingertips over the hard edges of the textbook in an attempt to stim. The other man—medical student, pretty far along, single, lives in a dorm nearby—raptly watches the movement with his eyes. An interesting reaction.

'Which book did you bring, then?' the blond says, meeting Sherlock's gaze for the first time.

JOHN COULDN'T PRETEND he was ecstatic about the person picking up his book being a bloke. It didn't even occur to him that was a possibility, except in hindsight it made perfect sense. It wasn't because the man was bad looking. If anyone were to ask, John would honestly admit he was attractive. He had an *under fed, under slept college kid* look about him, but aside from that he was tall, dark-haired and there was something adorable about the combined look of bewilderment and anger that was swirling on his face as he approached the table.

In the tense beats after the staff woman walked away, John tried to find a good icebreaker but was distracted by the way the other man's fingertips slid over the spine and edges of the Anatomy book. Unbidden, John imagined the hands of this stranger playing piano or another instrument that required long, dextrous fingers. In a mild panic, John cleared his throat and spit out the first thing that came to mind.

'Which book did you bring, then?' John pulled his eyes up and they made eye contact. Deliberately ignoring the bodily reaction to how very intensely the man across the table was looking back, John tilted his head to indicate he was waiting for an answer to his question.

'None. Why?' Storm-grey eyes squint at him. 'Which book did you bring?'

John blinked, breathing out a half-laugh. Instead of replying, he pointed at the book still being caressed absentmindedly on the table between them. Pulling his hands back as if the book was suddenly white-hot, his table companion stared down at it with the same confused, angry look from earlier.

'You have no idea what is happening here, do you?' John asked quietly, a smile slowly spreading on his lips. There was a negative shake of the man's head, so minute that John nearly missed it.

John couldn't help it. He threw his head back and laughed. As if his luck with dates could get any worse, this poor man came in to buy a book and was thrust onto a date with John against his will. When he started to flush from the laughter, John quickly held out a hand.

'Wait, I'm sorry. I wasn't laughing at you.' He stifled his giggles back and cleared his throat. 'Please, don't go, I'm sorry.'

THANKFULLY THE HOT feeling on his face dissipated as the Med student, John, explained the inane dating set up the bookstore was putting on, and why Sherlock picking up that particular book had led him to sitting here. That certainly cleared up quite a bit of the missing information.

'Why this book?' Sherlock inquired while pushing the book back in John's direction. He had theories. Maybe he had only wanted to date other students in his programme. Maybe John was only looking for a physical relationship rather than a romantic one and tried to cheekily make that clear with his book selection. Sherlock cleared his throat with a frown when that particular theory made his mouth dry.

John didn't seem keen to answer at first, rubbing his hands along the denim on his thighs, and it became clear to Sherlock that he had an unconscious tic of clearing his throat when he was thinking about sex. Which, then, caused him to mentally rant at his own epidermis for flushing again. He played it off as being too warm by removing his thick coat and draping it over the back of his wooden chair.

'I didn't have time to go back to my flat, so I went with what was on hand.' It wasn't a lie, but it wasn't the whole truth either. Sherlock smirked knowingly but let him have it. John was about to ask a question in return when a voice cut through, louder than the general noise in the café.

'What? That's disgusting!'

'It is not, how dare you!'

John peeked over Sherlock's shoulder to see Russ and his book date.

'Frodo and Sam are *not* gay. They're *hobbits*,' Russel cried. John couldn't see his face but could see his red-faced date standing up.

'That argument doesn't even make any sense, you fucking twat,' she responded, slamming a hand on the table. It took her long enough to extract her bookbag's strap from her chair that Russel got another jab before she was out the door:

'Whatever, pervert!'

The entire bookstore was thunderstruck and completely silent. All eyes were on Russel, who seemed smug when he got the last word. He looked around until he found John's face.

'That psycho bint writes *porn*, John, can you believe that? About *hobbits*.' Russel's voice dripped with contempt. He uttered a bitter high-pitched laugh as he waited, thinking John would take his side. There was more silence, and then everyone's eyes turned to John, including Sherlock.

'Frodo and Sam are not *gay. They're* hobbits,*' Russel cried.*

Sherlock watched as a kaleidoscope of emotions came and went from John's tanned face as it turned from a vaguely pink of embarrassment to a deep red of anger.

'Russ, shut the hell up.' John urged, shaking his head. His voice was pitched low, only just loud enough for Russel to hear, but had a hard, sharp edge that Sherlock found decidedly attractive. 'You are being such an arsehole right now.'

Russel seemed to finally catch on that the attention he was receiving from everyone in the café was not friendly. He flushed with shame and gathered his things in a rush.

'Fine. See if I come back here again! Filth peddlers!' Almost everyone in the room released a held breath soon as Russel was gone, the awkward tension leaving with him.

Slowly, conversations started up again. When John and Sherlock's eyes met once again, they noticed each of them have a similar *What the hell just happened?* look on their face and burst out in giggles.

'Friend of yours, John?' Sherlock drawled with an eyebrow raised.

'Ah. No, he's on the rugby team with me, but I wouldn't call him a friend.' John wrinkled his nose, vowing to have a word with the boys about this later. 'Don't think I want to be associated with him at all, after that little stunt.'

'You are a fan of hobbit porn, then?'

John choked on his sip of tea. Before he even had a chance to cough the liquid out of his oesophagus to defend himself, Sherlock was laughing. It was low and melodic, and settled John's ruffled feathers.

'I am not the type of date you had hoped for.' It wasn't a question.

'Ah ... No. Not exactly.' John hedged.

'Disappointed?'

All his previous dates, if one could call them that, were getting tiresomely predictable before this stretch of nothing. He went through people so quickly, John was beginning to get a bit of a reputation among his Blackheath FC mates. Apparently his 'conquests' were boasted about among the crew, much to John's chagrin.

Okay, sure, when this whole affair began, it would have been nice for a cute woman to pick up his textbook wanting a quick fling during the term break, but why not make the best of this truly odd evening? Sherlock was attractive, funny, and John was legitimately having a nice time. Maybe it was time to try a different approach, after all.

'Not really.' *Not anymore.* John cleared his throat self-consciously. 'What about you? Wish you would have picked up your required reading, instead?'

Sherlock tilted his head slightly and leaned in closer. 'If I wasn't the type of date you had in mind, why do you care? Indeed, why are you still here?'

'If you didn't come here for a date at all, I could ask you the same question.' John smiled, feeling clever and not-so-secretly revelling in the attention he was getting.

'You're interesting.'

'Wait, *I'm* interesting?' John's mouth dropped open.

'Yes.' Sherlock huffed, instantly regretting he had said it out loud, and launched into deductions as a defence mechanism. 'You're nearly done with Pre-Med, thinking about enlisting so the government pays for the rest up to being a surgeon of some kind. Your parents divorced when you were quite young, father had an affair, and you have at least one older sibling. Most likely brother, or else a sister who does not dress particularly feminine, since they gave you that jumper. You could continue going to school on loans and scholarships but are worried you won't be able to take care of your mum while under the kind of debt medical school can entail. Your sibling has a decent job but is … oh, don't tell me.' Sherlock's eyes rove over John's rigid form, trying to find the piece that will click neatly into the puzzle he was building, but there weren't enough clues. There's always something … 'The statistically most likely issue is alcoholism draining their finances, but not enough data to say for sure.'

John blinked. He was silent for just long enough that Sherlock thought for sure he'd stepped over a line.

'That …' Sherlock inhaled, ready for shouting that never arrived. John simply says: 'Wow.'

'What?'

'Spot on, really. How did you do that?' John squints intently at Sherlock. 'What am I thinking right now?'

Sherlock snorted and rolled his eyes. 'I do *not* read minds, John. I deduce things about people. Most read as easily as this textbook here.' This time, John rolled his eyes—medical textbooks were not exactly light reading. 'Did I get everything?'

John can't help but smirk. Apparently, Sherlock needed some validation despite the earlier praise. 'My parents did divorce early on, like you said. Harry is my older sister, and a pain in my arse in general. How you knew this used to be her jumper, I will never know. She got it for Christmas two years ago and never wore it.'

Sherlock watched John speak carefully, and at this pause he pursed his lips. 'What did I get wrong?'

'She's a fan of drink, but unless it's worse than I realised she isn't a full-blown alcoholic yet.'

The defensive way John shared this information told Sherlock enough—John loved his sister fiercely; John would not let anyone say anything untoward about his sister without dire consequences. John was perhaps skirting the fine line of cognitive dissonance involved with knowing one's loved one is struggling but not allow anyone else to say something disparaging about it. What other contradictions did this lovely, rugged man carry around in that head of his? How did this stranger in a bookstore café continuously prove to be fascinating? Sherlock had so many follow up questions.

'Folks, sorry to interrupt! We are so glad you had a nice time, but the shop is closing in fifteen minutes.'

They watched as other couples gather up their things. Some were clearly going off together to continue their conversation—or maybe an activity with significantly less talking—while others amicably shook hands and thanked each other for the nice chat.

'Um ...' John trailed off, seeming to struggle for words. Sherlock felt similarly lost. 'I'm sorry you never got a chance to buy your textbooks.'

The corner of Sherlock's mouth twisted as he mentally ran through multiple scenarios where he could continue to speak to John. He could steal his textbook and take off into the streets, John would probably chase him down. No, angering the man would not get the desired effect.

'What would you have brought?' he said instead, gambling on a conversation hook.

'Pardon?' John was standing, picking up the Anatomy & Physiology book from the table. Their connection was starting to sever.

'If you had time to go back to your flat. What book would you have brought instead?'

'Sherlock, we don't have time, they are closing.' John sounded sad, but Sherlock hid a smug grin. His plan was working.

As cool and casually as he could, Sherlock rose from his seat and gestured toward the door. 'Then, tell me on the way.'

John looked up at him with an open expression, equal parts excited anticipation and curiosity. Sherlock shivered with the release of adrenaline and dopamine when he realised John was following.

'On the way to ...?'

'Two two one B, Baker Street.'

IT GETS BETTER

ATLIN MERRICK

Those five? Gay. Those three? Bullied. That one? Both.

It is so true. If you look you really *can* see, John Watson thinks, eyes scanning the two hundred kids assembled in this gymnasium.

John has already done his career-day speech; now Sherlock is standing at the podium finishing his, and John is still surprised Sherlock volunteered them for this. Then again ... John glances at his too-tall, too-smart, too-*different* lover. Sherlock knows that for these kids, now, right now, at thirteen, fourteen ... it's the most important time in the world.

Sherlock Holmes turns; he's looking at him, repeating, 'Anything else, John?'

The good doctor steps again to the podium and veers off script. 'Yes, just one more thing.'

John looks a long while at the young faces. 'Know this: now is not forever. And you *can* do anything. If you're fat, skinny, short'—John gestures to himself—'if you're disabled, if you're gay, or think you're gay—' John isn't surprised when Sherlock's hand rests lightly on his —'if you're smart, not-so-smart, or just not sure what you are right now, leave here knowing one thing, just this one true thing: it gets better.'

John Watson tries to meet the eye of every single child he sees who's slouched, cowed, uncertain, confused. 'I promise you, I promise you on everything I know: *it gets better.*'

THE PLOT THICKENS
HOLLAND PARKER

W atson walked into 221b after his shift. It was quiet—Holmes was out or at the microscope. After climbing the steps, he saw dark hair on the arm of the sofa. 'Pondering a case,' thought Watson. Further into the apartment, he realized that Holmes's hands weren't right. Rather, a book was on his chest and he was asleep. He didn't recognize the book; the title surprised him. He thought Holmes really wouldn't want him to see this. *Please Select Your Gender: From the Invention of Hysteria to the Democratizing of Transgenderism.*[1]

Watson went to his room to change.

HOLMES WOKE THAT EVENING. Watson was walking around in his room and Holmes smiled, happy he was home. Then he remembered exactly which book was resting on his chest and was suddenly angry with himself. He hadn't meant to sleep. And he really hadn't meant to let Watson see it. He barely knew what was going on; he didn't want to share anything yet, if ever.

Watson came down carrying a book and greeted Holmes like any other day. If he was going to ignore the large pink and blue elephant in the room, then so was Holmes. He walked into the kitchen where Watson was making tea and saw the book on the bench. *Bisexual Men Exist.*[2]

'The plot thickens,' he mumbled, baffled.

ACT II: SUMMER

THE CASE OF THE POTENTIAL SUITOR

LF HOWARD

The day began as had the day before: sweltering and damp. The opening of a window brought little relief from the discomfort as it merely ushered in the moisture from outside. I paced through the flat, enjoying the feel of at least some air moving across my skin, and contemplating whether the norms of society would allow me to remove any more layers of clothing even in the privacy of my own home. Holmes appeared to be handling the temperature in his own peculiar way, reclining on the sofa, eyes closed, chest rising in a rhythm that hinted at sleep, even while a single drop of perspiration tracked slowly across his forehead towards his hairline. But he lay there without complaint, and in fact without even a sound; I found this to be a preferable alternative to his often-sarcastic demeanour. Even the tea Mrs Hudson served by mid-afternoon was hardly a comfort—someday a cretin would decide to put ice in the tea for a day such as this one. Holmes roused himself long enough for a cup and a biscuit.

After a socially appropriate time had passed, she returned to clear the tray, but graciously left us with a plate of biscuits. Only a few minutes later, I heard the door below open and footsteps ascending the stairs. Although I did not have Holmes' powers of observation, I could not mistake the tread of one of the two Scotland Yard detectives that Holmes seemed more or less to tolerate. Perhaps 'tolerate' was too low a bar for a proper description; I had seen a glimpse of satisfaction on Holmes' countenance on the handful of times Lestrade had offered a deduction or seen a piece of evidence before Holmes had. Although I graced our work together with my own helpful moments during our investigative outings, mine primarily filled in the gaps in Holmes' own unsystematic knowledge of anatomy, and sometimes in his rather incomplete understanding of human behaviour.

I glanced at Holmes, who had resumed his position on the sofa only moments before. His eyes opened slowly such that when Lestrade came bounding into the room through the open door, he was staring blankly at the ceiling.

'Mr Holmes, I need your help,' Lestrade cried immediately upon walking through our doorway.

My companion did not move, but instead continued his enigmatical study of our ceiling. I glanced up, briefly anticipating that I should find something unexpected or new etched into the plaster.

Lestrade waited, knowing the consulting detective's mannerisms well enough. He eyed the plate of biscuits on the table and then glanced at me, mutely seeking permission. I nodded, and he picked up one of the shortbreads and ate half of it in a single bite, flopping onto one of the dining room chairs.

'Starvin'. Haven't had anything since breakfast,' he mumbled through a mouthful of biscuit.

After Lestrade sat, I inspected his attire. He had recently visited a barber, and his hair was cut shorter than I had seen it. His hair normally flopped across his face in an unkempt—and sometimes not entirely clean—manner. He also wore what appeared to be a new white shirt underneath what I knew to be his best coat, one normally reserved for use at court appearances. Even I could deduce he had dressed for an occasion, but I could not determine what that occasion was. Thinking on that mystery, I turned to look at Holmes at the same moment he deigned to sit up, turning his legs so that his stocking feet touched the floor. It was at that moment I realised none of us was entirely dressed as normal; seeing Holmes in his stocking feet with his shirtsleeves rolled up to his elbows in front of a guest (other than Mrs Hudson) seemed almost intimate. And for once, Lestrade, in his best suit, uncharacteristically washed and groomed, may have outshone the two of us.

Despite spending most of the day in a torpor, Holmes focused on Lestrade, his eyes piercing as they roamed over him, taking in whatever extraordinary details he could from his appearance, possibly Lestrade's choice of breakfast or the name of his barber. I had long ago stopped trying to anticipate the sweep of the man's thought processes.

Lestrade, aware of being studied, shifted in his chair slightly; he likely shared some of my thoughts: what things was Holmes learning about him during this quiet study? I was momentarily grateful that Holmes rarely turned that focus on me, although he certainly had ample opportunity to deduce me during our daily lives.

Finally, Holmes asked, 'Which Lord has the current crisis?'

I raised an eyebrow, looking towards Lestrade. He nodded and uttered a quiet 'hmph' noise, obviously not surprised that the first question was on target.

'Lord Theodore Addington.'

'Who's missing?' came the immediate reply.

This question did startle Lestrade, whose head jerked back in surprise. 'I won't ask you how you know that; I gave up years ago.'

Lestrade looked at me, and I simply smiled and shrugged. It should be no surprise to him that I had accepted these wild surmises long ago. He pulled out his writing pad and flipped through his notes for a few seconds. I doubted he needed those for his report, but he likely did not want to miss an important point.

Finally, he continued, 'His youngest daughter, Lady Emmeline. Eighteen years old. Vanished without a trace two days ago. No signs of a struggle, no clothes missing, not even shoes. No diary, letters or personal notes to show a reason for her to want to vanish. Lord and Lady Addington report she had a disobedient younger phase but had grown into a well-mannered woman. She had a suitor ...' He flipped through his notes for the name. 'Mr Harold Giddens—his grandfather founded Giddens Transport—but he and his entire family have been in France for the summer. They reported through a telegram that they've not heard from or seen her since they left the country three weeks ago. We're checking with the rail stations and the ferries that service the coast of France.'

Holmes watched him quietly during this recitation. 'When was this reported?' he enquired.

'Yesterday afternoon. I was told to wait until this morning to meet with them because Lady Addington was returning from her country house.'

'Thus, the visit to the barber and your best suit.'

Lestrade looked away from a moment, absently running his palm along the hem of his coat. 'Don't meet a Lord and Lady very often,' he muttered. 'Used to a stabbing in a dirty alley behind a pub.'

'Clean yourself up, Watson. We're going to pay a visit to a Lord and Lady. Try to look as presentable as Lestrade here.'

'And am I to presume that Lord Addington and Lady Emmeline were staying in their London home?'

'Yes, they said that she asked to remain in London while her father was here conducting business for a few weeks, and then they'd travel together to Oxfordshire. They delayed reporting it because they thought perhaps she had decided to travel by herself there, but she never arrived.'

Holmes looked back up at the ceiling; he remarked after a moment, 'They did not want to risk suffering from the embarrassment of a missing, wayward daughter, even if it meant putting her life in danger from a kidnapping.'

'Holmes!' I protested immediately, as surely his general disrespect for all things political should not lead him to cast such aspersions on an unknown couple with a missing daughter simply because they had titles.

He rose, looking at me and taking in my generally damp appearance. 'Clean yourself up, Watson. We're going to pay a visit to a Lord and Lady. Try to look as presentable as Lestrade here.' Striding towards his bedroom, probably to take his own advice in changing his attire, he missed Lestrade's surprised expression. I caught his slight blush before he ran his hand over his newly trimmed hair. He saw me looking at him and glanced somewhat guiltily to the plate of biscuits.

'Good grief, man. Help yourself. I'll be back after I look as good as you do.'

I closed the door to my own room, splashing some water from my pitcher into the wash bowl to clean my face. 'Damnable, Holmes,' I thought, annoyed by something I could not entirely name. I stripped off my tie, shirt and vest—which was rather unsightly—cleaned a bit more, and pulled a thus-far dry change of clothing from my wardrobe. I buttoned my shirt, re-tied my tie, not looking forward to the woollen coat required by social niceties but not by the weather. I glanced at my reflection again after I had finished my ablutions. My hair was mussed from my efforts to clean it and from the day's worth of perspiration. I grabbed my comb and made desultory efforts to smooth it, ending with a rather unkept and greasy style. Not having any immediately better options, I determined that I too should see a barber in the near future.

I heard Holmes' footsteps shortly before I was finished and rushed to tie my shoes. Holmes had been known to leave me if I was not ready by the end of a period of time that was satisfactory to him, but undisclosed to me. After only another minute or two, I joined the two of them in the dining room, just in time to see Lestrade wipe his finger across the plate to pick up the last of the biscuit crumbs. Holmes looked me up and down, nodded, and strolled out of the flat, looking, at least temporarily, immaculate in his own freshened clothes. I wondered at the meaning of the nod, shrugged, and followed them downstairs into the cab that had brought Lestrade.

Lord Addington's London house was only a few miles from Baker Street, right at the edge of West Kensington. We arrived with few delays from the late afternoon traffic or inevitable congestion of pedestrians refusing to yield as they made their way home for the day.

The butler opened the door almost immediately after we knocked, clearly expecting additional visitors. Unlike Lestrade, I had been in the presence of the gentry from time to time, although the wide marble hallway and sweeping, spiral staircase in the centre of the room were impressive to me. After making our introductions to the man, we were ushered up the stairs and then the butler gestured for us to wait as he entered a room through a large, carved wooden door.

A portrait of the family, likely ten years old or so, hung on the wall immediately facing the stairs. Their youngest child appeared about eight or nine in it, a girl with lovely blue eyes and curly brown hair that hung in locks from blue ribbons, as was the custom for wealthy girls. I could hardly tell the difference between Emmeline and the girl who appeared to be her elder sister in any way other than height and dress colour, but then realised that was actually the way I frequently differentiated between members of the fairer sex. Those women with whom I normally came into contact, mainly those of a similar social status to myself, were fairly indistinguishable in terms of manners and behaviour. It was true, however, that those within my scope of acquaintance were primarily married to an acquaintance of mine, or a somewhat desperate and terrifying widow, or the wife of a crime victim. I had always endeavoured to have few patients of the fairer sex.

Holmes regarded the portrait with interest until the butler re-emerged and signalled for us to enter the room. It was a receiving room, meant for entertaining, with a small piano to the left of a large fireplace, thankfully not lit. Lady Addington paced along the windows, a few of which were open to admit the very slight breeze, and Lord Addington sat in what appeared to be his normal armchair near the fireplace, drinking some sort of dark golden alcohol from a crystal tumbler. He was an unremarkable man, brown hair, brown eyes, average height and weight; indistinguishable from thousands of other denizens of London by anything other than title and money. As we approached, he stood, setting his drink down on a small table, and coming forward to shake our hands, reaching first for Lestrade's hand in somewhat of a breach of custom. 'Thank you, Detective. Thank you for bringing Mr Holmes to help find our daughter. We appreciate the urgency and discretion in your investigation.'

'No, you do not,' Holmes remarked abruptly. 'You are pleased with his discretion but are quite lacking in a sense of urgency yourself.'

My shock from my companion's words prevented me from properly greeting either Lord or Lady Addington, and all of the rest of the room stared at Holmes. I became aware of my mouth hanging open

after a moment and closed it abruptly. Walking over to Lady Addington, I quietly introduced myself and escorted her away from her
husband under the auspices of my status as a doctor and her need to
avoid any further shock to her system. She and I sat on a sofa on the
far side of the room, and I assured her quietly that, although Holmes
had his eccentric ways, he was the most likely man in London to find
their daughter. That seemed to appease her, and she slumped
slightly onto the side of the sofa. She covered her mouth with her
handkerchief, and I hesitantly reached out to pat her elbow, twice. I
did not know how to further reassure her.

Holmes looked towards the butler and demanded to be taken to the
missing girl's room. The butler glanced at Lord Addington for
permission at the unusual request to allow a stranger to access the
privacy of her bedroom. The Lord nodded, reached for his drink, and
sank down into his armchair, tossing the remnants down his throat.
Holmes signalled for Lestrade to follow him and, as I made to stand,
he shook his head. 'Please do stay with Lady Addington, my dear
Watson; she has had quite the shock,' he said with a strange gleam in
his eye. He touched Lestrade's shoulder to usher him from the room,
a sight I do not believe I had seen before. 'What the deuce?' I
wondered to myself, as I turned back to Lady Addington and smiled,
uncertainly.

The Lord of the house seemed to take pity on my predicament and
met my eyes, asking, simply 'Whisky?'

'Yes!' I exclaimed, standing as if the sofa had caught fire. I followed
him to a sideboard with what appeared to be a fine selection of
cordials and spirits, and, when handed a glass, I murmured, 'To
finding your daughter.' He swallowed heavily, almost audibly,
clinked my glass, and drank. He reached into a pocket for a handkerchief to wipe the sweat from his brow. I drank as well and tried to
ignore the sweat trickling down my back. We stood together, wordlessly, two proper English gentlemen, as we waited for Holmes to

return. I tried not to think much on how I had abandoned my post as support for the Lady, as I looked around the room at the various paintings of fox hunts and gloomy English countrysides.

Only a few minutes later, the butler knocked and entered, followed quickly by both men. Holmes was smiling and his eyes glittered; he seemed delighted. 'Excellent work, dear chap. I agree completely.' He clapped Lestrade on the back to emphasise his point. I was aghast at both the compliment and the casual touch—nay, the touches—that I had seen today, and I quickly finished the remainder of my drink.

After glancing between the two of them, and worrying Holmes would, as he often did, keep his deductions annoyingly secretive or incomplete, I could wait no longer: 'Where is she?' I cried out.

'Why don't you share with Lord Addington our deduction?' Holmes asked, looking at Lestrade. My stomach clenched; neither these words—nor any words like them—had ever been spoken by the man.

Lestrade proceeded to explain how 'we' determined that the Lady Emmeline had likely formed a plan with a servant who had been dismissed from the household within the last year to leave the house, under stealth of night, dressed as a servant, leaving most of her belongings behind. Lestrade gave Holmes credit for his observation that a girl of her age would almost certainly have had letters from friends or a diary. Even if they had been well hidden from her parents and staff, they would not have remained hidden from Holmes (and Lestrade, apparently). The lack of any such items, as well as the lack of any sign of struggle, showed clearly that she left voluntarily. Find the dismissed member of the household, and you would find Lady Emmeline, he declared with an irritating amount of pride. I missed the exact flow of his words, as I was so disturbed by the choice of speaker in the summary of these deductions, which clearly originated in Holmes' sharp intellect. Why in all the name of everything good in the world was Holmes encouraging this?

Lady Addington inhaled sharply and exclaimed. 'Mr Porter! But he is twice her age!'

Holmes did deign to respond, rather than defer to his new partner. 'She was a rebellious youngster?' he asked, already knowing the answer,

'Yes, until about five or six years ago. We ran through more nannies and tutors with her than with her elder two siblings combined,' Lady Addington responded, still aghast at the idea.

'When did Mr Porter start with the household?'

She looked to her husband, narrowing her eyes, obviously trying to place the date. The Lord looked at the butler for guidance. 'About five-and-a-half years ago, sir.'

'Was he a man of some culture and education?'

'Yes. He managed our country estate. He was mostly self-taught but may have had a better head for figures than I do. I showed him a few fundamentals of French and discovered him reading one of our books in French a few months later. But he wasn't dismissed, he resigned with grace, saying he had a chance to manage an estate with a vineyard and a substantial winery in Provence. I could not keep him in Oxfordshire upon hearing that.'

'Then I think you know where your daughter is. Also, I suspect he may be a mentor for her, and might allow her to use her mind running the estate, rather than sitting quietly here and being asked eternally to obey someone.'

Lord Addington nodded to himself as his wife walked towards him, resting her head against his chest. He lifted an arm around her shaking shoulders. 'But I don't understand,' he asked after a moment. 'Porter left months ago. There's no sign that they were even in communication.'

'Exactly,' said Holmes, turning on his heel and walking out the door. Lestrade and I looked at each other, surprised, but made our leave quickly before Holmes absconded with our cab.

We were almost silent on the cab ride back to Baker Street, my annoyance apparently clouding the otherwise happy case resolution. The cab stopped, and Holmes and I exited, with the cab waiting apparently to return Lestrade to his home, wherever that was. Perhaps he had paid for a day's use with Scotland Yard funds.

After Holmes and I stepped down from the carriage, he turned back, reaching out to shake Lestrade's hand. 'Good work today, old chap.'

Lestrade shook his head, smiling, but looked puzzled. 'You as well, sir. Good day.' Holmes shut the door, rapped on the side to signal the driver and they left.

I stormed up the stairs, still not entirely knowing why I was unhappy to the point of being angry at the man. They had solved a case, determined that a young girl was safe, and they had done it in a way that set my teeth on edge. I tore off my coat and flung it across the back of my chair, reaching up to loosen my tie. The heat had dissipated some as the afternoon had bled into evening. I stalked across the room to fling upon a window, hoping for some breeze, as Holmes started to quietly laugh.

I turned to him, suddenly furious. 'How dare you!'

'How dare I what?' he parried, calmly, leaning back into the sofa. He had slipped out of his coat without my notice.

I realised I was not entirely sure, so I gestured wildly around my head. I shouted: 'Today! That! With Lestrade!'

'If I did not know better, my dear Watson, I would say that you are jealous.'

'I'm not jealous!' I yelled, then remembered that Mrs Hudson could likely hear every word spoken at volume. 'I'm not jealous,' I repeated at a more conversational volume.

'Then what explains your behaviour? Deduce yourself for me.' He stood, walking to our sideboard to pour two glasses of brandy. He handed me one wordlessly, as I gaped at him. He returned to his seat on the sofa, calmly sipped from his snifter, and repeated, 'You are jealous.'

'Of Lestrade,' I said dumbly, and not in the form of a question.

'Of Lestrade,' he answered. He seemed to be fighting a grin.

'I am not ...' I paused, as the events of the day rushed through my memory. I drank heartily from my brandy to stall for some additional time, which worked exactly as well as expected, which is to say, not at all.

Holmes crossed his legs, staring at me from the sofa. He gestured for me to sit in my normal armchair, and I walked across the room to flop gracelessly upon it. 'You have already deduced it,' I said quietly. 'Tell me what you think.'

He looked up at the ceiling again, as he had done this afternoon, apparently able to read some secret message from the cracks in the plaster, or the slight discolouration that comes from age. 'You have little regard for the fairer sex. You can barely tell them apart, and I heard you rise from your place next to Lady Addington almost before I left the room.'

I felt cold for the first time in days. I glanced at my drink in my hand, resting on my knee. I was no longer certain I could lift it to my mouth without shaking. I finally managed a single syllable, 'So?'

'I thought the events of today could prove a valuable experiment and they did. Otherwise, it was not a particularly interesting case,' he calmly stated, still staring upwards.

My hand rather involuntarily grasped my glass harder until I could see my knuckles whiten from the pressure. I took a breath and eased off, not wanting to provide him with any other fodder for his deductions. 'I do not know what I can say.'

'You can say that I am correct, as always.'

'Almost always,' I managed the comeback immediately.

'Today I am correct in every respect.'

'About me?' I asked, shakily.

His eyes finally left the ceiling and focused on me. They shone with something that might be certainty of purpose, much as he looked towards the end of a challenging case.

'No,' he shook his head. 'About us,' he corrected.

I finished my drink and set it on the table in front of me. I looked back at him, realising I had no grounds whatsoever to further debate the subject. I simply nodded, and he did as well.

RAIN

KYNDALL POTTS

The wind gusts and dry leaves swirl around their feet as they walk. A shadow falls across Regent's Park as the temperature drops and the chlorine smell of ozone signals the approaching storm.

'We should go,' John says, looking up at the dark clouds roiling above them.

'No, let's stay,' Sherlock says, and his gloved hand brushes John's.

'But It's going to rain, we'll be drenched.'

'I know.'

All around them people are hurrying to exit the park.

'But ...'

'I've always loved rain, dear Watson, especially the petrichor.'

'Pardon?'

'The smell of raindrops liberating organic molecules from the grooves and pores in rock or cement. It's called petrichor, and it's my favourite smell. Well, my favourite after the smell of you.'

John blushes, and as he does, the first raindrops fall, and there is a gentle rumble of thunder. They stop on the path and look up at the sky as the cool rain pelts their faces. They are alone now, safe from judging eyes and are indeed getting drenched as they stand together in the pouring rain.

They listen to the sound of it hitting the pavement and the summer-green leaves of the trees. *Patter patter.*

Sherlock takes John's wet face in his hands and bends to him. As their lips meet, lightning illuminates the sky with a jagged blaze.

LOVE BLOOMED
LINDA M. CRATE

love blooms in peculiar places,
but i knew it as soon as i felt it in
my bones;
i couldn't ignore the truth
when it stared me straight in the face
i have never been the sort of man
who leaves a mystery unsolved—

but it is so peculiar that love
should grow here
between two who spend so much
time together?

sixty cases i've solved,
only being bested four times;

and i do not care to make it five—

so here i am standing before you
offering you my heart, hoping
that you'll take it, because if i am left
here alone for another moment i fear
i may perish from the heartbreak.

COULD HAVE

LF HOWARD

Holmes paced across the floor of our flat, hands clasped behind his back, muttering to himself. I tried to ignore him, contemplating taking a respectable dose of morphine followed by a small brandy before bed.

Finally, I could stand it no longer, crying out, 'Will you sit down?'

He threw up his hands. 'You were stabbed today!'

'Are you angry with me?' I asked quietly.

His eyes flicked towards the sling holding my arm in place. Shaking his head, he answered simply, 'No.'

Waiting for him to continue, I looked towards the vial of morphine, which seemed a very long way off. Readily reading my thoughts, Holmes measured a dose into the nearby spoon. 'I am angry at myself,' he said as he carefully handed it to me.

'I don't recall that you stabbed me,' I answered, grimacing at the bitter taste.

'He could have killed you.'

'And if our positions had been reversed, he would have stabbed you instead.'

He laid the spoon down and sat gently on my good side. 'This is how you feel every time I do something reckless,' he said miserably, staring into the middle distance.

I reached up with my good hand, turning his chin gently so that he would look at me.

'Yes, it is, love.' I pulled him closer and kissed his brow.

A CORRESPONDENCE
SHAI PORTER

My Dearest Brother,

I wish to offer you and Dr Watson my congratulations on your latest romantic adventure. There was, indeed, a time when I would have read such an account with a degree of contempt: a notion we may, at some point in our lives which grows ever more distant with each passing year, have shared. But they say with age comes a degree of wisdom. (As your senior by some seven years I can attest to the veracity of this aphorism.)

There is yet another aphorism I wish to call to your careful attention. I, and in fact the whole of this great nation, owe our security to men like your Doctor Watson, as well as a debt of gratitude to his skill in wielding a sword on behalf of the Empire, but I am well aware that, in your view, it is eclipsed by how mighty his pen is. It is one you have long held. This view, perhaps somewhat unusual but no less valid, comes as no great surprise to one who has known of your nature from the start.

It has also been brought to my own careful attention, in light of some unfortunate events, that you might come to question my willingness to assist you in future endeavours. Let this letter, then—which I will admit has gone through sufficient drafting as fits one whose talents lie in numbers far more than letters in hopes of ensuring its lasting service as a keepsake—confirm that you have, as ever, my pledge of assistance in whatever form required, and, as family should never have to call into question (though far too often are made to do so), my love.

MH

~

MY DEAR BROTHER MYCROFT,

My partner wishes me to begin my reply by advising you that your letter has been the subject of much amusement within our household. It seems your ability to balance the sacred—for indeed we have undertaken, as you have deduced, our own version of a sacrament—with the profane is unparalleled. As I am the one with command of the ... pen ... at present, I will ask that you delay basking in your humour for just a moment more whilst I arrange my narrative in order of importance.

First, I must thank you. Not simply for the sentiment expressed, though that is certainly most appreciated, but for not following through on what I believe was your initial inclination—to publish a more heavily-coded version of your letter within The Times's agony column.

I have no doubt that I would have found such a message with ease—as would have one or two of the more clever and literate members of my Irregulars, and possibly the very brightest of the Yarders—but it was indeed a risk unworthy of taking despite your rather pedestrian notion that such a step requires a public announcement of some sort. As I have no wish to call upon you to expand your sphere of influence in an attempt to protect my person, you have my gratitude for exercising due caution.

In a similar vein, there is only so much of a blind eye which one can turn. Know, then, that it was this, rather than my inability to judge your character as worthy of my trust, which has led me to keep such information from you—in as much as anything could be successfully kept from your notice.

I also will not find fault in your assessment of my previous lack of interest in such matters, as I offer to you my own version of a merging of the sacred and the profane, though, in truth, it is not a profanity: For it is like a mustard seed, the smallest of all seeds on earth. Yet when planted, it grows and becomes the largest of all garden plants, with such big branches that the birds can perch within its shade.[1]

SH

∼

Mr Mycroft Holmes,

I have been assured, in no uncertain terms, that this letter is entirely unnecessary; that I should not expect to receive warning that my conduct must remain above reproach, lest I find myself in something akin to permanent exile; indeed, that it is perhaps inappropriate that I should send this at all. Still, it is my desire to convey a far greater degree of respect than I have hereto demonstrated during our all-too-brief acquaintance. My dear Holmes has also informed me that he is, in your eyes, no delicate blossom in need of protection courtesy of thinly veiled threats (though he did chuckle and say that, if such threats were to be made, they would not be idle ones).

My Dear Brother Mycroft, My partner wishes me to begin my reply by advising you that your letter has been the subject of much amusement within our household.

It is of little consequence to me whether they are idle or not.

Your brother has my heart.

It is a simple statement, which speaks to a greater truth.

My own brother had no abundance of concern for my well-being, be it in matters of love or of any other subject, so perhaps that is why I have been remiss in my attention to duty. I, therefore, beg your forgiveness and seek to honour your position, in as much as your younger brother might be considered your charge. I offer my apology for any slight I may have committed in following through with what likely seems, upon its surface, a hasty action. I wish to assure you that it was nothing of the kind, but instead the natural progression of our growing affection.

My actions would be the same, blessing or no, but please do not think that having such is entirely without meaning to me.

Yours in Faith,
John H. Watson, M.D.,
Late of the Army Medical Department

Found amongst reactants at 221B Baker Street

Sherlock, I do believe I have frightened your Army Doctor. His signature line has spoken volumes. Am I truly such a force to be reckoned with?

Found in the Transactions of the Honourable Society of Cymmrodorion periodical in the Diogenes Club

Do consider sending John an intimidating letter. I am told it is a fashionable way in which to express one's concern.

S

~

SHERLOCK STOP I SHALL NOT ENGAGE IN UNNECESSARY THEATRICS STOP I HAVE WORK ABROAD STOP DEVISE YOUR OWN THREATS IF NEED BE STOP

-M

~

MY DEAR SIR,

Sherlock is my junior and, as befits the situation, matters of our estate and other petty family concerns fall to me. That is the full extent of my role in loco parentis. I am not in possession of his hand to impart to you, and whilst I am assuredly a man of strong traditions, they do not extend so far as this.

Concerning your letter, I find no discourtesy in your actions to date. I can picture the smirk upon Sherlock's face, knowing its content. In truth, Sherlock's only need for tradition lies in his having something against which to rail. Though he will simply find it amusing, please know that I am indeed touched by the gesture, as I am also touched by his refusal to have tampered with this or to have disposed of it altogether.

That he should choose to spend his life with a man was foreseeable; that he should choose to spend it with one in possession of honour, surprising. Please do not think this means I find my brother dishonourable in any sense ... simply unconventional in the extreme.

Your partnership has endured, and that it should continue to do so is my fervent wish. Truly, I cannot see one of you thriving without the other by his side. A symbolic acknowledgement of this fact is more appropriate than any of the pomp to which I am a near-daily witness. It was already inevitable. Whether you have met my own standards of approval or not (though you have) is inconsequential.

Yours in Deepest Regard,

Mycroft Holmes

THICK AND THIN

SC TAYLOR

They've made their way here in fits and starts, through hard times, and thick and thin.

In a garden behind an old Sussex cottage, Holmes glances at Watson, sitting at his side, a singular constant. He takes in Watson's quiet existence, breathing it in alongside the scents of lilacs and lavender. The hot and pollen-thick air tastes heady on Holmes's tongue.

Watson speaks, his voice earning a lazy smile from Holmes. 'Eleven years,' he muses, making Holmes hum through upturned lips.

Their hands dangle, fingers brushing in a seeking touch. Across the yard, Holmes's bees dart from hive to flower and back, filling the backyard with their bustling noise.

'Eleven years,' Holmes repeats. Turning his head, he catches John's hand and brings it to his mouth. His lips drift along Watson's weathered knuckles with the ardour of a worshipful man, eliciting a quiet sigh.

'Any regrets?' Holmes asks.

Watson's eyes shine with fond devotion. 'Could have met you a little sooner, I suppose.'

A faint chuckle escapes Sherlock's lips. 'Now, my dear Watson, don't be greedy.'

Watson grins. 'God forbid.'

Still smiling with the sun warming his face, Holmes closes his eyes and listens to the drone of the bees.

HOLMES ON HOLIDAY

SHAI PORTER

'Vermissa Valley,' Holmes said in response to my clarifying the location he had in mind for our 'impromptu holiday.' I should have known he was being facetious.

Perhaps it was a sign of advancing age, but there was nothing appealing about a last-minute transatlantic steamship journey in the dead of winter. I was well aware the murder of a Pinkerton agent linked to the arrest of Boss McGinty—proceeded by some mudlarkers' discovery of a body Holmes insisted was Porlock—merited further investigation. If there was any chance that an American had risen from the ashes of the late Professor Moriarty's organization, or, as much as I hated to think it, that somehow the man himself had survived his descent into the falls of Reichenbach, I knew Holmes would leave no stone unturned. Still, I grimaced.

'All of his known agents have died or are still imprisoned. There is simply no one who remains to act on his behalf with any authority. His ties in the UK are severed. It is the only other location where he has shown any significant influence.'

'A soft place to land, so to speak,' I said, 'if he did indeed land in one piece.' Holmes chuckled at my dark humour. It was all I could do to prevent a wave of despair at the thought of his somehow having navigated that abyss.

'Fortunately, a man such as he cannot go to a place such as that without leaving obvious traces,' he said. 'When I am there, Watson, I shall know.'

By now, I am also all too aware that when Holmes sets his mind to something, there is no question he intends to see it through. The only choice in the matter, then, becomes whether or not I should accompany him—and his use of the singular communicated my participation was indeed a choice. In truth, it had ceased becoming one long ago.

'But ... now?' My mind wandered back to the vivid descriptions the man we later came to know as Birdy Edwards had provided for us. A cold, miserable, wretched place. I was not an overly religious man, but I enjoyed our carollers and puddings, and the fortnight's travel time alone seemed ... if not exactly excessive, then at least disheartening.

Holmes read my mind with his typical ease. 'Needs must. And as compensation for journeying to what the late Mr Edwards described in his memoirs as resembling hell, perhaps a brief visit to Philadelphia as well?'

'Hardly sufficient compensation, but I am, as ever, by your side.'

He grinned and sprinted to the door. 'I shall inform Mrs Hudson! Be sure to pack your warmest clothing. Layers, my good fellow! Layers! We will certainly need more than an Eley's and a toothbrush this time! The Red Star Line bound for Philadelphia leaves to-night!'

And so it was that we made our way to Liverpool and onward on an eight-day crossing bound for Philadelphia.

I had never been to the States. My previous experience on other continents was limited to Asia and Australia, but I had read a great deal of Philadelphia, and of Boston as well. They were said to be steeped in history, and I thought I could cure my ignorance of the finer details of American Independence. Still, it was the newness of the States which held their appeal. Their amiable, unpretentious charm.

The vessel was also new, and Holmes had secured us a well-appointed first-class cabin with a double berth. It was surprisingly similar to a simple country inn, with brass rails upon the beds and a washstand between them. Opposite the door was a wardrobe, and astride the port window, a small writing desk. That would have been more than sufficient for our needs, but what I had thought a water closet was actually a door to a second sitting room with a small sofa, which Holmes immediately claimed, stretching his long frame upon it and sighing.

'Have you ever been aboard a luxury steamer?' asked he.

I called out to him from the other room as I unpacked a muffler and a heavy coat. 'Certainly not. When I went to Australia, it was alongside my brother in little better than steerage. The cabin floor flooded on occasion.'

'I have never been. I hope the waves agree with me.'

'They have some periodicals,' I said, sitting at the writing desk, which was as much my domain as the chaise was Holmes's. 'Care for some light reading? It may serve as a distraction to the motion of the vessel.'

'No, my dear fellow. I wish to think. It remains to be seen if that is possible.' I heard a creaking sound as he settled into what I knew to be one of his poses best suited to contemplation, so I perused a copy of *The Cosmopolitan*, which my dear Mary had read regularly and had shown me was not without literary merit. It was between its pages that I had discovered H.G. Wells's mystical piece, whose title eludes me, about a journey to Saturn. I remember it had affected me greatly, shortly after I had lost Holmes, to read of the main character feeling outside of himself. 'It is not you that is reading, it is Bedford—but you are not Bedford, you know. I was something quite outside not only the world, but all worlds, and out of space and time, and that this poor Bedford was just a peephole through which I looked at life.'[1] So, although some might have dismissed it as a mere woman's homemaker journal, I was not at all surprised to find myself engrossed in a Mr Henry's *A Retrieved Reform*, when Holmes bounded into what I had just determined was my room.

'I believe a stroll upon the deck may help me get my sea legs. Care to join me on a quest for the smoking room?'

I nodded and slipped my *Cosmopolitan* inside a copy of *The Anglo-Saxon Review* for appearance's sake.

'Holmes, something about that whole Birlstone affair has always puzzled me.'

'Yes?'

'Why should Moriarty have been involved with goings on in the United States at all?'

He stopped and leaned against the ship's railing. 'Why would I be interested in the cases of Pinkerton's Mr Leverton, hero of the Long Island cave mystery? And why should he have followed our notorious friend Gorgiano in ... you called it 'The Red Circle', I believe? From New York to London? It's a small world, Watson, and mark my words, it will only get smaller. We are on the edge of an interdependence so great that we will find ourselves drawing this planet together in the tightest of bonds, for good or for ill.'

I nodded. It seemed somehow fitting that in these first years of a new century we should make our way to America.

'I should like to travel to Chicago sometime and visit my namesake's murder castle. I am told it survived an arson attempt more or less intact and simply sits there. Boarded up of course, but that is of little consequence.'

'Holmes!'

Breaking into a hotel designed to murder World's Fair tourists was exactly the sort of thing I expected from Holmes on Holiday, and I was suddenly immensely grateful for the distance between Philadelphia and Chicago. He laughed at my obligatory indignation, as I knew he would, and we headed into the smokers' lounge, settling in the fine leather chairs.

I had nearly finished the story when a young lad in uniform burst into the room calling for Holmes. The boy handed him a telegraph and with a single unbroken movement of his right arm Holmes handed it to me.

'It appears to be from a senior member of the Pinkerton Agency,' I said. 'Culprit has been apprehended. You may question him upon your arrival.'

'I have my doubts he is the true criminal,' said Holmes, 'but it will take no time at all to ascertain if it was he who orchestrated the deed. If Mr Edwards's account is accurate, and I have little reason to believe it is not, I think it likely Ted Baldwin was the only one to escape the policeman's net. As Boss McGinty did not survive the ordeal, someone would have needed to tell Baldwin to go after Edwards. It is possible it was his own vendetta, but a second agent continued to pursue him after Baldwin's demise at Birlstone. As I had mentioned previously, those were the brush strokes of a Moriarty. One can only hope the man in custody is capable of being the true successor and had somehow been elsewhere during the raid.'

The week went by in much the same fashion, with Holmes spending his days in relative isolation on his chaise and myself either reading or writing, and occasionally staring out the porthole, contemplating the vastness of the ocean Holmes thought to be metaphorically shrinking.

Once, in the dining room, a young lady sheepishly wandered over from her family table and asked Holmes to confirm his identity, amidst several blushes and false starts. When Holmes said that yes, he was the well-known detective, she asked him what he thought of Mr Gillette's portrayal.

'I have not seen it,' he replied, 'but I am told he will star on the West End this summer. Perhaps then I will be able to make a determination as to its accuracy.'

'He seems rather like you. The you in the stories, that is. I don't know if you are like you.' She blushed once more.

Holmes smiled graciously.

'Is there a real Miss Alice?' she asked.

'I have no wife, despite what Mr Gillette implies. But I am indeed spoken for.' The young lady smiled and struggled to ask another question so as not to seem as if that was her sole purpose for interrupting our repast. 'Well, I ...' her voice lowered to a whisper. 'Does Inspector Lestrade truly resemble a ferret?'

Holmes laughed, and I felt a pang of guilt for having garnered him a reputation as a man lacking in mirth (but little for permanently linking Lestrade to Rodentia). 'Yes, my dear young lady. Yes, he does,' he said.

She retreated to her table.

'I owe you an apology, Holmes, for perpetuating the notion that you are a man without emotion.'

'And I you, for once again not acknowledging your importance in my life.' He rested his hand upon my thigh beneath the draped table.

'Well, that cannot be helped. But as for my writing ...'

'You would think that your mentioning my coldness and disdain for women would serve to keep them from me, but I fear it merely poses a challenge to the more intelligent amongst them, bored with their lot in life.' He picked up the menu. 'Oh well, so be it. Now, I do believe the Wellington to be excellent if that man is a good indicator.' He gestured toward a tuxedoed gentleman at the Captain's Table. And so, the conversation turned toward the meal and away from our regrets.

We were undisturbed by fellow passengers for the remainder of the trip, though Holmes did take pains to go for his constitutional in the evening hours, when there was less of a chance of recognition, and we dined in our cabin as often as not, despite the lack of a true dining table. Holmes handled the hardships of the sea quite well and enjoyed looking at the vast ocean and the countless stars above it.

On the night before we were to arrive in port, I joined him as he gazed up in unguarded wonder. 'Beautiful,' I said.

He laughed. 'John, I am no maiden to be wooed by double entendre, nor am I beautiful.'

'And here I was, thinking you the most observant man on the planet. You should know I find you beautiful.' I kissed him. A simple kiss, nothing which would make him feel ill at ease, and I knew him to be aware we were quite alone.

'And here I was, thinking you had an eye for beauty,' he replied. 'But it is fortunate for me that you do not.' He kissed me this time, his lips pressed against mine for longer than I had dared. Kissing was not uncommon for us, but not frequent either. Physical intimacy, the likes of which I had had with my Mary, was certainly on offer, should he wish it, for we had long ago cleared the matter up over wine and a night-well-into-morning's conversation. What we had might not make sense to many, but it was perfect for us. It was of our own unique creation.

PHILADELPHIA DID NOT DISAPPOINT. On the way to our hotel, I passed the former residence of Edgar Allan Poe, which surprised me, as I had believed his residence to have been in Baltimore. It was here where he had written 'The Tell-Tale Heart' and 'The Gold Bug'. I resolved to pay a visit. As we walked on, I stopped to better examine a poster upon the brick of an alleyway which had caught my eye.

'Holmes? Holmes, if I'm not mistaken ...'

'Well, well, well. Yes. I do believe we know this ... Lily Lament.' The poster showed her with an exaggerated frown, and this was a far cry from the halls of La Scala indeed, but the former Miss Adler, turned Mrs Norton, was now, unmistakably, Miss Lament.

'The final performance is this evening, Watson. Shall we?' His eyes sparkled with mischief. 'That is, if you are not threatened by my reunion with the unrequited love of my life?'

I smiled. 'I should love to, Holmes,' said I. 'And I did tell them, rather directly, I recall, that you had no emotion akin to love for Irene Adler.'

'There was romance between the lines. It had to land somewhere.'

Miss Lament's persona promised melodrama, and the clothing of the dancers in the background promised ... something else ... but I had no doubt we would hear a fine voice emerging from even the bawdiest of performances.

'It might be quite distasteful,' I cautioned.

'It very well might. But I can weather your Gilbert and Sullivan as well as my Norman-Neruda.'

We purchased our tickets at the elaborately decorated booth, which was operated by a woman who, despite her advancing age, still clung to a certain dignified beauty. Holmes tipped his hat. 'Madam, might you have Orchestra Premium seating available?'

She smiled broadly and said, 'Certainly, Sir!' brightly in a voice brash enough to wipe away any façade of gentility—surely the American version of Cockney slang. Sliding the tickets forward, she said, 'That Miss Lily's really somethin' ain't she?'

Holmes turned toward me and gave a quick grin. 'I'd say she eclipses and predominates the whole of her sex, wouldn't you agree?' I hit him upon his hat with a rolled program guide.

The seats must have been quite expensive, as there was only one person seated near us—a rather handsome gentleman who quietly eyed first the stage and then down the aisles of the audience, gazing anxiously. I deduced he was awaiting his companion. As the house lights dimmed, Holmes leaned into me, and I felt the comforting and energizing warmth of his body. He took my hand in his as the curtain rose. Yes, readers will take what they wish from my stories regardless of my intent, that much is certain, but that they had never quite gotten it right, and never would, created an incomparable intimacy.

After some rather standard dancing girls of little interest to me and a magician of mild interest to Holmes only in the ways in which he might improve upon his act, the theatre went pitch, the raucous music changed to the saddest of violins and Holmes leaned forward in his seat. A spotlight grew upon the stage to encompass Miss Lily Lament, a sort of Pierrot figure. She looked just as stunning as I had remembered, though her chestnut hair was pulled back and her stage makeup gave her a melancholy air.

He took my hand in his as the curtain rose.

Miss Lament began a pantomime with musical accompaniment of a young lady getting ready for an elaborate ball, but her clothing was too large and her hat far too floppy, and her struggle to maintain decorum as adjusting one element caused an opportunity for another to malfunction soon brought even the most empathetic of souls into fits of laughter. Finally, disappearing behind a screen, the gown was tossed over the top and into the fire, and the spotlight faded out in much the same gradual fashion with which it had come to life.

A comedian followed, then more dancing girls, then a mentalist with whom Holmes seemed to take personal offense, and then Miss Lament appeared once more, in a solemn plea to her audience.

'As it is the holiday season,' she said, 'a time to rejoice! Let us not leave poor Miss Lily on such a sad note! But first, some well-earned applause for my musicians and our many friends behind the scenes who have worked so hard to bring you this show to-night!'

As the applause stilled, a stagehand wheeled in a dressing table with three large hat boxes upon it. She took from the first a washrag which she set upon the table and some cold cream. The second contained another exceedingly large ostrich-plumed hat, and the third a man's bowler. She angled the mirror toward herself and began her magic.

In a moment's time she had transformed herself into something resembling a child's doll, complete with a heart-shaped smile, large eyes, and dotted cheeks. 'I'm here to audition for your leading lady!' she said, her cacophonous voice alone bringing about much laughter. Her vapid portrayal of Juliet was filled with carefully crafted errors and ended in a squeaky soliloquy. She then turned back toward the mirror, wiped off her smile, and donned a moustache and the man's hat, transitioning to the casting director with remarkable ease.

In this guise, she went through a series of pained expressions and finally offered Miss Lament, in a voice surprisingly masculine sounding and lacking artifice, 'a role in the theatre which you were born to play!'—that of a cigarette and candy girl.

She whipped off the moustache at startling speed and did up that heart-shaped mouth to accept the position with gratitude.

Next, she donned the plumed hat and far more sophisticated makeup and mimed a leading lady preparing to go on stage, having a coughing fit, and presumably losing her voice.

Quick change back to manager, who had no choice but to use Miss Lily as a replacement. Yet another character, a chorus girl by the looks of it, suggested he change the crowning finale from the anticipated heart-rending ballad to a comedy routine, using the horrid voice of Miss Lily to great effect, before rapidly switching to the manager to have him say 'yes,' whilst leaving bits of the chorus girl costume still on deliberately for comedic effect. It was a brilliant move, and Holmes and I both laughed aloud. She combined the face of Miss Lily with the hat of the leading lady and cleared her throat as we all waited for her squeaky voice to belt out the finale. Everyone but Holmes, that is ... who released my hand to clasp his together at his celiac plexus, closed his eyes and stretched out his feet, preparing for the sound to wash over him like a wave. The beauty of her first note took the rest of us by surprise.

Holmes had heard Miss Adler sing when he had observed her from the stables when disguised as a groomsman, but I, having never heard her before, gaped at how such a full, rich sound could come from such a petite woman. I do not exaggerate when I say her voice was one of the most beautiful things I have ever heard.

I did not recognise the song, and admittedly the lyrics seemed largely inconsequential, though I remained somewhat aware that they were of kindness and hope and finding one's place. I was deeply moved. Her voice elevated the words from well-meaning prattle to a plea on behalf of all humanity.

As we rose to our feet, lauding the performance, Holmes shook off his languor as quickly as Miss Lily had changed personas, and we were both so absorbed that I jumped when someone behind me laid his hand upon my shoulder.

'Dr Watson, Mr Holmes, I should think Mrs Godfrey Norton would be pleased to meet you both backstage, if you have the time?' He had aged. Hadn't we all? But I felt the fool for not having recognised that handsome yet restless man in the front of the house as Mr Norton. His smile was genuine, his tone earnest. Of course we would meet with the celebrated contralto. I couldn't help but wonder if anyone in the audience would ever be aware of just what they had been privileged to have heard for their cheap holiday entertainment.

As we made our way through a maze of interconnected paths to the green room, Norton thanked us. 'It was such a gift to us, your having written, 'the late Irene Adler.' The King offered me his condolences in a rather elegant letter—and yes, the paper was the very same which you had described, Dr Watson.'

I nodded. 'After she had treated the disguised Mr Holmes so kindly, only to have us both betray her good nature, we felt it a simple gesture which might make your new lives just a bit more pleasant.'

'Watson deserves all the credit here,' said Holmes.

'That it did, gentlemen, that it did! We returned to New Jersey without incident. Irene even said she found being thought to be dead quite freeing. After reassuring Irene's grandfather that she was alive and well, that is.'

That Holmes's features still registered the tiniest traces of a guilty conscience at the mention of a shammed death remains pleasing to me, though it has been years since we had put the matter aside. I was far more intrigued by Mr Norton's expression, however. He showed not even a trace of jealousy when much of the world seemed to think Holmes and his wife an ideal couple.

'What brings you two to Philadelphia?' No air of suspicion lurked behind his words, merely an amiable curiosity.

Holmes was reticent. 'The case is closed, but I wish to examine its origins more closely. There are loose ends which, should they prove to still be present, need to be snipped.'

'Is it one of which we are all aware?'

'I had written it up some time ago,' I explained, 'but my literary agent seems to think the market favours short stories at this time over a longer novel and has refused to publish it. It does concern the late Professor Moriarty, however.'

'Ah. An entirely more sinister form of dubious and questionable memory.' I blushed, realising my words had been less than flattering. 'I ... apologise ... for my—'

'Not a bit of it, Sir, not a bit of it! My wife worked hard to leave a dubious and questionable memory; of this I assure you! And though there is no better woman for me in existence, I would not have her entirely reformed. In fact, I am glad she has deigned to share me with her first love—the stage. I will admit I am cut of more conventional cloth, but I have grown to appreciate her for all that she is.'

It did my heart wonders to see this unexpected confirmation of a happy ending. He turned a final corner and pushed open a sliding door, gesturing to some small settees amongst a mountain of discarded costumes and props. Holmes and I took our seats, and he joined us.

'Yes, there is an entirely different meaning behind 'questionable' in this particular instance,' said Holmes. 'It is perhaps beyond the limits of pure reason and entering into the realm of the spiritualist, but I do somehow feel that had the Professor survived, I would sense it.'

'You think it possible he may yet be among the living? That he may be in this very city?' Norton was equal parts intrigued and alarmed.

'No, not here. We are merely enroute. And so long as it remains possible, it warrants careful examination.' Holmes smiled. 'I do not wish myself to be derelict in my duty to civilisation.'

'Nor do I. I hope it ... draws to a suitable conclusion.' I felt as if Mr Norton and I shared the same uneasiness, a lingering fear that a part of Holmes would wish for his nemesis to be alive, if just for one last meeting of those formidable minds. But it soon became clear to me Mr Norton's lack of ease came from a different source.

'Gentlemen, I feel it appropriate to inform you that I was seated in the dress circle as well, as is my custom during Irene's performances. I do a final count of the number of occupied seats just before the curtain rises. I was ... observing both of you as the house lights dimmed.' He coughed lightly. 'Please feel free to express yourselves as is most comfortable to you in our establishment. There is no judgment here. I will admit it is new to me, coming from the legal world as I have, but Irene has been in the theatre for some time, and I assure you neither she nor any member of the company will so much as bat an eye.'

In the past, I had made a grave error. A rather inebriated man who was groping his equally inebriated male companion informed me that within those particular walls Holmes and I were free to do the same. Expected to, in fact. I informed him that that was not the precise nature of our relationship. Though true—such an act was not Holmes's preferred way of expressing physical intimacy, and therefore would of necessity not be mine—the disclosure through which I intended to have made Holmes feel more at ease clearly had the opposite effect. It took a great deal of effort for me to coax the information out of him: any attempt at clarification was not only unnecessary but served to make our relationship appear considerably less intimate. This time, I simply smiled and took up Holmes's hand in response.

'I'll see if Irene is out of costume,' Norton said, and slipped through a heavy velvet curtain.

'Your mind is filled with worries of all sorts tonight, my dear Watson. While the show was enjoyable beyond a doubt, I wonder if the burden of conversation will prove too much. Shall we take our leave?'

I gave the offer some thought and concluded I'd no desire to avoid Mrs Norton. The performance was remarkable, and I wished to tell her so. I expressed my thoughts to Holmes.

'Good,' he said, 'for I do as well. And there is no need for Moriarty to have any influence upon—' He stopped as Mrs Norton entered through the curtain.

'Mr Holmes! Dr Watson! How remarkably good to see you both! I trust my husband has informed you of our gratitude?'

'Yes, my dear lady, but we were the ones with the debt to repay,' said I.

Mr Norton joined the room and sat beside her as she responded to my statement. 'Nonsense! All's fair in love and war. We were on opposite sides, Mr Holmes. I have no doubt I would also have done whatever was necessary to protect my own interests and reputation.' She glanced at my hand grasping Holmes's just long enough to ensure us that it had not escaped her notice, then took up her husband's hand herself. There was some hesitation before she finally spoke the question which had clearly been forming.

'I have often wondered if the rest of your story is accurate, Dr Watson?'

'Well, a certain degree of embellishment is often necessary for ...'

'I have the photograph, if that is what you are asking,' said Holmes.

Irene bent her head down demurely. 'The one I had given the king as a replacement.'

'Many have interpreted it as a romantic gesture. Far too many,' he continued.

It was a surprisingly awkward moment. Both Nortons clearly had not known what to make of this information for some time. I daresay I had been unsure as well. And as such, I was responsible in part for the confusion and rumours which spread amongst the public. I confess I had assumed the request for Miss Adler's photograph to have been somewhat romantic in nature, using my own frame of reference. I have since found that rationale to have been extremely unlikely and did edit the opening pages to reflect such at the same time I had made the decision to portray her as deceased.

Holmes paused, then turned to me. 'Your position is blameless, Watson.' I should be accustomed to Holmes's ability to break into my thoughts after all this time, but in truth, it never failed to catch me unawares. I simply nodded.

'To understand fully, one must first possess some vital information. A reminder: the year was 1888. I had been growing my singular profession for just over 7 years. Long enough to feel myself an expert, but not long enough to actually be one.' He now looked at our hosts in earnest. 'Forgive me, Mrs Norton, for much of what I am about to say does not view you in the most favourable light. I ask for your grace. I no longer subscribe to all of these beliefs, but to explain my position, I must present them, bare and ugly.'

She brushed it aside, but there was genuine curiosity in her eyes, and perhaps a hint of trepidation.

'I had a great deal of sympathy toward womenkind, but not a great deal of respect. I stand by my decision to have not informed Miss Sutherland of her situation in full during the months before your case, though she may have recognised her circumstances once they appeared in print and made the connection. I pray she did. How does one tell a woman she has been having ... whatever intimate manner of relations she might have been having ... with her stepfather? But I am now focussing on that uncomfortable confession and straying from my own. I justified my legitimate concerns with some nonsense about removing a woman from her delusions. I would not have spoken those words had that case occurred a few months after yours and not before. And I remain certain I would not have been able to solve the case Watson referred to as 'The Second Stain' at all, had it not occurred after the events of 'A Scandal in Bohemia.''

A faint smile appeared on Mrs Norton's lips.

'In any case, that I could be thus thwarted in my plans was a hard lesson for me, as some have, in fact, speculated. But that is not why I wished to keep the photograph.' Holmes paused and sighed, then turned to face me. 'This did not appear in print, so I am somewhat reluctant to disclose it.'

'I hold no secrets from present company,' said I.

'Watson, do you recall how I questioned taking the case at all, and explained how I should only do so as the lady's safety was at stake, for the king would surely escalate to greater violence, having both burgled her home and had her twice waylaid?'

Mr Norton shifted ever closer to his wife's side.

I remembered it all too well. I thanked Holmes silently for not disclosing my part of the conversation, where I expressed incredulity that Holmes should wish to sympathize with a 'woman of that sort.'

'Yes, indeed. I could tell the king did not leave a favourable impression upon you.' Mrs Norton laughed.

'I had said to you, if you recall, that to live a successful life outside the conventional boundaries of society requires intelligence as well as bravery.'

I nodded.

'And that was the start of it. I had intelligence. There was ample proof of that. But did I have bravery? In some ways, I did not.' He cleared his throat. 'Mrs Norton, you had not only won against me, and the King of Bohemia, but you had won a far greater victory. You have led your life as you saw fit. Sang in concert halls in Warsaw. Took photographs with a Crown Prince. Fended off his attempts to force you to return them. Followed me to the outside of my very home in a convincing disguise and wished me goodnight! Whereas I ...' He shook his head. 'I was losing myself within my cases with little success. Watson explained it quite succinctly.' Here, he adopted the steady voice of a narrator. 'Holmes, who loathed every form of society with his whole Bohemian soul, remained in our lodgings in Baker Street, buried among his old books, and alternating from week to week between cocaine and ambition. I travelled a great deal. To Holland. To Odessa. Yet, my existence was a miserable one. You interpreted this as engagement in my work, Watson, but in reality, it was coping with the loss of what I had come to see as a part of myself.'

Yes, I had seen little of Holmes (and he little of me as well, my mind protested) during the early years of my marriage, but I had never thought of it in quite this manner. I had always considered the depth of his feelings toward me to have been a more recent development. Certainly, after he had left me to take on the near-impossible task of dissolving Moriarty's empire. Had that been punishment for my having rejected him? Had he witnessed my devotion to Mary and saw no place for himself in my world? Did he choose to let me think of him as dead out of the selfishness of not having me to himself, or the selflessness of removing Mary's competition from the scene? Whatever the reason, I was dumb-struck by my ignorance.

'Watson, guilt is the enemy of reason and I do not begrudge you a single second of your time with the former Miss Morstan. But it is important to acknowledge that this case arrived just as you had, though I had not in any way deserved it through my self-imposed isolation, returned to me.' He turned back toward The Woman. 'From start to finish, Mrs Norton, your case was what set me upon the right path, wherever it might lead. Conventional society be damned. So, it was not for a romantic purpose. Nor was it solely as a reminder of the cleverness of women—though I am eternally grateful for that. It was also an admonition that one could live life on one's own terms if one had courage enough. Perhaps the situation one had expected, even counted upon, would never arise, but, in its stead, there might arise something no less joyous. And so, my dear Watson, the following month, at the beginning of what you would later title 'The Stock-broker's Clerk.' I made the brash decision to ring you up, throw in some meretricious chatter regarding summer colds and slippers, and whisk you away with our client waiting impatiently in the hansom.'

My heart grew light at the memory.

'Mrs Norton, I trust that answers your query, and before I lead us too far afield, I must tell you that your performance was extraordinary. To master quick-change requires countless hours of practice, but to master comedy can only be done with natural talent.'

'And your voice ...' I added, unable to even find the right words to express my amazement.

'Godfrey runs the theatre, giving me time to work on my performance.'

'I may run it on paper, but you found the location, trained the staff, and continue to manage the daily activities ...'

'It has always been my dream. Now I am free to live it. I'm glad Wilhelm decided I was not proper enough for him. If he had made me his wife, I shudder at the life I may have been forced to lead, the compromises I would have had to make for the sake of 'respectability.' You are right, Mr Holmes. Life does not always deal the hand you are expecting, for it is often a far better one.'

'And now we must retire to our comfortable room, for to-morrow, we are off to Vermissa Valley. Goodnight ... Mrs Godfrey Norton.' And with those parting words, Holmes tipped his hat, and we walked arm in arm, as had long been our custom, to the Continental Hotel.

ONE DAY

LISBETH KING

He's told him he loves him in so many ways, without ever using the exact words. Holding doors open for him at crime scenes. Listening to him reading from the gossip columns of *The Illustrated London News* while warming his feet under his thighs. Playing the violin in the dark when a nightmare's tormenting him. Making sure he's sufficiently dressed when the weather's bad.

He's pledged his love for the madman with every praising adjective in the book. Of his brilliance out on a case. John relishes what emanates from that. The lovely blush on his cheekbones, placed there by John's endearments. In bed, overwhelmed by the description of his beauty.

His doctor understands that it's difficult for the great detective to express his feelings. But he knows that Sherlock Holmes loves more fiercely than most people. He considers himself privileged to share his life with this wonder of a man.

When John says 'I love you', Sherlock reciprocates in his own way, calling him 'my conductor of light'. The intensity in his eyes speaks volumes. Sherlock knows it's enough, but for John, he'll always try to improve. One day he'll be able to say those three words back.

THE HEART IN THE DETAILS

EM ROWENE

My friend's voice cut through the morning's quiet: 'I can't imagine what you've found in your own writing to distress you so, Watson. You've been eyeing the same page for the better part of an hour.'

'I most certainly have not,' I said. 'It hasn't been twenty minutes.'

My friend keenly eyed the leather-bound journal in my hands. I could see the curiosity ignite behind his eyes at my lack of denial, the furrow between his brows that spoke of frustration—frustration that he couldn't simply *deduce* his answer, perhaps.

My cramped script told of our latest adventure—more precisely, a lull in the tale where we had gone to St James's Hall for some music. Re-reading the account, I discovered a secret nestled between the words—one even the great Sherlock Holmes has not observed.

My account did not describe the music, pleasant as it was. Rather, it described Sherlock's enjoyment of it. It described his eyes, his form, his beautiful hands. It praised his mind, his talent, his nature. Reading it back, my secret was hardly a secret at all.

Still, I had not known.

Wordlessly, I offered the book, letting him take it with a delighted grin, knowing it was tantamount to a confession, knowing he'd see past my words to the heart behind the words laid bare.

BODY

BOOKER WEGNER

'I am my brain,' he says.

He has said this before. Still—his hands are long and spidery and sturdy. I take the risk—join mine to his. I run my thumb over his knuckles. 'Do you feel that?'

His eyes narrow. 'Of course I do.'

'I wonder,' I say, inspecting the calluses on his fingers, 'what these are from.'

Rather thrown off guard, he says, 'Violin playing, obviously.'

'Obviously. And this?' A white blotch on his beloved palm.

'Chemical spill. You were there.'

I huff a laugh. 'That I was.' The scar on his thumb now. 'Here?'

As if anticipating my reaction already, his pretty lip curls. 'Caught a suspect's knife.'

'Bloody madman,' I say with a wife's affection. 'A miracle the moss-rose didn't stab you too.'

'Your point?'

Oh, obstinate man. 'Other hands could do what yours do, but these are yours. What is a brain without a body to live through? You have played concerts, conducted experiments, caught killers. You have held—roses.' (In the dark, hiding from thieves and murderers, he has held my hand. I leave this unvoiced.) 'You are more than your brain,' I end lamely. 'You've got to be.'

He is quiet. Abruptly I remember that my hands encircle his and move to release them, but he tightens his grip.

'I've got to be,' he echoes. His eyes latch onto mine, and in return he slowly caresses my thumb.

SOLUTION

S.C. FRASER

This was the second time Holmes had barged into my bedroom in the early hours. Not that I begrudged him the liberty, but ... perhaps there was a more practical solution.

To my pleasant surprise, Holmes was amenable. Now, if he desires to wake me, he need only reach his arm across the bed. And I fancy that he sleeps better.

I AM YOUR MAN

ELEANOR NEWELL

I t was not long after my return to Baker Street that I remarked something of a change in my old friend Sherlock Holmes.

After my marriage—a marriage for which I still feel considerable contrition, both for my long-suffering wife and my desolate friend—there had been too few occasions for me to assist Holmes in his curious pursuits. I had almost always been able to make some little contribution to his endeavours; whether he had experiments to conduct, mysteries to solve, or villains to face down, I was his man. While we'd shared rooms in Baker Street, I had been available at any hour, night or day. At the first cry of 'Come, Watson! The game is afoot!' I became instantly alert, instantly prepared, and if instructed, instantly armed. Indeed, I did not like for Holmes to pursue his dangerous métier without my assistance and protection.

My marriage changed all that.

I had expected—no doubt naively—to be able to fly out of the door of my new home at a moment's notice, whenever Holmes might need me. No doubt it would have been wise to confer with a married man on the subject before proposing to Mary; but at the time I did not feel wise. Or rather, I thought I *was* being wise in marrying and moving out of the rooms where I had been deeply happy; for the temper of the times was becoming grim and, I believed, dangerous for my friend as well as myself. When Mary Morstan gave a gentle but clear hint that a proposal from me would be most welcome, I resolved to take a step which would secure the safety and respectability not only of Holmes and myself, but also of the lady.

I have always found it unfair that marriage is the only avenue open to women of a certain class. But now I learned that it was the only one available to men, as well.

Holmes had looked stricken when I told him, but he maintained his composure and wished me well. He later described this change in my circumstances as the only selfish gesture I had ever made in his regard; how I longed to make him understand that it was, if anything, the most selfless gesture of my life! I would go to any length to defend him, not only with a weapon, but with any necessary sacrifice.

Mary respected Holmes, was fond of him, indebted to him. She declared that she intended to make it possible for me to work with him just as before—indeed, with little difference noticeable between John Watson, bachelor, and John Watson, husband.

But it was not possible. Not because Mary was a harridan, or a clinging vine, or a shrew; far from it. But I had not fully realised that one has *obligations* to a living-companion. One cannot share space with another without falling into either a harmony or a disharmony of activities, of meals, of presence, of rest. Disharmony was alien to Mary, and repugnant to me; our marital home was then harmonious, but this meant that a thousand tiny threads bound me to that home as surely as Gulliver to the Lilliputian earth.

Did Mary constrain me? Not voluntarily, I believed and still believe; but her gentle voice asking if I was going out, where I was going, when I might be back, when she should see me again, was enough to make me constrain myself. Thus, many times when Holmes summoned me or solicited my assistance, I was obliged to excuse myself. I could not be forever leaving Mary alone in our house for unpredictable numbers of days while Holmes and I raced about London or beyond, tempting fate or playing pirates.

And I needed to support her, which meant that I had to build up the medical practice which I had allowed to become regrettably desultory.

It felt, in many ways, like slowly turning to stone. A companion in my home for whom I had real regard, but no devotion; a profession for which I had qualifications, but no true dedication. And on the other side of the ledger: a person, and a life, infinitely loved and agonisingly missed. Every day that passed without Sherlock Holmes, every week that passed without a collaboration, made me certain that I was going to simply disappear.

And the separation was hurting him, too. I could see it. He tried to receive each refusal cheerfully, or indifferently. But I knew him, and I saw his energy dimming with his confidence and his motivation.

At last, one day, it was enough for all of us, and Mary said—still gently—that our marriage had been a mistake, and that she would leave England for the continent. There, she said, she could begin a new life and dedicate herself to her true loves: the piano, and composition. She would support herself giving music lessons and live inexpensively and discreetly. This would leave me free to live the life I missed, and to dedicate myself to my writing. There did not seem to be the smallest sting in her words, as I would have expected had she known where my heart lay.

At last, one day, it was enough for all of us, and Mary said—still gently—that our marriage had been a mistake, and that she would leave England for the continent.

We parted, with some tears but without regret; had I not been so bound up in my own selfish sorrows I should have noticed that our marriage was as thoroughly constraining to Mary as it had been to me. I shall always remember her as a noble soul and, if such a relationship is even possible in an estranged couple, as a true friend.

Likewise, I shall always remember the look on Holmes' face when I opened the door to his flat, laden with two heavy cases and my medical bag. With no other creature in the world would I have been so bold as to assume an unequivocal welcome.

At that moment I was morally certain that he had been as desolate in his solitude as I had been in my companionate marriage.

'My dear fellow, I cannot tell you how very welcome you are! Your room awaits you. While you stow your belongings, I will make us up a hot toddy: you look to be perishing with cold.'

And with those warm words, that unexpected gesture—and with barely a hiccup in our usual compatibility—my friend and I resumed our accustomed cohabitation.

But something, so slight as to be for some time quite impalpable, had changed in him.

I HAD many hopes for our renewed acquaintance, our restored—dare I call it—intimacy.

I hoped that the fact of my *having been* married would suffice to quiet any talk about us, though any such talk would have been as inaccurate as it was indiscreet. Though when has that ever stopped a determined scandalmonger?

I hoped that my having left him voluntarily for another person might in time be forgiven; for without a word spoken between us, I had seen how deeply it had hurt him.

And I hoped—oh, *how* I hoped—that I might find the courage to tell him both why I had left, and why I had come back.

He certainly gave me encouragement to hope. In an altered mien, a more solicitous manner, in an occasional friendly gesture. Indeed, Holmes had always been free with the last of these; but now I detected a slight reserve, a shade of awkwardness, that had not been there before. And this, paradoxically, bolstered my hope: that the new touches to elbow or nape had a meaning that had not been there before, or that had been carefully concealed.

And for long weeks, that was all it was: the faintest stiffness on his side, a burgeoning hope on mine, that he understood me as at last he had brought me to understand him.

Whenever I dared to dream of a rapprochement, I sometimes imagined it prompted by the excitement and relief of a danger narrowly averted. Other times I imagined it borne of the exhilaration and triumph of a difficult case successfully resolved. I never had the courage to imagine it prompted by nothing at all except contentment, and a galvanising intensification of a quiet moment between us.

Yet so it was. We were enjoying a fairly rare night in, like so many that I had known with Mary, yet with Holmes, how very different! The silences were companionable, the occasional murmurs reassuring; the glances we exchanged were amused or contented, never anxious. Our nights in were to be relished, not endured.

I was sitting in my armchair before the fire, and he was sprawled on the red velveteen sofa a few feet away; I was reading, and all at once I became aware that he was looking at me. Staring at me. I felt a private little smile, a smile of satisfaction, tug at my lips, even as I felt a tingle of anticipation skitter along my spine. The atmosphere in the room had gone from placid to electrifying in less time than it takes to write it.

I felt myself compelled to look at him, as though he were mentally commanding me (a notion he would undoubtedly scoff at). With my eyes locked on the book on my lap, I held out until I could no more— knowing that when I did look up, my eyes would instead lock with his.

And so it was. His piercing gaze, his wildly ruffled hair, his—I could hardly believe it—outstretched hand, all made me set aside my book and rise from my chair.

I thought about saying something anodyne, to break the tension. A 'What is it, my dear fellow?' would put a hearty, manly distance between us, and restore the balance.

I didn't want to restore the balance; I wanted no hearty distance. I lay my book on my chair and moved toward him, my eyes fixed on his. Even as I rose and extended my own hand, I felt a chill. *And if I have misconstrued?* But that tender gaze, that turned heated as I advanced, reassured me.

His fingers flexed and I reached for them, touched them in a fashion unmistakably caressing. He pulled me down to sit on the empty portion of sofa, tucked into the S-curve of his body.

'John.' And with that one word—my given name, one banal syllable, a leap of a hundred miles toward intimacy—my last doubt vanished.

'Sherlock.' I could say no more.

A small sound escaped him, and his eyes closed, involuntarily, I think. Again, he said, 'John—!' his voice broke on my name, and I felt broken as well, as the stuff of my endless daydreams about him became real, as tangible and as warm as his hand in mine.

'I have missed your company so very much, my dear.'

'And I yours, my ... very dear friend.'

'Might we resolve to not repeat the experience? Truly, I think I might not survive it.'

He kept his tone light, I think with some effort; my own went husky with emotion, and I gripped his icy hand tighter.

'I know I would not. My dear ... my Sherlock.'

Again, his eyes fluttered closed for a moment, then opened, his usual hawklike focus restored. 'May I, John?' And to my tender amusement, the permission he was asking was only to kiss my hand.

'Of course you may; if I may do the same.'

'You may do anything you wish, my dear. You are the expert here. I rely on your guidance in this area in which I am a novice.'

Giving the lie to his claim, he drew my hand to his lips and traced over my skin and joints until I was trembling with anticipation. Oh, brave new world, that has such touches in it!

As long as I had known my friend, we had never permitted ourselves so much; and intimacies much greater, in my varied amorous past, have affected me much less.

'And I—may I?'

And his dark, speaking eyes smiled as he echoed me: 'Of course you may, if I may do the same. And thus the first time our lips met, we were both smiling.

His hand slipped my grasp and cupped my face, stroked my cheek, and he surged up to bring our mouths together again. It was a kiss so long dreamt of, so hotly desired, that I felt myself as aroused as if we had begun tearing at each other's clothing, grasping for each other.

'Take me,' I murmured, 'to your bed,' between one kiss and the next, and shakily we both rose and retired to his room.

AND WITH THAT NIGHT, my new life began with my dearest friend, my … dearest. It was a life lived half in the shadows, of course, and that brought its own occasional bitterness; but for the most part, we were so enchanted, so euphoric, that for long periods we were able to forget our forced concealment.

I had never known this kind of ecstasy, and nor I think had he. We were not merely lovers, we were in love; and we had been for so long and so hopelessly that the simplest gestures and touches were overwhelmingly stimulating, overwhelmingly gratifying.

Only one thing happened to give me pause.

I am a simple man, Holmes has always said, and for myself I can attest to my very simple tastes in the matter of coitus. The fact of our mutual—I should not say infatuation—but captivation added all the spice, all the mystery that I could have dreamed of.

But not, apparently, all the spice that *he* could have dreamed of. At first his murmured proposals were tentative to the point of bashfulness; but as he saw that I was invariably enthusiastic about anything he suggested, he became gradually more confident. More daring.

More, shall I say, adventuresome.

At first the activities he broached were familiar to me by rumour, if not always by experience; and they were a source of exhilaration and delight of heart and body alike. Indeed, it was a thrill to learn that my beloved had desired me in all the ways that he had, and all the ways that I had, and then some. Perhaps the forced secrecy of our congress, of our sharing a bed, promoted a sense of transgression that encouraged experimentation, even wildness.

I cannot say just when I began to grow uneasy—or rather, just when I *recognised* that for some time already, I had been growing uneasy. Not at the matter or substance of his little initiatives; though some were surprising at first, all turned out to be delightful and delicious. No, my unease was of a different, and timorous and perhaps selfish sort.

Was the man of my dreams going to grow bored with me? With what we did together? Were my uncomplicated desires, my elementary emotions, not enough to satisfy him? Was I *already* beginning to pall on him? I could not bear the thought; having finally found my bliss, I could not contemplate with serenity having it snatched away because I was (am) too ordinary, too tame, for a man of such infinite curiosity and energy.

He began to sense my growing apprehension, naturally, which manifested itself in a new circumspection. No man alive is more observant than he; and my unexpected reticence may have generated resistance in him, just as my own fears did in me. In response he became, if anything, more daring in his desires to experiment, to vary things, to try fillips and enhancements that left me frankly concerned that he was already bored to tears in our intimate life.

It all came to a head late one Sunday evening. Sundays were the time we could reasonably expect to be uninterrupted, to take advantage of what privacy we could to enjoy and to cherish one another. I was slowly, tenderly, unbuttoning the shirt he wore under his dressing-gown, when he put his lips to my ear and whispered something that I'm quite certain made me blush.

'My dear fellow—!' I expostulated vigorously, without even reflecting what a rejection such vehemence must convey to him.

He froze, then turned away and clambered off the bed as though he couldn't get away from me fast enough. This would not do. From perfect complicity we had blundered into perfect misery, and I pursued him into the sitting-room and caught him by the sleeve.

'My dear, please—tell me what I must do to please you, to satisfy you. I've a dreadful fear that you must be thoroughly bored with my attentions, and I never wish to disappoint you, but I fear that—' and I could not, honestly, I could *not*, continue, and speak my worst fear aloud: that he would leave me, after having shown me the only true rapture I had ever known.

He turned back with an expression of the blankest astonishment. 'Bored with your—my own John, you *cannot* think so. You, the man of the world, experienced in all kinds of amorous activities with—with—both sexes, in all corners of the world—! How could *I* be bored, with so experienced and solicitous a lover? It must rather be the reverse!'

He looked so honestly shocked and perplexed, so distressed even, that I forgot my own fears and thought only of reassuring him.

'Oh, my dear, oh no, I could never be bored with you. You have been the light of my life from nearly the first week of our acquaintance; and knowing each other as we do *now*, has only made you all the more essential to me. If anything, it is I who must have led so much more sheltered a—a love-life than you, that many of the things you urge that we try—several of which I have cravenly avoided—are not only entirely new to me, but unspeakably *intimidating*. Forgive me my hesitations and my avoidances, I beg you. I will try to take courage; I do assure you.'

Now he looked even more astonished, though I've no idea how he managed it. '*Your* experience of love more 'sheltered' than mine? How can you think it when you *are* my entire experience of love? My heart, I was afraid that you must be concealing a growing impatience with my inexperience, my naïveté; so I was trying to rise to the occasion, to your greater knowledge of the Olde Daunce, as they used to call it. To show you I am willing to learn, to try new things with you.'

A mighty relief seized me. Each of us had been attributing to the other a breadth of experience and of curiosity that was if not wholly absent, then at least grossly exaggerated. And both had been fearing a waning of interest in the other that was even more illusory.

Out of that very relief, I threw my head back and laughed. Sherlock was disconcerted at first, and a bit offended; but as he saw that my laughter was at us together, not at him, he began to join in. Soon we were teasing each other, plying each other with ever more outlandish suggestions between kisses and caresses that may have been bland in comparison, but which were all we needed for perfect happiness.

'You could dress yourself in Mrs Hudson's underdrawers, my dear, and burst out of a cake!' he warbled, in a creditable impression of the lady herself.

'Better,' I cried, 'we could invite her to burst out of the cake for us!' And instantly we were howling at the terrible irreverence we were showing our kindly and irreplaceable landlady.

'Speaking of inviting, we could have a few fellows in and make a regular orgy of it!' And we were off again, until our faces were red and hot from laughter.

'Oh, who needs them, my boy, let us simply coat you with honey and I shall—'

'Well, we *could*,' he interrupted, speculatively.

'Your sweet tooth will be the death of *me*, in that case.'

And when we had regained our composure, I assured him solemnly, 'Your presence, your affection, your *hunger* is all I need, my dear, for perfect happiness. For now, let us learn each other gradually, and simply; let us take this journey together. Should one of us come to feel the need for more elaborate stimulation, he may bring that up in the clear understanding that his own curiosity motivates the proposition, not an imagined dissatisfaction in the other.'

He looked at me with that startling gratitude and tenderness that have made me the happiest and luckiest of men.

'You are a genius, John, honestly you are. Of course you're in the right of it. We need no devices or costumes or stimulants,' and here his voice sank low, 'when everything about you excites me beyond my self-control. Thank you for relieving me of anxieties I now see were foolish. And now—if we may start again?'

We were soon back where we had started, just the two of us, without the spectre of exotic or acrobatic feats of prowess. And that Sunday night, like all our times after, constituted a supremely joyous joining of our hearts and bodies, as we learned and taught, gave and took, shared and exchanged, *the love that moves the sun and the other stars.*

MOMENTS

LISBETH KING

J ohn Watson has many favourite moments with his beloved
Sherlock Holmes.

Watching him deduce crimes, clients, even the good doctor
himself.

Sitting by the fireplace in companionable silence, Holmes smoking
his pipe, John reading the newspaper or a book, glasses filled with
fine port at hand.

Chasing criminals through London or at the countryside, his pistol
ready, the adrenaline singing through his veins.

The most treasured ones are when they lie in bed together. When
John calls him Sherlock, sweetheart and my beloved, and Sherlock in
return calls him John, my dear boy and darling. The love and affection between them are so strong and intense. John's heart fills. It's an
exquisite sort of pain.

John loves to observe his lover in the afterglow. All limp and pliant.
His features smooth, his beauty conspicuous.

Sometimes he's quiet, other times talkative, like tonight.

'My dear boy. I think we will have a splendid retirement in Sussex when the day comes.'

I play with his hair, which he enjoys immensely. He leans into my touch like an agile, gorgeous cat almost purring.

'Pray tell, what we will do there, my beloved,' I say quietly.

'You will grow vegetables and write our memoirs. I will tend to the most fascinating creatures,' Sherlock says lazily.

'Ah, and what creatures are those?' I inquire.

'Bees.'

ACT III: AUTUMN

THE TEMPEST

CARISSA WING

'Damn this storm,' Watson said in a low mutter.

The whole of London was blanketed in a dark and dismal pall. It was weather better suited to the bleakest days of winter rather than a temperate fall, but the equinoctial winds were indifferent to our expectations. All day and all evening, the gusts had battered the city. In our flat, the glass panes trembled and rattled, and the thick sheets of rain falling from heavy clouds obscured what little might be seen beyond them. From where I sat working on my commonplace book, I watched as Watson pulled his dressing gown closer around himself, although the room was warm enough. He stared out the window, his mood as foul and his expression as dark as the tempest that beat against the pane.

In truth, since we returned to sharing rooms at Baker Street, he was often morose and distant. This was a John Watson I did not recognise, a disquieting departure from the genial bonhomie I had been used to. Even more disquieting was his unwillingness to discuss the cause of his ill temper. I was, of course, hardly in a position to point an accusatory finger at his churlishness, the pot being considerably blacker than the kettle in this regard. I suppose his changed disposition was understandable and might even have been expected: the good doctor had endured enough tragedy over the past three years to break the fortitude of even the most stalwart of men.

However, the source of his grim mood tonight, at least, was readily apparent to me.

'Yes, Openshaw's death was a senseless tragedy,' I said aloud.

He turned to look at me, his eyes wide.

'How did you—' He stopped and sighed. 'Why your ability to read my thoughts surprises me, after all the years I've known you, I cannot fathom. Then again,' he continued with a slightly enigmatic twist to his lips, 'your very presence these past few months, raised from the cauldron of the Reichenbach Falls, has yet to lose its novelty.'

With a sigh, he returned his gaze to the window and the storm without. 'Seven years. It does not seem possible that so much time has passed since John Openshaw stood in these very rooms. I remember the young man so clearly.'

'No doubt it is because you recorded the case in *The Strand* only three years ago,' I said.

'Perhaps,' he replied, although his tone indicated he thought otherwise. 'At the time, it was very important to me to recall the particulars in as much detail as I could. I felt I owed Openshaw that much, at least.'

'I confess I thought it odd that you chose to include that particular tale in your chronicles. It was ... not one of my more successful cases,' I said.

His eyes shifted in my direction. 'No, it was not. It was a singular one, however.' He moved to his armchair and lit a cigarette. The familiar tobacco scent was comforting, but the smoke hid his expression from my view.

'I suppose that is true,' I said with a shrug. 'We do not often cross paths with the Ku Klux Klan on this side of the Atlantic. It would have been more singular indeed, had we been able to lay hands on James Calhoun and his accomplices. It is a shame Openshaw was careless.'

'Oh, come now,' he said, nettled, 'you cannot possibly blame the poor soul for his own death!'

'Blame him? Hardly. But I warned him, did I not? I made it quite clear that the threat to his life was real and imminent, and urged him to take every care.'

'Yes, you did. Even so, I would imagine that his death weighs heavily upon you, regardless.'

'Should it, still?' I queried, at something of a loss at his assertion. While I am not the uncaring automaton he makes of me in his stories, neither am I given to pointless regrets. 'It was not I who pushed him into the Thames.'

'Of course not. But surely in hindsight, you will agree that something more should have been done,' he cried. He jumped up and flung his cigarette into the fireplace, quite upset. In fact, excessively so.

'What would you have done, pray tell?'

He lost all patience, and with it, any semblance of dispassionate discussion. 'What would *I* have done? Well, instead of sending him off on his merry way, alone and unguarded, I would certainly have gone with him and protected him. I knew that his enemies were dangerous, ruthless men, for you had made that very clear. I knew that they were desperate and cunning and would stop at nothing to destroy the object of their hatred, the man responsible for their downfall. I knew, I was forewarned—'

His agitation was rising, and with it, my unease. I arose and crossed the room to where he was standing. 'Watson—' I said, but to no avail; he ignored me and continued his tirade.

'—and yet, I lost focus at the critical moment and allowed myself to be distracted by the flimsiest of deceptions, allowed myself to be stupidly drawn away from the man I had sworn to protect, with my own life, if necessary, fooled like some gambolling pup into abandoning my post.' Grief and self-loathing rose up like a wave, a force of nature, relentless and implacable. 'I abandoned you.'

'No! My dear fellow—' Thoroughly alarmed, I tried again to stem the tide, but he would not be dissuaded.

'"She could hardly live a few hours, but it would be a great consolation to her to see an English doctor." What puerile rubbish! It was so bloody obvious, the most transparent ruse, and I was completely taken in. I even saw the figure of a man hurrying in your direction, and instead of sensing the trap, I dismissed his presence as inconsequential. At the most critical time in your life, I was useless.'

I grabbed him by the upper arms and shook hard. 'Stop this nonsense at once,' I said. 'You were most certainly not useless. You did not see the truth because I hid it from you, because I needed you to believe the lie. I needed you to be out of harm's way.'

'Yes, so you have already said. You must pardon my lack of gratitude for your chivalry,' he said in a biting tone. He pulled himself out of my grasp and turned towards the door, but I would not let him pass.

'I do not expect your gratitude, nor do I deserve it,' I said. 'You have every right to be angry.'

If I thought my *mea culpa* would soothe his outrage, I was quite mistaken.

'Yes, I do.' His voice hardened. 'I categorically refused to leave you, as you will recall. Can you imagine how I felt when I realised I had been tricked by Moriarty into doing the very thing I was dead set against? And that you knew, and allowed it?'

I prided myself on having a very good imagination. Watson's anguish and shame became my own, burning and twisting inside me.

'Why was I even there on the Continent,' he continued, 'if not to assist you? Why did you have me accompany you in the first place?'

'I—' Suddenly our positions were reversed, and I was the one in treacherous waters.

My hesitation was my undoing. Watson narrowed his eyes. 'Why, Holmes?'

Rallying, I said, 'I desired your company. I said as much at the time if I recall correctly. It was unconscionably selfish of me to expose you to such peril, but in my hubris, I ignored the possibility that the snare I had laid for Moriarty and his gang might fail, and did not anticipate the repercussions—'

'No.' Watson shook his head decisively. 'That explanation will no longer suffice. You would never have undertaken such a daring enterprise without considering every conceivable outcome, and you cannot convince me otherwise. You knew better than to underestimate the man you called the most dangerous and capable criminal in Europe. For God's sake, you put your affairs in order before you left London!'

'That was merely a precaution—'

'And that is precisely my point! You were clearly aware of the risks. So again, I ask, why did you take me with you? And do not repeat that fiction about the pleasure of my company.'

'It was not fiction,' I said, wounded but determined not to reveal how deeply. 'I did desire your companionship, as I still do. As I always have. I am not in the habit of lying to you.'

Watson barked out a harsh, unamused laugh. 'No? I suppose that would depend on how one defines lying. A lie of omission, then.'

'Please, there is no need to revisit my faults, which we can both agree are legion.' Once again, my attempt at self-disparagement fell flat. The desperation edging my brittle words was clear and unmis-takable.

'Enough!' He struck the window frame with a force nearly equal to the furore raging on the other side. 'What else have you omitted, Holmes?'

I felt the blow as though he had struck me, its vibrations reverber-ating through my body, insistent and demanding, brooking no further resistance, no further denial.

'Enough!' He struck the window frame with a force nearly equal to the furore raging on the other side.

'Nothing! When I said I desired your company, that is exactly what I meant. Your companionship in my work, your presence in my life, your unwavering and undivided loyalty—I keenly felt the loss of these things when you married. Where I once had you in abundance, I was now deprived, in want. So yes, this was a chance to have you exclusively at my side again, and I found I could not let the opportunity pass, despite the dangers.' I shut my eyes and heard myself say, 'I omitted nothing. I was, I fear, rather obvious.'

For long moments, there were only the sounds of the crackling fire and the wind-driven rain. Then a short, rueful snort drew my eyes open.

'You forget yourself, Holmes. "Obvious" to you is a complete mystery to the rest of us mortals.' Watson was not smiling, but his anger appeared to have dissipated, replaced by bafflement and ... something else, some emotion I could not identify. 'I had no idea you felt this way. You never said a word.'

'It was not something I cared to admit to myself, much less to anyone else. Especially not to you.'

'But good heavens, man, it wasn't as though we had cut all ties. I was still interested in your work. I always came when you sent for me, as soon as I could arrange matters. There was never any question of my refusing to participate in your cases. Mary understood and never begrudged the time I spent with you. Why—?'

Why? How could I possibly explain that I wanted the whole of him? Or as close to the whole as I could have.

From the early days of our acquaintance, Watson chose to court the feminine sex rather than pursue illicit pleasures with the masculine, although I had long ago deduced that he had experience of both and even preferred the latter. My own inversion I kept well hidden behind a façade of clinical detachment; a façade bolstered, as fate would have it, by Watson's portrayal of my unfeeling persona in his stories. It was an exaggeration for literary effect, but one I had encouraged. Better that everyone, and Watson in particular, thought of me as disdainful of the softer passions, lest they suspect I was tortured by them.

In this manner, we had forged a life together. We were partners in all but the carnal: this, while less than satisfactory on several levels, had been sufficient. Cherished, even.

But then he plighted his troth to Mary Morstan, pledged to her those parts of him that were beyond my reach: his love, his ardour, his fidelity. And that was beyond unbearable. I was unable to sever the relationship completely, as my addiction to the man was stronger than any drug that ever flowed through my veins; and indeed, Watson would not have countenanced such a break in our friend-ship. However, for the sake of my sanity I had put as much distance as I could between us, for as long as I could stand it. Until the threat of Moriarty, until the possibility of meeting my match loomed large and real, and I could stand it no longer.

'I am a conceited sort of fellow,' I said finally. Another lie of omission, if truer than most.

'No,' he said slowly, more to himself than to me. While I had been pondering on how to answer him, he had apparently been doing some thinking of his own. His eyes were distant, focussed some-where beyond this place and this time.

'No?' I asked dryly, though only half in jest. His intense concentration was slightly unnerving. It was as if—

'Eh?' He blinked, then looked at me in the here and now. He let out a slight huff. 'Well, yes. You *are* a conceited fellow. However ...' He stepped in closer and examined my face, studied my expression, as though seeing it for the first time. I felt my breath catch.

'I think ... I am finally observing that which I have seen and deducing from that which I have observed.' He reached out a hand, slowly but deliberately. I stood, mesmerised, as his fingertips came to rest lightly on my dressing gown, directly over my heart. For several moments, we were frozen in this strange tableau.

'Oh, Holmes.' There was wonder in his voice, and no small amount of contrition. 'How long?'

'I ... cannot recall,' I stammered. Indeed, I could not. How long *had* my heart been his? When had I relinquished it? Was it when he so readily agreed to accompany me to Lauriston Gardens, our first case together? Or was it in the early weeks of our joint residency here at Baker Street when I realised he enjoyed a mystery and so I endeavoured to make myself as intriguing and enigmatic as possible? No, it was earlier; perhaps the moment I first laid eyes on the invalided soldier Stamford brought to the laboratory at Bart's, improbable though that may seem. I no longer remembered a time when I had not been madly in love with him, and when you have excluded the impossible, whatever remains, however improbable, must be the truth.

'I see,' he murmured, and his sympathetic gaze made it clear that he understood what I had left unsaid. 'Forgive me, my dear boy, for being unforgivably obtuse. My own epiphany was a far more recent event; precipitated, ironically enough, by your apparent death. After I lost you, *I* was utterly lost, inconsolable, for a very long time.' His hand settled more firmly against my chest, the contact a tangible assurance that I was not a ghost. 'I did not consider my grief unnatural, mind you. It was natural that I felt bereft, I thought, considering our long and intimate acquaintance, and the guilt I carried for having failed you. And then Mary .... It was after Mary had gone, God rest her soul, and I mourned for you both, when I began to comprehend that the depth and breadth of what I had felt for you was far beyond mere friendship.'

My heart thudded painfully, and I looked away. Whilst I had been abroad, Mycroft kept me apprised of Watson's situation as best he could through our sporadic correspondence. When word of his wife's passing reached me, I felt the weight of his sorrow from afar, but the realisation that his pain had been magnified by my deception—

Watson touched my face, drawing my gaze back to him. 'You did not know,' he said. 'How could you? I had not known.'

I pressed my hand to his, marvelling at the feel of his warm fingers against my cheek, solid and real. He smiled, and I marvelled also at his capacity for empathy and forgiveness.

'When you returned,' he continued, 'I was overjoyed. For the obvious reasons, of course, but also because you wished to share rooms with me again. All would be well; all would be as they once were. I thought that was what I wanted.'

'But a door once opened is hard to shut,' I said, speaking from bitter experience. He nodded.

'God, yes, deucedly hard. I found myself growing more and more dissatisfied with how things were between us, yet I was unable to see my way clear on how to change them.' He shook his head again, but his eyes were twinkling now. 'You have often said that it is a capital mistake to theorise in advance of the facts, but an argument can be made for taking too long to theorise, I think, and you are as equally at fault here as I am. The truth was right in front of us, all along.'

My mouth went dry as he moved his hand to cup around the back of my neck, the other wrapping around my waist.

'You will excuse me if I dispense with ... formalities,' he said, his voice dropping low. 'Now that I have applied your methods and reached the correct inference, I find I am eager to be getting on with things. We have wasted altogether too much time.'

An impartial observer, had there been one, might have been hard-pressed to say which of us closed those final few inches between us, whose lips sought out the other's, whose arms demanded surrender, and won. As there was no such observer, I shall simply say that while Watson is arguably more experienced in these matters, I too have ... travelled to several continents. In any case, this was a joint victory, the outcome, a partnership full and equitable in all things.

The tempest continued to rage outside, violent and unabated, but in the haven of our flat we were warm and dry, safe in each other's embrace. Home, at last.

DESCENT

S.C. FRASER

I have grown so accustomed to work that I hardly know what to do with myself now that the chase is done. A black cloud descends upon me; I have no appetite. Neither music nor mystery can rouse me.

But one thing can. My stalwart friend, my Watson. He will find the means to deliver me from this dark pit.

SOLACE

KYNDALL POTTS

I stand in the dark outside his door.

Raise my hand to knock.

All is quiet.

I let my hand fall.

I put my ear to the door.

The sounds that woke me from my fitful sleep have ceased.

The sounds of fear. Of pain.

I turn to leave. I want to stay. I want to stand by his bed and watch him sleep, but I don't.

He moans.

I turn back.

'Watson,' I say.

He whimpers.

I open the door. Just a crack.

'Watson,' I repeat.

He doesn't answer, and now I hear his rapid breathing. Fragments of words.

'Murr ... Whaa ... No!'

I push the door open.

He's tangled in the sheets, and the moonlight shows the sweat on his brow. His torment makes my heart ache. I can only imagine what horrors live in his dreams.

So much pain. So much loss.

My brave soldier.

I sit on the bed. Place my hand on his shoulder.

'John.'

His eyes open. Wild and searching.

But I'm not the enemy.

He relaxes.

I lie beside him. Pull him to me.

He lets me.

I cradle him against my chest. I stroke his hair.

He sobs.

'You are safe,' I say. I kiss his forehead, then stop, afraid I have overstepped.

'Don't stop,' he whispers. 'Stay.'

And I think my heart might burst.

FALLEN

CARISSA WING

'**M**y dear Watson,' Holmes's final message began.

I fell to my knees, the letter clutched tightly in my hand.
I do not know how long I remained there: frozen at the edge of the
path, surrounded by the incessant roar of water, staring down into
the very pit of Hell itself. Long enough that I was soaked through
from the dank and clammy mist; long enough for my cries to hoarsen
to ragged whispers, for darkness to claim me. How many minutes,
how many hours? I cannot recall precisely, but it does not matter.
Too long, yet not long enough.

Part of me is there still. The best part of me, perhaps.

'*My dear Watson.*'

He frequently addressed me thus in the past, but for the first time,
the import of those words became clear, shockingly apparent in
hindsight, as Holmes's deductions often were.

I was his. I belonged to him.

Dear God, had he known?

Of course he knew. You were the one who could not see what was in your own heart. You damned fool.

I cursed my blindness, my stupidity. If only I had realised sooner ... or not at all.

But it is too late for regrets. I know it now and will carry the knowledge to my grave: I am his. I suspect I always will be.

UNRAVEL THE TANGLES

LINDA M. CRATE

all the mysteries i accompanied
you on,
and all of the emotions i have
seen in you;
i didn't realize your love
until now—

you'd probably tell me 'it's elementary,
dear watson' as you were always
so fond of saying to me,

but i guess i am not always good at
picking up on the subtle clues
you left me;

and so i am here
heart pounding in my chest as if this
is a mystery that might just
kill me—

i don't know what to say, i must confess;
you were always the clever one—
so unravel the tangles of my heart and put it back
together.

THE FOURTH TIME ASKING

ANNA GRAHAM DOE

Each time he was caught, Holmes believed Watson would never agree to his sarcastic prodding in response. It took only four attempts to be proven wrong.

'Yes, fine, let's see just what is so bloody wondrous you're willing to throw your mind and life away for it. Our life. No, I don't need help.' He ripped the morocco case out of Holmes's grasp. 'You're not the only one experienced in administering injections.'

'Watson, don't.'

'Now you don't wish me to try it? Worried I'll like it as much as you do?' He pulled back the plunger to fill a serious dose. 'Or you worry you'll have to share? I wonder which you'll miss more having all to yourself, the drug or me?' The loop around his bicep brought a robust blue vein, pristine and untorn, to the fore.

'Stop. You don't want this.'

'You do.'

'No, I made a mistake.'

'Asking me to share in your only joy anymore is the sole mistake you'll admit.'

'I make many mistakes. Asking you to partake of my poison is but one. Believing my only joy is this chemical is yours. It's true I know of only one thing genuinely good in this world, only one thing worth living or dying for. But it isn't cocaine.'

'Prove it,' Watson said, and Holmes was bound.

SONNET FOR JOHN

EC BOSS

my John. your name is all. with you I live.
fortress of mind built strong to conquer crime
but your regard reveals the true captive
fled pain and loss; the towered heart is mine.

to you the world stands wide, to me closed round
from sentiment; to sense, an open book.
deduce the culprit, crook, all traces found
glass clear; yet you eclipse me with a look.

despite all risk you joined my side, my Work
tho shelled and scarred in battles far, and home,
transformed both lives with deeds and words
twin lights saved by plain gift of being known.

virtuous and virtuoso, we soar we two
yet each breath I breathe unfettered, owes alone to you.

THE LETTER
S.J. LOCK

Dr Watson,

I don't know why you have left the greater London area, but I hope this letter finds you in good health.

It is not my way to write to you in this fashion, but I fear I must. He needs you. I know you don't think that he does, but I know better.

Please come see him soon.

Regards,

Mrs Hudson

This is the letter that had me packing my bags before I had time to think better of it. This is the letter that said very little but very much at the same time. She knew something was wrong, it was the only reason she would write to me in this manner. As she said, it was not her way ...

He needed me, and against my better judgement I would go to him. As I always do. The train journey gave me time to think back over my reason for leaving. It had been after a particularly bad case that had left him with a mild concussion and three cracked ribs which he disregarded as though it was just another day. We had fought over his care and his refusal to lie still and let his ribs heal. My temper being what it is, well, there you have it. He told me to go, and I left.

I didn't plan to stay away as long as I had, but the doctor I was filling in for at Bristol Royal Infirmary had been slow to return, thus causing me to stay away for well over a month. Holmes must have thought I was never coming back. I had thought about writing him a letter, but I was unclear on how to start or what to say. It was better to speak in person about such matters.

He had been aloof about my leaving, much as he always was; there are times that I would think the man cared for no one. But then there were the times it was just us, alone, and I knew he cared for me more than anyone else on this earth.

BAKER STREET. *Home.* It is good to be back in London after a long time away. I wave down a hansom cab and give the address.

'221B Baker Street, on the double if you please.'

It's not long before the street comes into view, and I am awarded the first glimpse of our home. I should have written to him ... What will he say when I waltz in the door and up the stairs to our flat? Knowing Holmes as I do, he will most likely say nothing, but ask for a cup of tea and continue as though I had never left.

I can hear his voice in my head already. *Watson, tea, if you will.* Most likely without even lifting his head to meet my eyes. Never in all of my years have I met a man like him.

'221B Baker Street, on the double if you please.'

From the very beginning, the world appeared to circle around him, at least mine did. It took me longer to realise that it was more than friendship that I sought from the man. But he showed no feelings for the matter, and I tried to put those thoughts behind me. We have worked together for many years now, and each day it grows harder to be near him and not touch.

Being the British men that we are, one might say that I should push these feelings down deep and forget they are there. But I can no longer continue this way. It was part of the reason that I left after our argument. He seems to care so little for his own life that there is no place for me.

I stand at our front door, staring, unable to bring myself to open the door and walk in. I cannot say how much time passes as I stand there, bag in hand until Mrs Hudson appears. She appears to be heading to the shops and is caught by surprise to find me standing there.

'Oh, Dr Watson, are you back? How wonderful.' She smiles before continuing down the street.

To my surprise, she says not a word about what has happened. I watch her for a moment before entering the building and starting up the stairs. There is an eerie silence from our flat on the second floor, and the stairs creak loudly in the quiet. I find myself holding my breath and I climb to the top. I place my bag on the floor of our sitting room, but looking around I can find no Holmes about.

Mrs Hudson made it out that he was in real trouble; most likely he was out on a case and fit as a fiddle. I let out a sigh, shaking my head, not knowing what to think at this rate.

'Mrs Hudson? Is that you? Back from the shops already? That can't be right.'

The voice is coming from down the hall. Holmes's room. He sounds in bright spirits. It twists my heart to hear. He has no more need for me than he did before I left. Once more into the breach.

'No, Holmes. It is not Mrs Hudson,' I say, removing my coat and hat.

'Watson?' There is a quiet gasp that one could have missed, had one not been hoping for a sound of wanting from the host of the voice. There was a flutter of activity down the hall before Holmes appeared in his silk dressing gown and slippers. 'It is you.'

'Yes, I have returned from Bristol,' I announce, taking a seat in my chair.

'Ah, well, yes, very good.' Holmes seems flustered, which is unlike him.

'I was under the impression that you were in some sort of distress?' I prod, while watching Holmes move across the room to fuss with his violin.

'Oh? I assure you, I am quite well.'

'I can see that. My mistake.' I huff a bit. Under my breath I scold myself for returning.

'What is that?' Holmes asks. His hawk-like eyes are watching me very closely now.

'It is of no consequence,' I wave a hand dismissively, picking up the copy of *The Strand* that sits next to my chair. There is movement out of my sight and before I know it, my paper is gone, and Holmes is very close to me.

'If it matters to you then it matters to me.' He says with enough force for it to ring true.

I take a moment to reply, choosing my words carefully. 'I was merely thinking that I should not have returned, that is all.'

'Why? Why would you think that was better?' Holmes looks at me slightly distressed, searching for clues. I hope there is none to give my true feelings away.

'Just leave it be.' I sigh, and in standing I have to push him back a bit. As I do so he grasps my hands and refuses to let them go.

'I will not leave it be, my dear Watson, for something is bothering you, as it was before you left. Won't you tell me?'

'As though you can't deduce the truth yourself,' I assert, trying to pull my hands free. The warmth of his hands is almost too much to bear. I want to wrap my arms around him and pull him close. I want so many things that I cannot have, and it hurts deeply.

'You could though,' he whispers, leaning toward me.

I stop struggling against him. 'I could do what?'

'You could act on those thoughts.' He releases my hands and I miss the warmth instantly.

'I could not,' I state. 'For it is not something you would want.'

'And you know this to be true?' He gives me a look that has me rethinking all I know about the man.

'Yes,' I say, but with less certainty than before.

He gives me a look, leaning forward. 'Are you willing to test that theory?' His voice is low and his eyes twinkle with the dare he lays before me.

I step back from him. 'I am not.' I say, though my heart is breaking in my chest.

He pauses before taking a step towards me, his mouth opening to say what I may never know, for at that time there is a knock. Since Mrs Hudson is away, it leaves me to answer the door, as we both know Holmes will not.

I open the door to greet a man who has come for help from Holmes. I see him up the stairs and take my seat across from Holmes. He sits, hands steepled under his chin as though he knew there was a client at the door. I marvel that he can look so at ease after the conversation we have just engaged in. I envy him.

'Mr Holmes, my name is Charles Bradford,' the man says.

'What do you have for me, Mr Bradford?'

'I am not quite sure.' Charles Bradford seems ill-at-ease, and I feel sorry for him.

'Walk me through your dilemma first.' Holmes closes his eyes and waits.

There is a sigh from the man before he begins his tale. I listen to the details while studying the man sitting across from me. Most would say he is an unfeeling, cold-hearted man, relying only on facts and deductions, caring not for the people around him. But I have seen another side of him, a side that does feel sadness, pain and hurt.

He is not the cold, calculating machine the whole of London believes him to be. Maybe he does feel something for me. But can I trust it? I trust this man with most things, my life included, but can I trust him with my heart?

I come back to the conversation to find Holmes regarding me with his deductive stare. I look away, hoping my heart is not on my sleeve. Bradford has finished his tale and Holmes has already uncovered the truth without even rising from his chair. He is quite brilliant in that regard.

Before long, the client is gone, and we are left alone again. I realise that Holmes expects to continue speaking with me about what I feel, and I stand from my chair.

'Well, I'm afraid I must—' I pick up my bag and walk down the hall to my room without finishing my sentence, mostly because I don't have an answer to where I am headed or why. I only know I need to leave the room. He lets me go without a word, and I close the door to my room with a thankful sigh. Setting my bag on the bed, I begin to unpack my items and put them away. This will keep me from the sitting-room for some time, but I will still have to face him. Teatime is soon and I am too British to miss that.

At three o'clock on the dot, I hear Mrs Hudson carrying up the tea. I can no longer hide in my room and relinquish its safety for the call of tea. Holmes is where I left him in the sitting-room, still in his chair. I wonder if he has moved at all. His eyes are closed, his hands still steepled. I take my seat and thank Mrs Hudson for the tea. Five minutes pass before he opens his eyes and picks up his tea. I try to continue reading my book and sipping my tea in the silence. We finish our tea without exchanging words and for that I am thankful. I don't know if I can continue our talk today or ever.

A knock at the door sees Detective Lestrade in our sitting room with a case.

'Holmes, Watson.' Lestrade nods to us both.

'Afternoon, Detective Lestrade, what brings you by?' I ask, offering him a chair and a cup of tea, he declines both.

'Murder, I'm afraid.' Lestrade answers with a look towards Holmes.

I follow his eyes and find Holmes barely contained in his chair.

'Do tell us particulars of this murder.' Holmes sits forward, his eyes gleaming.

Detective Lestrade walks us through what he knows of the case.

Holmes decides it's of the utmost importance that we see the scene, and we soon find ourselves donning our coats and heading out of the flat. Holmes is almost giddy in the cab, and I find myself reminding him with a gentle hand to the forearm that some don't find murder a happy affair. Though I do enjoy seeing him this way. It's a softer side of him.

The time it takes for Holmes to look over the scene and come to his conclusion which puts all other detectives to shame. I marvel as always at his brilliance. The moment passes quickly as Holmes is in pursuit of the killer and I follow as best I can. We are well past the age for such things, but he continues, and I try.

Once cornered, the killer turns on us quicker than a flash flood and Holmes is struck. I pull my pistol and wound the man before kneeling beside Holmes. My mind flashes to a month ago with a similar injury. I am furious that it's happening all over again.

Holmes shrugs off my care and stands with minimal shaking. I huff my anger at him while Lestrade takes care of the killer. Since he needs no more from us, I bully Holmes into a cab and direct the driver to Baker Street. With me seething, and Holmes knowing my temper as he does, it's a silent ride.

Inside Baker Street I can hold my tongue no longer, peeling off my coat and shoes, I pace the room. 'You should not be taking such chances.' I fume.

He watches me from his chair, coat discarded beside him.

I continue as he remains silent. 'This cannot keep happening. You cannot disregard your life in such a way.'

'Why? Is it not my life?' He asks.

'Yes, it is. But what will I do if you are gone? It is not a life I would want.' I stop speaking instantly, knowing that I have said too much.

'Are we now going to speak of the matters you wish not to speak of?' He stands, walking over to me.

I shake my head. I cannot put into words what I feel. He stops in front of me. 'Tell me why you left and remained away for over a month with no word.'

'I had to replace a doctor on leave in Bristol,' I say quietly.

'That is not why you left. That is what you found to keep you busy.' He is standing very close to me now. I imagine reaching out and touching him. Holding his hand. Anything.

'I was angry,' I say, barely above a whisper. My heart is pounding so hard in my chest, I know he must hear it at this distance.

'At me?' he asks. 'Because you thought I was injured?'

'You *were* injured,' I snap back.

'I have endured worse,' he pushes. 'So have you.' Again he takes my hands gently and my breath catches in my throat.

'This was different,' I say, my voice shaking. I am staring at our hands where he holds them against his chest.

'How?' he asks softly. We are so close, I can feel his heart beating and the warmth of his hands. I have experienced this gentle side of him only a few times over the course of our friendship. I want to tell him, to share my feelings. But can I trust the expression on his face?

I take a deep breath. 'I could not lose you, Sherlock,' I say softly, his given name slipping past my lips.

'Nor I you, John,' came his hushed reply.

I gasp at the sound of my name. He has always called me Watson, as I have called him Holmes. My heart leaps at the sound, and I look up to meet his eyes. What I see is unmistakable: he does in fact care for me; I can feel it.

He leans forward slightly, his lips nearly touching mine. 'May I?' he asks.

'Yes, please,' I whisper, I can feel him close the distance between us and it is heavenly.

∾

TWO DAYS LATER, on our way out of the flat for a case, I stopped Mrs Hudson in the hall before leaving. 'I must thank you for your letter,' I say. 'If not for your letter I may not have returned as I did.' I smile.

Mrs Hudson has an odd look of surprise. 'Letter, Dr Watson? I am afraid that I have not sent you a letter.'

I pause. 'You did not send a letter while I was in Bristol this past month?' I am rightfully confused.

'No, I am sorry to say that I did not know you were in Bristol, only that you were away.' She looks apologetic.

'My mistake.' I say, allowing her to pass with the shopping.

I turn to Sherlock waiting by the door and his look says it all. He had sent me the letter in her name, and it made me love him even more. My darling Holmes had sent for me, and I had answered.

GLIMPSE OF TIMES
JACO MISMEANDER

It happened in the haze of one of my favourite drug-induced comas. I use such excursions to exempt myself from the constancy of my observation and inference; the sight with which I am gifted can at times burden me tremendously. I see everything, and it is my duty alone to make judgements on each of these millions of surveys. The sifting is exhausting and ceaseless during my sobriety, so it is no surprise that I am irrevocably drawn by the needle and its liquid components when they allow me sweet silence.

There was something which felt distinctly more real than my casual hallucinations in this episode, however. I found myself craving sobriety for the chance to hold my own observations accountable. I must have known this was real and wished to understand how.

I reclined in my armchair, and the good doctor was resting at his desk beside the fire. The shine of my syringe case shone my own countenance back at me. A mirage flickered across my own face, affecting his too; I could not explain it, but I had the strangest sense that I saw us across different times. There were times we looked inexplicably different, with features that did not match ours, yet I knew it was the pair of us, sanctity throughout the ages in our bond.

RETURN

LILITH INKWELL

There is an inexplicable surrealness about returning to a beloved place following a long absence. As I sat in my old chair at 221B, the right side of my body warmed by the old fireplace, and my erstwhile friend sitting just inches across from me, I wondered, for the umpteenth time that month, if I hadn't finally succumbed to delirium.

His eyes were closed in despair, and his forehead rested upon his left hand as if preventing a headache. I observed him silently with my heart lodged in my throat, the two of us scraped so raw we could hardly look at each other.

He'd come back from the dead a month ago, and I'd told him then I could never forgive him. He'd summoned me to his place that same morning, promising to finally leave me alone, if only I listened to what he had to say.

He'd confessed his love for me, his secret inappropriate desire, and the fierce jealousy which led him to flee as soon as he saw the opportunity.

His words were an echo of what I've known for long to be my own feelings. Would that they'd been enough to relieve our old wounds! There I sat torn between the impulse to kneel before him, vowing eternal devotion, and my inability to withstand more betrayal.

SHE UNDERSTANDS I LOVE YOU

LINDA M. CRATE

all the cases
i have solved,
but i have yet to
crack you open;

i suppose people are
harder to solve than cases
especially when you
care about them too much—

but here i am pining away,
dear doctor,
you have always been my
dear watson;

and yet i cannot seem to find
ways to express my feelings for you
in any meaningful way that you can
understand—

& so i sit here melancholy as an angry
moon watching the woman who loves
you hate me because she understands
i love you.

HOPE

RONIT SILVERSEEKER

It is only after Moran is stopped, after this final threat has been removed, that Holmes allows himself to unwind. He sags against me, three years' worth of exhaustion boiling to the surface, and I half-carry him back to our rooms, to our bed, tuck him in and climb under the blankets next to him.

In his haze he reaches for me almost blindly, clinging to me like a drowning man to his salvation, and I suppose I do the same—he buries his face in the crook of my neck, I run my fingers through his hair, and we breathe each other in. *Alive,* I weep with joy. *Safe,* he trembles in relief. Tomorrow there will be gaps to cross, bridges to rebuild over three years of mourning and peril, but for the moment I am content to simply have this. I wrap Holmes in my arms and press feather-light kisses to his forehead and temples and the crown of his head, whisper soft promises of love and forgiveness and a future. Holmes returns the sentiment by making a tiny broken sound and clinging to me even tighter, and I trust in tomorrow. I trust in him.

A Hive of 221Bs

Shai Porter

'CAN YOU FEEL THIS?'

He has waxed poetic on the state of my hands more than is fitting, both for the sake of propriety as well as for accuracy; it is his hands which are by far the more remarkable. They hold a weapon steady to fire, true-to-target, at a remarkable distance ... and yet wield a pen with an equally remarkable grace (though I am reluctant to admit it, lest I give my own hand away in the telling).

In truth, both talents have saved me—thwarting violence directed upon my person and providing the notoriety which has kept me in work—freed from my penchant for self-destruction. My hands are not prone to acts of healing where my own self is concerned.

A relief, certainly, to be tended to by one so skilled, but there is far more than this.

As my hand rests in his and he numbs the area between finger and thumb, prods alongside torn skin with a needle and queries, 'Can you feel this? Is it numb?' I cannot help but wonder what exactly it is I do feel. It is a singular emotion, one to which I am quite unaccustomed. He looks at me with an uncertain gaze, as I have neglected to answer the question, lost in the moment. I nod, and answer, 'Yes. You may begin.'

'PEOPLE LIKE YOU HAVE NO IMAGINATION.'

'That ... would never have occurred to me, Holmes.'

'Of course not. People like you have no imagination.' The words seemed innocuous enough to my ears and I've said far worse to the Yarders on numerous occasions, but there remained something in Lestrade's countenance which gave me pause.

He looked at me quite directly, with a shocking earnestness. 'If we in the official police force lack imagination, it is because we are trained to rely solely upon the evidence,' he replied. 'Is this not one of the lessons which you have sought to impress upon us? Or has Doctor Watson chosen to put false words in your mouth when expressing your desire to never theorise before facts?'

'I had not anticipated your following my counsel.' I blinked in surprise for I had not.

How to explain the intricacies of deduction? The myriad potentialities which flit about within my mind like a swarm of insects, pestering me with the seemingly endless possibilities, until they are eliminated as the facts present themselves. It had been a kindness to advise anyone wishing to take on this profession to disregard them, for it is not a fate I would wish upon another. The noise is grating and endless until the creatures depart one by one and at last all I hear is a single remaining buzz.

'Is this not one of the lessons which you have sought to impress upon us?'

HOW CAN I TRUST YOU?

Another shift in his chair, eyes fixed upon the crackling fire. 'You work for Scotland Yard. How can I trust you?'

I bristled at the very thought. 'I do not work for Scotland Yard. I'm a consulting detective. I work for myself alone and am not obligated to report to the police, save at my own discretion.'

I had hoped it reassurance enough. Still, he hesitated.

These moments are dangerous ones. The temptation is great, but I've more than my own security holding me back. Many would dismiss me from serious consideration given my Bohemian ways. 'That is all it is', they'd reason, 'a penchant for the eccentric.'

Gregson is likely quite aware; Lestrade would never entertain the notion; Jones has not a clue—I could take a companion for the evening right in front of him; he'd be none the wiser. Hopkins is … well, much remains to be seen regarding Hopkins. He could very well be a companion to take, should I wish it.

But to speak plainly to the client who sits before me? A risk I would gladly suffer, but for the scrutiny Watson would face—the strain upon his marriage and consequently upon his health. That he would be innocent of the charge and I guilty, the supreme irony. So I remain silent. I think it best.

WILL THAT BE ALL?

The tread of footsteps upon the stair dragged me away from my swirling thoughts.

'Will that be all?' my tireless landlady asked with a smirk, gathering up the serving tray from which I had removed every available scrap of food. Post-case hunger was upon me, soon to be followed by post-case lassitude. Watson would be arriving shortly, however, so I had my hopes that reaction might yet be postponed while I shared with him the details of the newly solved case. Workman's logic, but he doubtless would be spinning it into some romantic tale. I frowned as she tucked the tray beneath her arm; my hunger was conspiring to make me an exceedingly poor host.

'If you should happen to have additional portions on hand—'

She smiled sweetly. 'It doesn't take a consulting detective to notice Doctor Watson joins you most Thursday evenings. I have prepared extra, of course.'

I do not know what I would do without dear Mrs Hudson. She has a knack for interrupting me at the most inopportune moments, but it does serve to break my isolation into more manageable periods by simple visits designed to look entirely utilitarian. This does not fool me in the least, but I remain grateful.

I stretched my every nerve and could just hear a hansom approaching. I waited for the bell.

'TAKE WHAT YOU NEED.'

'So. You'll take what you need—'

'Enough to confirm my suspicions.'

'—leaving the rest for the official force?'

'Should they know where to look. I wouldn't wish to impede their investigation.'

'You intend to burn this substance, I presume.'

'Having first taken reasonable precautions. Open window and door should suffice.'

I recall scraping the residue off Tregennis's lamp and placing it within a small envelope. The rest of the evening's events are considerably more hazy.

I do know three things. I know Watson pulled me from that death trap, filled with far more potent fumes than ever I could have imagined. I know I apologised for having put his life at risk. And I know, in my delirium, I used his Christian name.

I cannot tell with certainty if he heard it or no, but it was no quiet thing. I shouted it with all the strength of one whose cherished companion had vanished into thin air, for this is exactly what I believed he'd done.

I've never counted the psycho-active medicines amongst my vices, lest my senses be compromised. I did, however, bring my Morocco case with me afield. As I struggled to make sense of my new surroundings, the deep cuts of my heels in the fresh grass, I knew beyond all doubt I would not be bringing it back.

'I HEARD ENOUGH, THIS ENDS NOW.'

I apologised once more at Baker Street for endangering his life—an unacceptable risk, made considerably moreso for having placed a dear friend in harm's way. He had made no mention of my lack of propriety, but I could scarce believe he hadn't heard. 'I also deeply regret any other ... inappropriate gestures ... I might have made,' said I.

He gave a brusque nod.

'The drug caused a certain degree of ... I was responding to what I thought was reality, but was, in fact, a twisted interpretation of events. I fear I may have reacted in a rather haphazard way. I do hope that you will find it in your—'

'I heard. Enough. This ends now.' He sighed. 'No one else could have, save myself, and I took no offence at so minor an ... impropriety ... under such circumstances. Do not let it trouble you any longer.'

'I see. Thank you, Watson.' I also found I had little else to say. He did not wish to speak of it, nor did I, lacking words to convey whatever it was I wished to impart. That he meant a great deal to me was obvious, surely the rest must be equally so. Though perhaps not. Of all the talents Watson possesses, observational skill was not one of them which Divine Providence had chosen to bestow.

'NO WORRIES, WE STILL HAVE TIME.'

'The very same room her sister ...' Watson puffed out his chest. 'Well, she shall have fewer worries knowing in the morning we shall be joining her at Stoke Moran.'

'I intend to leave her no worries. We still have time, Watson. The last train leaves in an hour.'

'What shall we bring?'

'A revolver.' Watson patted his coat-pocket, indicating the need for that particular item had been anticipated. 'And ...' his eyes darted around the room, considering my next request, 'a toothbrush.'

What followed is well-known. I'm told by Watson's literary agent it remains the most popular of his stories. Still, what was known to myself alone were the dark thoughts which haunted me during that interminable stretch of time.

I suspected a snake, given the efficiency and elusiveness of the poison and need for a rope, but was prepared for novel techniques for the second victim. Vents could just as easily serve for poisonous gas; a less detectable creature (spider?) might be employed. Joining her at Stoke Moran might take on a different meaning.

If Roylott knew full-well of our presence, he'd murder his step-daughter for her betrayal—and we'd never be found. It was well I should be consumed with such thoughts, for never once did I consider Watson and myself, alone in the darkness, the only sound our breathing.

I KNOW YOU DO.

When the Swiss youth arrived, bearing a letter upon hotel stationery, I knew.

'I have to return to the hotel.'

'I know you do.'

I hastily requested the messenger accompany me to Rosenlaui, and Watson meet me there. I did not trust the boy, only content with my fate secure in the knowledge that my dear friend was not in immediate danger. Watson made as if to speak, then turned up the path toward Englischer Hof alone.

The youth vanished and, leaning against the sheer rockface, I waited. A figure was visible upon the spray-slicked path.

'Might you permit a note?' I shouted above the din. 'Watson shall return from his fool's errand and attempt to catch me up. I shouldn't wish him never to know what became of me.'

'Indeed, it would be entertaining to read a proper eulogy, Mr Holmes, featuring my prominent role. Of course you may.' I hastily scrawled as Moriarty lamented, 'A formal duel would have suited, but I am too tired for elegance. My only wish is that you trouble me no more.'

'I have to pursue you. To do what I must to counter your every step.'

'I know you do,' he mocked, and I found myself charging him, armed though he was—myself with nothing save my walking stick and knowledge of Baritsu.

YOU SHOULDN'T HAVE COME HERE.

You shouldn't have come here. You should have clambered down from your hiding place, or called out, instead of watching from 200 feet up. Coward.

If I had done, there would be no need to rise every two hours to ensure my limbs still functioned in these inhospitable temperatures. I'd be back at Baker Street beside the fire or, if he had chosen to join me, there would have been two of us generating warmth upon this hillside. And not in some prurient manner.

How much of this is disabling Moriarty's network and how much your need to disappear in the most dramatic manner possible?

I will never forget Watson's face upon finding my Alpine-stock and the message tucked beneath my cigarette case.

Holding that note in my hands, after my unexpected survival, I found myself contemplating life, death, and the precarious nature of it all. Watson, his wife, their child on-the-way. Their future and the complications I would certainly create. Not only was I better suited to this task alone, but perhaps in subsequent endeavours as well. Mindful, I rewrote that note several times until it betrayed far less and began my climb upward.

Could anyone have asked for a more rewarding exit? Watson retracing my steps admirably, to confirm my sacrifice had rid the world of a most terrible blight.

YOU THINK THIS TROUBLES ME?

'My visitors have lost something they did not wish to lose, or wish to lose something they cannot avoid. But you, my friend ...?'

'I believe I have managed both.'

'With the same person, yes?'

I paused. 'Yes, with the same person, I'm afraid.'

He sipped his milk tea and nudged a bowl toward me.

'It is in our desire for a specific outcome that we suffer. I offer ... exceptional advice, for an exceptional person.' I took my offered bowl and held it in my lap. 'Self-hatred, fear ... manifestations of delusion and dukkha. Enemies of happiness. Perhaps you should inform him of your situation and let him decide what path it is he wishes to take.'

I was speechless.

'You think this troubles me? I am a student of human nature. Gyalwa Yang Gönpa writes of Ma ning—the abiding breath between male exhalation and female inhalation.'

'I meant no offence. I am quite unaccustomed to being read so easily. Typically, I do the reading.'

'Yes. But far more importantly ... the issue you face is one of rebirth. You have pretended to be dead so long, you feel as if you truly are. I say you live. Your troubles will find you; there is no need to hunt them down. Return to the things and people you love, and the joy they bring.'

I WILL NEVER FORGET!

'Mary Watson has died.' Why does that sound kinder to my ears than 'Mary Watson is dead'? Mycroft's telegram stated the former. One could almost delude oneself into believing it some event in the long-distant past, until the subsequent line no amount of semantics could disguise: 'Daughter unlikely to survive.'

I know John would have been with Mary during her final moments. I cannot comprehend what it would be to see someone you love beyond saving. And having lost not one, but two? No, I am getting ahead of myself. The child might yet live. A reminder to us of her mother's exceptional pluck. It was so long ago that we accompanied her to Thaddeus Sholto's home, but I will never forget! I am, perhaps, the only other to know how remarkable Mrs Watson was, yet my condolences would be most unwelcome.

A second telegram arrives, and I fear the worst, but it says, 'You are a fool to think he would not be grateful for one less loss, regardless of circumstance.' Mycroft's damnable omniscience strikes again. I have already been planning my return, for there was truth in the Dalai Lama's words. Colonel Sebastian Moran is awaiting me in London.

It would be three months yet before I found myself in a hansom, directing the cabbie to 221 Baker.

WHO COULD DO THIS?

'Who could do this?' Colonel Sebastian Moran surveyed the charred remains of a chemical laboratory in Montpellier.

'Law enforcement can be quite ruthless. Why when I was—'

'I didn't mean it like that. I meant who is capable of tracking us to here, of getting through our security. Get me a list of new employees!'

Woodhouse shrugged. 'Paperwork would have been destroyed in the fire. I recall a research scientist we had at the lab a few months ago, though. Simple fellow. Working on coal-tar derivatives.'

'Tall?'

'Six feet?'

'Take precautions. I need to get back to London. I've an appointment.'

Moran collapsed his paper, safely in his armchair in the club's sitting room. He had been wise to leave the Continent; it was no longer safe, as evidenced by Woodhouse's arrest in Arles.

I'm the only one left. What was it he said in those stories? Once you rule out the impossible you are left with the truth? Well, Holmes has to be alive. No one else could have done this so neatly, and in such a short amount of time.

They'd meet again. Holmes would turn up somewhere in London and Moran would be ready. While he was waiting, why not enjoy himself? But he needed money. Well, there was always a card game at the Bagatelle.

TRY HARDER, NEXT TIME.

I rose. 'I only agreed to inform you of my whereabouts to obtain access to funds, in exchange for intelligence concerning Khartoum. And, occasionally, to assure you of my health and well-being. What I did not bargain for were telegrams filled with unsolicited advice, like some ridiculous alienist-philosopher!'

'One telegram. And your emotions were both conspicuous and compromising your assigned task.'

'No, they weren't! On either count!'

'Try harder, next time, Sherlock. And do pay him a visit.'

'Perhaps I already have. Perhaps he did not wish to see me.'

'You most certainly have not.'

'You find that reaction impossible to imagine? But yes, I have made no attempt to contact him upon my return. I wouldn't be surprised if he punched me in the face for it. I made no attempt to contact him when I was travelling either. I wrote to him. Many times. But how can one write such a letter? And then to learn he is twice-bereaved—'

'Thrice-bereaved, Sherlock. Yours is another death. But it can be undone. Do not hesitate.'

'Watson is a more emotional man than you or me, Mycroft.'

'Is he?'

I had no doubt I was being far more emotional than I had intended. 'Very well then. I shall observe him and then I shall reveal myself to him. Now let me be.'

SOME PEOPLE CALL THIS WISDOM.

Some people call this wisdom. Surveying the terrain, as it were. Reconnaissance. Others would call it fear.

Was I afraid? Yes.

I had bungled this. Badly. I would approach him incognito. If he were in good spirits, appeal to his pawky humour and make light of it all. Explain how critical it was to my success to have absolutely no indication that I was alive. Watson is a military man. Surely, he would understand the need for absolute secrecy in carrying out a mission. Then I would regale him with tales of the Far East. The Frozen North. The Forbidden City. The ground I had tread where an Englishman has scarcely ever set foot. He may bear ill-will toward me for my distance and deceit, but he cannot resist hearing of the adventures of Sigerson.

Now, what titles for my decrepit bibliophile? Britain, Worship. Catullus—immoral and immortal.

I offer Watson #96:

If anything pleasing to silent sepulchres

> *is to be done by our grief,*
> *by this longing we renew old loves*
> *and we lament sent-away friendships.*

But, ashamed, I think only of #48:

> *If I could play at kissing your honeyed eyes*
> *as often as I wished to,*
> *300,000 games would not exhaust me.*

I stared in the mirror and dabbed more spirit gum beneath my scraggly beard.

I THOUGHT YOU HAD FORGOTTEN.

'Colonel Moran! Good to see you again!'

'My dear Milner! And here I thought you'd forgotten me.'

'Never! You're always welcome! I'm afraid your usual partner's ... indisposed.'

I smiled. 'He won't be joining us for years yet.' If he makes it through gaol in one piece. 'I'm sure I can make a few new friends, though.'

'Young Adair over there could learn a thing or two from someone like you. Due to come off his losing streak any time now.'

'Is that so? Always good to play the odds.' Or improve them. I headed to his table. 'Adair, my good man, fancy a rubber?'

'Colonel! I'd be honoured.'

It was clear why Adair was losing; he was playing an honest game. I did my best to compensate. We took home £420 that evening, and he was none the wiser.

When we met again weeks later, he was quite eager to join me once more, and watched me carefully. After he played miserably enough to lose £5, despite my best efforts, he asked if we could discuss something privately, at his home in Park Lane.

I'm no fool.

I watched him from across the street as he took out his ledgers, tallying how much ill-gotten gain was his and how much mine. I solved the issue with a bullet.

THIS IS GONNA BE SO MUCH FUN!

'Got y'self another case, Mr 'Olmes?'

'Not exactly, Billy, but an adventure nonetheless. First, I'll need you to retrieve an item from a Monsieur Oscar Meunier. A guinea for speed. Mind you, it's a bit heavy ... and quite fragile.'

'The 'Regs and me ...' Billy stopped in the doorway and coughed a bit. It was good to be missed. 'Well, we's so glad you're back, Mr 'Olmes.'

'Thank you, Billy.'

He nodded his head sharply and scampered off.

He returned with Wiggins, each boy grasping opposite sides of the package. I paid them a guinea apiece, then sent Wiggins away and called for Mrs Hudson. Some might think it reckless to ask a mere boy and an elderly woman to take on this next burden, but I trusted them implicitly. Moreso than any Yarder.

The plan was simple. Tuck the bust securely within my dressing gown—the faded mouse one, should it become damaged—and create a convincing silhouette for Moran's target practice. He'd aim for my head, of this I was certain; so long as my accomplices approached on all fours to rotate the facsimile, their safety was ensured.

'This could go throughout the night, so I believe it best if you work in shifts.' They both were more than eager to assist.

'This is gonna be so much fun!' said Billy.

I'LL TELL YOU BUT YOU'RE NOT GONNA LIKE IT.

The paper's description of the body might as well have been a signed confession from Moran (it could have been done by no other ... I had no need to examine the scene), and it was clear to me my purpose in heading toward 427 Park Lane was not professional, but personal. I was confident Watson, who had retained his interest in the work after my ... departure, couldn't help but be drawn to the Adair case. The confirmation by my Irregulars that he was indeed present made it seem as if fate were drawing us together.

'You want to know who done it?' A tall, thin policeman, attempting a rather pathetic disguise with his coloured glasses, was speaking to the eager crowd of onlookers gathered round. 'I'll tell you but you're not gonna like it.' I ignored his babble about anarchists, the severe temperature drop resulting in the rise of the All-England Women's Hockey Association. That is when I spotted Watson in person for the first time in so many years. I was so stunned that I must admit, I froze and simply watched him. The grief was easy to observe, as were his attempts to overcome it. Though I certainly should have, in truth I had not orchestrated for him to back into me and knock down several of my books.

YOU SHOULD HAVE SEEN IT.

I followed him. Of course I did. And without stopping to form a serviceable excuse. I found myself knocking upon his door whilst hastily fumbling for some explanation as to why an old, hobbled book peddler should track a stranger all the way to Kensington. I mumbled something about my having overreacted and wishing to apologise. A weak justification, and he knew it. I sought reinforcement with my imaginary bookshop, located off Church Street. Had I been just ... wandering through Park Lane? It is so very clear when one wishes to be found out.

That is when I spotted Watson in person for the first time in so many years.

I called his attention to a small gap upon the shelf, and as his back was turned, I stretched out to my full height and removed my side-whiskers. Once more, my tale is told more or less accurately in the public account. I reached for brandy and offered my apologies. When he had quite recovered, I told him, briefly, of my adventures.

'You should have seen it, Watson! Pilgrims making prostrations, incense burners taller than a man bringing forth their scented clouds to challenge the ever-present juniper, performing the kora—a clock-wise circumambulation of sacred sites whilst turning a prayer wheel. Women with their long tresses smeared in yak butter and men with tassels of red yarn braided through their hair and a dagger upon their belt.'

OH, PLEASE, LIKE THIS IS THE WORST I HAVE DONE.

It was immediately apparent I had placed my foot squarely within my mouth, and once my brain had managed to catch up, I found there escaped from out that be-footed mouth a quiet, 'Oh.'

'Please ...'.

Like this? Is the worst I have done in this three-year-long absence ... Are the flaws inherent in my very character which I attempt to conceal to be dredged to the surface? I know too well Watson would have given anything to have been there with me, and I with him. And, yet, what do I choose to say? I am ashamed.

Though the original act was rapidly shifting from ill-advised to unconscionable, it remained in the telling where I was cementing my fate. There were other things—far more important things—I wished him to know of my time in Tibet.

Not of the bitter cold, nor the hunger felt keenly even by one as accustomed to self-denial as I, nor the acts I had committed which required perhaps more moral justification than I had a right to lay claim.

'Watson, this is ... somewhat remarkable, but I assure you of its veracity. The cobbled path which hosted the market I have described, as well as my lodgings, was called Barkhor Street. I spent every moment alongside a cruel reminder I was not where I longed to be.'

I HOPE YOU HAVE A SPEECH PREPARED.

He turned away, as if my countenance pained him. 'I should allow myself to feel only gratitude. You are alive. That is more than enough.'

'My dearest friend, recently I've spent time alongside philosophers and mystics ... unintentionally reinforcing my Bohemian reputation. That aspect of the journey has not left me unscathed.' I hoped for a smile. None came. 'I've learned allowing oneself leave to feel or not feel a thing is utter nonsense. Tell me what it is you feel. And I'll endeavour to simply listen. For I have done you a grave injustice.'

'You acted as you thought best, perched upon that fearsome precipice. That is all any of us can do.' Watson shook his head. 'Besides. We are not men of words. We are men of action.'

'Then I offer you the gift of action. This Adair affair is far from over. A starring player will make a second entrance upon the stage.'

I removed my index from its shelf, turning, again, to 'M'. 'I hope you have a speech prepared,' I mumbled to the smirking photograph. 'We could use some light entertainment.'

I faced Watson. 'I have a piece of work for us both which, if brought to a successful conclusion, will in itself justify a man's life on this planet. Tonight, we hunt a wild beast.'

IMPRESSIVE, TRULY.

From here on out, there is much Watson does not address or simply manufactures. And rightly so. But what is impressive, truly, is when he writes of my leading him silently through a maze of streets and back-alleys, past mews and stables and deserted yards, only to arrive in Camden House. Then, in that musty old building with the peeling wallpaper, I directed his gaze toward our old rooms, 'the starting point of so many of your little fairy tales, so we might see if my three years of absence have entirely taken away my power to surprise you'. I will have you know I did no such thing.

Instead, I turned to him and said, 'I owe you a distinct lack of surprises, Watson. I confess I had once thought it charming.'

'It was charming, in its way,' said he.

'You're too kind! I now prefer openness to secrecy, having exhausted my allotment of deception. We shall take a circuitous route, as I expect, hidden amongst the evening street crowds, none other than Colonel Sebastian Moran—the one responsible for the death of Ronald Adair—and the Late Professor Moriarty's right-hand man. Our destination is Camden House. Once there, you shall witness the murder of a wax dummy of myself, like me in every aspect, save its possessing far more brainpower.'

I KNOW HOW YOU LOVE TO PLAY GAMES.

Watson was right. We are men of action. I grasped his wrist and guided him through the darkened corridor, whispering close in his ear, 'It really is rather like me, is it not?' As intimate a gesture as I dared, but upon observing a certain welcoming aspect, I longed to try more.

'I know how you love to play games, Holmes, but this is an exceptionally dangerous one. Have you not just learned your lesson concerning ill-advised decisions?'

It had been my intention to quit these urges during my travels. To give Watson a more conventional life. 'I am sorry,' I said once more, in the safety of darkness. 'For the loss of your wife and child. The loss of all the promise that life held.' My emphasis on 'that' was ... unexpected.

Watson was silent for some time before uttering, 'You think I ... yes, you think had I not been turned widower, I'd have preferred your continued absence.'

My turn for silence.

'When you left, you thought yourself gracefully stepping aside to let me become a father! Dignified. Not someone who ... followed you down dimly lit alleys into empty houses to track a killer. You said Moran had some flaw which isolated him from respectable life. I'm no murderer, but that aspect applies to us both.'

THIS IS NOT NEW; IT ONLY FEELS LIKE IT IS.

'My Mary was a wise woman.'

'That she was.'

'I'll have no platitudes from you, Holmes.'

I fell silent.

'My Mary was a wise woman. She gave me leave to chase criminals down alleyways because she understood to do so was within my nature, and acknowledging this would not take me away from her but rather, brought me closer. To all the things which made me feel whole. To all the things I loved. And she knew she would always be part of that love. As will you, Holmes.'

'I wish you would not include me in that sentiment, Watson.'

'However do you mean?'

'To speak of me in terms of love.'

'I see nothing amiss. And this is not new.'

'It only feels like it is acceptable because you do not see it as I do. My lens is distorted. I do not see things in the same manner as others.'

'Certainly not—you see far more.'

'That is not what I meant.'

'But Mary saw far more than you.'

I let him humble me.

'You believe I chose Mary for what she represented, rather than for the woman herself. If true, she'd have been gravely disappointed. A husband and wife ... have occasion to discuss things. She was far less concerned than I. In time, I learned she knew best.'

YOU KNOW THIS, YOU KNOW THIS TO BE TRUE.

'I've found many men attractive—even acknowledged this publicly in my stories—but I've not disclosed I've loved a fair number of them. And if I love Mary as well, it should not be taken as proof I loved either any less. You—I certainly felt this way about you, but believed you counted yourself above such emotions. Now, I feel I may have been in error. I witnessed what seemed to be cause but was actually effect.'

I am glad I was incapable of viewing the expression of shocked ignorance I must have presented. Doubtless Watson managed it somehow, for there was a smile in his voice as he said, 'I shall not say something akin to "You know this, you know this to be true," for the very last thing I should wish to do is speak for you on such a delicate matter. But it is a near thing. So, what say you?'

'I say it's a remarkably accurate deduction.' I moved closer to him, taking his hand in mine, grateful for the darkness to conceal my blush, when I heard an echoing creak. It could only be Moran, seeking our hiding spot for his own. I placed my hand upon Watson's lips with quivering fingers and we both saw within the blackness a crouching figure just a shade blacker.

GO FORWARD, DO NOT STRAY.

As he moved forward with single-minded purpose—hunched low, the light hitting his face as he raised the grimy window—it was apparent he was entirely unaware of our presence. Go forward, do not stray. Ye shall not turn aside to the right hand nor to the left. Though I suspected Moran was not taking his technique for attempted murder from Deuteronomy, Joshua, Proverbs or Kings.

I waited patiently for his shot, then sprung upon him. He was a large, powerful man, and I was grateful Watson was but a moment from striking him with the butt of his revolver. We both held him in place as I summoned aid with my whistle.

'You fiend! You clever fiend! You cunning fiend!' said he.

'I see words escape you, Colonel!'

'You may or may not have just cause for arresting me,' he said to the officers, 'but at least there can be no reason why I should submit to the gibes of this,' he hesitated, 'person. If I am in the hands of the law, let things be done in a legal way.'

'Ah, your eloquence has returned! I had been hoping for a speech! Come, Watson! Let us retire to my sitting room. That is, if you don't mind a draught. I'm afraid my window is broken.'

BUT IF YOU CANNOT SEE IT, IS IT REALLY THERE?

His words, my actions, his responses, all circling round my mind. What had we been moving inexorably toward within that darkness? Something like love ... but no, not love, for in truth we already had love, of that I am certain. Something like attraction. Dare I say, like passion? Impossible to define, to confirm, whatever was manifesting between us—but if you cannot see it, is it really there? If you cannot hear it, nor smell it, nor leave it to any empirical evidence gathered from infallible senses—how can you ever be certain of its existence? And certainty was a requirement.

He had been direct. Remarkably so. And yet, I was still incapable of taking those words at face value as we sat quietly in the cab on our way back to Baker Street. He turned toward me, and I felt the heat of a blush once more. It was humiliating, to appear so weak next to one so strong. I had pushed my emotions down so relentlessly that it was no surprise they should find their way out in strange ways during unguarded moments. I resented it nonetheless—the relinquishing of control. It was then that he took my hand and kissed it gently. It was never a question, between the two of us, who was the braver.

REMEMBER, YOU HAVE TO REMEMBER.

Up all seventeen steps without a word, though Watson couldn't help but chuckle as the seventh squeaked beneath his weight, as always. Mrs Hudson had lit a fire in anticipation of our return.

'Remember.'

'You have to—'

'Remember. All that I said.'

'But when you said—'

'Holmes. Are you implying that I do not know my own feelings on the matter?'

'Certainly not. I'm merely ... Well ... in truth, I have no idea what I am seeking to accomplish.'

'Do not be uncertain on my behalf. If on your own behalf, then by all means take the time to assess your feelings. The confidence you demonstrated at Moran's capture, in addition to being rather compelling, led me to an incorrect assessment.'

'You are confusing the end of a case with the beginning of something else entirely. That they should occur at the same time does not make said confidence transferable.'

Watson gave a firm nod. 'Well then. My only concern was your labouring under the misapprehension I would not reciprocate your interest. We should let it be for now and discuss other matters.' He smiled and sat down in his old armchair. 'Mrs Hudson has kept up your rooms admirably. There is not a trace of dust.'

'Brother Mycroft had requested she preserve the rooms as—no! No, this is bootless!'

I FELT IT. YOU KNOW WHAT I MEAN.

'I'm not suggesting we pretend we've nothing to discuss. I'm suggesting you first consider what you want, or do not want ... privately.'

'Unnecessary! I know what I want! There is no logical reason why we should not proceed!'

'You are apprehensive.'

'No, I am perfectly willing to enter into a ... more ... physical aspect of ...'

'I felt it. You know what I mean.' He sighed. 'Well, we agree you are open to the possibility. That is all we need know for the time being.'

'Watson, I—'

'I would quite prefer "John".'

'John, I ... John.' It felt extraordinary, deliberately addressing him in that more intimate manner. I wanted to repeat the name several times. Use it at breakfast over the morning paper. 'John, please pass the marmalade.' 'Tea, John?' Our sitting casually together during the morning meal was hardly a novel occurrence, but my mind traced this seemingly commonplace moment backward in time. We'd have been arriving at the table simultaneously, after a night spent together. Possibly. Probably. That would be my preference, in any case. But his ... John's, John's! John's past associations might not be in keeping with the dyadic implications of a shared room. Yet another point to address in this wholly new arrangement. And what of Mrs Hudson? Any observant woman would notice we were sharing far more than breakfast.

AT LEAST IT CAN'T GET ANY WORSE

One of my worries had been removed. And by removed, I mean had increased tenfold. Mrs Hudson was fully aware of the situation in which we found ourselves. We had scarcely done more than confess our interest to one another, yet all the same she had brought up supper—having prepared a careful mix of both our favourites. It was transparent. And because she knew I knew, she winked at me!

At least it can't get any worse in that respect. She found it somewhat amusing, which I should find condescending in the extreme, were it not for the fact I found it so as well.

I had made a habit of being unconventional, and yet here I was, still standing on the precipice of the relationship, alternating between eagerness and hesitancy. I was not afraid in any truly limiting sense; I was simply determined to do this correctly. And therein lay a hesitancy which must have been clear as day.

Ever since she delicately removed the charred remains of Watson's ... John's ... tennis shoes from the fireplace and had disposed of them whilst on holiday in Kent, I knew she had no qualms about our law-breaking for the public good. Apparently, that extended toward the private good as well. I looked at the tray once more. She had even made biscuits.

DO WE REALLY HAVE TO DO THIS AGAIN?

Upon offering Billy and Wiggins a guinea apiece for the delivery, I heard a rather put-upon grumble.

'Do we really have to do this again?'

'A precaution. Count Sylvius was a big game hunter. They've similar modus operandi.' I removed the bust. 'This one's by Tavernier. I hadn't wished to inform Meunier of his work's fate, so I contracted another artist.'

'Was that it, or did you just enjoy another sitting?'

'Watson, while there are things I am quite vain about, I assure you my profile is not one of them.'

Palpable tension. A flash of discomfort that I should, of necessity, refer to John as 'Watson', and Billy's uncertainty if one in his position might laugh at his employer's expense. Wiggins obliterated both concerns, laughing so boisterously everyone was obliged, then relieved, to join in.

Once alone, I attempted to reassure. 'Is it different ... John ... when facing one who does not merely wish to avoid capture, but wishes me dead ... given our deepening bond?'

'Sherlock ... there's scarcely room for an increase in worry witnessing you placing yourself in danger. I pray you only take necessary risks.'

'Well, had he known I was the dainty thing he chivalrously handed a dropped parasol to this morning ...'

He sighed. 'So, we are to witness the destruction of another perfectly good bust.'

I'VE WAITED SO LONG FOR THIS.

'I've waited so long for this.'

'As have I.'

John raised his eyes to meet mine and smiled. 'And just in time! We're nearly out of that foul smelling vinegar, oak and tobacco concoction of yours.' He lifted the latch which separated the hives from the garden to join me, though still at a prudent distance. 'I don't expect I'll ever get used to them, but I knew they'd get used to you ... eventually.'

'Well, you can testify as to my slow acting, yet irresistible, charm.' I returned the super to the hive. 'Pity I couldn't simply perform some remarkable service for this queen to earn her trust with as little effort as it had taken for the human variety.'

'How long has it been?'

'Four hours, John! Four hours and not a single sting!'

'You'd think they'd do it out of boredom.'

'Ah! Yet another way in which we prove similar!'

'Enough with the bees! Time for bed.'

'But it is another hour till darkness stakes its claim upon the world, and I'm far from tired,'

'I did not say time for sleep, Sherlock. I've been watching those graceful hands and forearms of yours arranging and rearranging those slat boards going on four hours now. I choose my words with a writer's care, and the word I chose was bed.'

He lifted the latch which separated the hives from the garden to join me.

HOPE, WHICH FREED BEGETS
ALEXANDRA FOX

hope, which freed begets the only answer to death: love.

do not speak of a fate worse than death.
i have faced the devil and watched as angels fled the
    precipice, the very edge of my mind, where he plunged
    to darkness and committed me.

yet even that abyss could not hold forever that one most
    treacherous and noble truth: in the heart of man,
    there is hope.

hope, which freed begets the only answer to death : love.

do not speak
of a fate worse than
death. i have faced the
devil and watched as angels
fled the precipice, the very edge
of my mind, where he plunged
to darkness and committed
me. yet even that abyss
could not hold

forever that one most treacherous and noble truth: in the heart of man, there is hope.

ACT IV: WINTER

BUT SWEETER STILL

ALEXANDRA FOX

They fell like prayers at my feet: snowdrop and olive, rosemary, rue, yarrow petals waiting to be swept off the snow by the barest wind. The passing of two years had done nothing to abate my sorrow for her. My mind conjured her face, wiped clean of the desperation to become a lady of London, that artificial pallor which led to such an early demise. It was said she had a Good Death, but these ideals would not serve her nature. She was a daughter of the Empire true enough, yet she was also a daughter of the sun. To hide her wit and strength beneath the winter chill was an unconscionable act. It is one I shall hold against God and his Angels evermore.

'Alas, poor Mrs Watson. Would that I had known you better.'

Sherlock Holmes, returned from the grave of my mind not nine months hence, stood solemnly at my shoulder. They were his, the blossoms. It might be a shock to those who imagine the man to be more mind than matter, having only seen him in his performances and glories. For a man such as myself, who has been privy to his silent storms and paralysing sadness, the poetry of his actions was well-suited to his heart. He was a person of far more romance than any other I've met, and his intentions were not without kindness. Indeed, he was a greater man than I.

'Holmes,' I began, not yet knowing what I was on about, 'do you believe it is time?'

A sharp inhale sounded in my ear. It was a sound I had not thought to miss, a simple intake of breath through the nose, and it stung like a dagger to the chest.

'It has never been any other time for me, dear Watson.' His footsteps crunched a minor retreat in the snow—a gentleman's gesture indeed.

'Be well, sweet Mary.' My hands brushed her headstone, beneath which my remains might someday lie, and I indulged myself in a final view of the flowers gracing her tomb.

'Alas, poor Mrs Watson. Would that I had known you better.'

'Home, then?' I asked, studiously avoiding Holmes's eye for fear that I might yet be speaking to a ghost.

He nodded, pausing to remain a step behind.

'Home.'

THE SOUND of uncertain footfalls broke the silence which encompassed my sorrow, softened but not removed by the passage of another year without the influence of Mary's laughter. It had not been a time without joy of its own, and I chose to believe she would be pleased by my progress toward restoration of spirit. My wife had never fully understood the penchant for excitement which coursed through my veins, first in Her Majesty's Service, and then in the wake of my most unusual friend. Yet, for all her pleasure in simply living day to day, she never sought to dowse that flame with which I was enamoured.

'You were a good wife, darling Mary.'

A hum escaped Holmes's throat, which he attempted to disguise by coughing into a gloved wrist. The pitch was elevated too slightly for anyone else to discern—had anyone else been present—but after passing twelve months in the confines of Baker Street with the man whose customs had once been intimately familiar to me, it was sufficient to pique my curiosity. Casting a raised eyebrow in his direction, steam filled the air as I opened my mouth to speak.

'Forgive me, Watson.' His breath tangled with mine in the space between us. 'They are predicting a fierce storm by Christmas. I suspect they are not wrong.'

Holmes's eyes were possessed of an emotion I had only observed once in the man. Following the departure of Mrs Adler, now several years past, my friend exuded for many days an aura of regretful longing. Not as a man possessed by the desire for marriage; that was never his way. His mood suggested that he was a man who had instead beheld a treasure which he would never encounter again. In this way, his gaze met mine, and I felt my mind stirring with an incomprehensible warmth.

Coughing once more, Holmes tore his eyes from mine, and I was surprised to discover my lips still parted for words that had never come. Deft flicks of his fingers plucked apart the flowers held bundled in his hand. Petals and leaves floated silently to the earth, pure white jasmine, forest oak, royal purple hyacinth, and the gentler Nile lily in a tidy row adorning the ground like an offering of jewels for the forgotten nymphs of the land. Would the coming snow bury them until they melted into the grass and mud, or would some wisp from before the birth of our God weave them about her neck and carry them away?

'Mary, I believe you would be proud,' I said, tucking my bare hands into my pockets. 'Yes, yes, I know, the gloves. But without you here, who will scold me into remembering? My life is feeling more and more like it should be lived, Mary. Baker Street is breathing purpose back into me. I am renewed in my eagerness to face each day, and I cannot take any credit onto myself for that. You know I questioned it for years, my dear, and after your departure, my confusion only deepened. But I believe it now, though I cannot pin down the exact nature of it just yet.'

My fingers flexed inside my coat as I surveyed the graveyard. A dusting of snow had fallen in the night which now reflected the defiant sunlight back toward the sky. I could not recall having seen such cheerful weather in a place of death. Perhaps eternity was simply this: the living remain living.

The noise of displaced crows sounded behind me, and a smile crept unbidden across my lips.

'You're late,' I chided lightly as Holmes pulled up at a rapid pace. He took a few steadying breaths and folded his hands behind his back. 'I almost believed you had forgotten me.'

'Forgotten you, my dearest Watson? Such a thing could never come to pass. I dare say you will forget my very name before I should ever lose a single detail about you.'

'Is that a proper vow, Holmes?'

I admit I do not know what came over me at that moment; perhaps my senses were obscured by the scent of warmer days held in my friend's hidden fists or by the glint of the sun off the powder-dabbled earth. The flush that raced to the surface of my skin must surely have been visible to as observant a man as my companion, yet my embarrassment at that did not compare to the overwhelming misery of waiting for his reply.

'It is better than a vow. It is the truth.' He stepped forward, closing what little gap there was between our shoulders. 'I shall remember you always.'

My courage failed me woefully then, and I turned my face away toward the clouds.

'What have you brought us this year?' My voice was wrested from my chest by sheer will, and I kept my eyes trained on the ground before me, grateful to have managed an excuse for evasion.

Holmes brought out the small bouquet in one hand and shuffled sideways to access it with the other. The loss of body heat against my arm was like falling. I gripped the insides of my pockets and fought back the urge to protest as he plucked the petals roughly from their stems. Lilac and orange blossom, violet and edelweiss, and mint cut through evening primrose lay in the frosty grass, and all at once I saw it. The man's heart appeared cast open before me. Could this be?

'Come, Watson,' he said, tilting his head toward the gates. 'The light will not last forever, and you are without your gloves again.'

ALL THE SKIES were engulfed in white as though Heaven itself has forgotten how to laugh, and I stood beneath them, blasphemously untroubled heart beating red. Holmes had followed me up from the cemetery gates on that occasion. Had it been my hands clutching a shivering bouquet, there is no doubt he would succumb to his nature and remark boldly upon the fact, announcing to my great agony the meaning behind such erratic movements. Fortunately, it was I who did the observing. It would serve neither my nature nor my desires to point out the surprising vulnerability betrayed by his body, and so rather, I had modestly averted my eyes and led us up the familiar path.

'Hello, sweet Mary,' I whispered, fearing full speech would betray the strangeness of the day. 'The passing years have begun to feel whole again. I would not allow dust to settle over your memory, but only a lovely patina which describes your impact on my life.'

'Indeed, Watson, if I may be bold enough to speak to this?' Holmes's voice did not carry the waver of his extremities. I swore I would be impressed with his composure until the end of my days!

'My dear friend, you have been at my side through more than any other man would endure. For you to speak here is no boldness; it is a right, well and truly earned.' A stirring ran the length of my spine as the words left my tongue. For the first time since my arrival in London those many years ago, I felt the ground dropping away from my feet.

'Mrs Watson, when upon my return I learned of your death, I harboured a selfish fear. Your widower, if he would deign to forgive me my absence, might never again allow that part of his heart which you held to bloom. Even another woman would not displace you in his memory, and I am glad for that—he would not be the John Watson we have both held in high esteem if it were possible. And yet, I was sickened by a self-administered poison. If my friend, the dearest I had ever known, could not be restored fully to himself, what was to become of me?

'I am a man of grand sweeping ideas and precise measurements. I am a man immersed in colour and darkness. Without the careful attention of the man whose sole idea of family had been buried with you beneath the frost, I might never find myself centred again.'

Holmes stopped speaking and bowed his head to his chest. His words raced through my mind, rearranging themselves to reveal the spaces between them. What had he tucked inside those crevices, those pockets of meaning brimming too full for him to continue? And had my idea of family gone away with Mary to eternal rest?

A spark of colour caught my eye, a blossom blown against the headstone by an errant breeze. He was dropping them by the fistful, his usual grace abandoned. Purples, greens, and reds spilt across the December earth, an insolent act against the blank slate afternoon. A cascade of gemstones spoke where it appeared Holmes no longer could: pansies, larkspur, eucalyptus, azalea, sweet William, and elderflower. Suddenly my chest constricted with that old horror, and I watched his body fall over the cliff face once more. My legs forsook me, and I lurched forward over the grave.

'—son!' A manic voice met my ear tearing through the nothingness. Barren branches merged into steady lines before my eyes, and I blinked hard to regain control of my senses. Arms were wrapped around my torso. The lack of pain in my knees suggested I had never collided with the ground.

'Holmes?' My voice did not sound like my own, though as I met the eyes of the man reluctantly releasing me, it elicited a response suggesting it was. Relief and guilt swirled in those sharp irises— emotions I cared for far more than my own.

'WATSON,' Holmes began, settling into his annual position by side, 'have I offended?' He was of course referring to the message I had sent to him by way of one of his Irregulars. I had never been known, at Baker Street or any other place, to engage in the dramatic; however, just this once, I could not restrain myself from what I felt to be a rather spot-on imitation of the recipient himself.

Holmes shoved his hands into his coat pockets with more noise than any man of the theatre could have mustered, making the point that he had complied with my request to arrive empty-handed. A small pang of remorse plucked at my heartstrings, but it was wrapped in a giddy pleasure that I had finally outdone the man.

'You have given offence to many a client, a witness, and an officer of the law. It would be useless to deny that you have even, on multiple occasions, given more minor offence to me. In this instance, though, it is not you who would offend. Not in the slightest.' My fingers curled lightly in my pockets, fighting the winter for blood flow.

'You cannot be suggesting that it is you who have caused offence,' Holmes said. Allowing myself to examine his expression, the whirring of my possible sins through his brain was nearly visible through his forehead. 'I cannot find a single way in which you would be to blame for at least the past week.'

'Pray, what crimes have I committed the week before this?' I asked, a grin tugging at the corners of my mouth. 'Never mind. I did not say I had caused offence, but merely that I was in danger of doing so.'

Holmes knitted his brow, then turned toward the headstone before us.

'Please pardon us, Mrs Watson. My confusion, and your widower's reproachable joy in it, do seem to be intruding on your remembrance. We are here, as always on this date, to honour you.'

I watched him as he spoke, as I often did when assisting him with his work, but never before had I been filled with the same degree of pride and tenderness. My hands began their mission before my mind had finished instructing them, so overwhelmed was I by the character of my companion. Pale white petals fell at our feet, broken only slightly by dignified reds and yellows. They had been plucked before I left the horrified florist, for I knew I would not manage the grace and dignity with which it had been done in years past. I was dropping the final blossoms before he noticed my activity.

'Why, Watson! You scoundrel! What trick have you decided to play, on this of all days?'

'Ah, my friend. This time it is you who does not observe. I would not purport to be as skilled as you, yet I daresay I am not a complete dolt. Read them to me, then, these jewels of the earth.'

Surprise passed across those sharp features as he stepped back for an improved view. Amaryllis. Lily of the valley. Wheat. Apple blossom. Yarrow. Snowdrop. His mouth formed each name silently, lower lip quivering as his eyes trailed over them a second time.

'Five years, Watson, and I have been grateful every moment. My messages had been intended only to release pressure in my own heart, though I suppose I may now confess I had hoped to share them openly one day.' His eyes slid upward to where Mary's name was etched in stone. 'I fear I may have been unforgivably selfish. Dear Mrs Watson, please forgive me.'

In a moment of bravery, which I likely should have summoned long ago, I wrapped my hand firmly around Holmes's upper arm.

'I think we've had enough of that,' I suggested gently. 'Mary, you darling soul. You believed a family should be carved out of love. I believe you were right.'

Holmes's gaze was still fixed on the headstone, but any man would know that all he saw were the contents of his own mind. With my hand steady on his arm, I could feel the quickness with which his breaths came. The numbness crept along my fingers, and I determined to buy a set of gloves for each coat.

'Is that a proper vow?' he asked, voice cracking on the last syllable. I leaned closer until our shoulders brushed.

'It is better than a vow, Sherlock. It's the truth.'[1,*]

---

* See 'A Guide to Flower Language' for details regarding the code Holmes uses.

REMEDY
RONIT SILVERSEEKER

'Rest.' Holmes kisses my cheek and disappears farther into our cottage.

'Really, Holmes ...' My protest dissolves into a fit of cough. 'It's nothing but a common cold. There's no need to fuss.'

'Doctors truly make the worst patients,' Holmes chuckles. The cupboard opens and closes; a lid is removed from a jar. I resign to my fate and call out, 'Are you destroying the kitchen?'

'Not without you!' comes the reply, and somehow it isn't reassuring. After a beat, when I expect to hear an explosion, Holmes continues: 'I'm brewing a remedy!'

I sigh, my head falling back on the fluffed pillow. Brilliant though he is, my husband couldn't have possibly found a *cure* so quickly. It simply needs to run its course, then I'll be ... good as ... I ...

I am stopped short of drifting off by the kettle blowing, and soon after my Holmes returns to the bedroom with a steaming mug in hand. 'Careful,' he warns as he passes me the mug. 'Wouldn't want you to burn your tongue.'

'Wouldn't you?' I raise my eyebrow in a half-smile and take a sip, instantly warmed by the rich beverage. 'It's cocoa!'

Holmes smiles. 'Had you read my monograph on comforting ill doctors you would've known exactly what to expect.'

AFTER ALL THESE YEARS
LINDA M. CRATE

i have always
loved our banter,
and our friendship;
but i am glad
something more blossomed
from all the chaos and mayhem
of the cases we've solved
together—
i cannot imagine anyone else
that i would want knowing
me so well as you,
and when we shared that first
kiss i knew that it was the beginning
of the end;
i wasn't going to let you evade me
like the woman did—
irene adler may have been clever,
but she was not the one that's saved
me time and time again;

that was you my friend, my doctor,
my soldier—
and i am so happy to finally be yours,
giddy that you are mine finally
after all these years.

Anchors for the Afterlife

Narrelle M. Harris

Sherlock Holmes was thoroughly annoyed by incorporeality. Offensive enough, against all logic, to become a ghost, but he had no *cases*.

Happily, he still had John.

John Watson found disembodiment less frustrating. They could slightly influence the physical world; he could still hold Sherlock's hand and kiss his cheek. Even as a mere feat of imagination, it was enough.

What were they now but the persistent imaginings of their most intense emotions? Sherlock's burning curiosity and John's devotion to Sherlock, which had survived all manner of discouragement until finally, Sherlock reciprocated that love, with fewer words but unmistakable fervour.

Their spirits had returned, never heard and rarely seen, tied to each other and to the keepsakes Wiggins kept in John's old despatch box.

But then tiny Annie had taken John's pen to write a letter to her Poppa Billy. Small, ferocious whirlwinds had wracked the cottage until the pen, containing John's spirit, sat again alongside Sherlock's magnifying glass. Wiggins had bricked the box into the foundations of refurbished Baker Street, binding them there now.

Sherlock theorised that with time, its precious contents might eventually allow stronger manifestations. He longed for greater *form* and *presence.*

Actually, John thought that Sherlock, who delighted in the theatrical, simply longed to speak directly to a living person, even if it was just to say BOO!

HAUNTED HOUSE
NARRELLE M. HARRIS

Caitlyn, an architect, had questions about her new flat: the refurbished, very irregular 221b Baker Street.

The building was shorter than expected, each floor's ceiling lower than the high Georgian original. Planned extra storeys had not eventuated. Blueprints and materials had frequently vanished, along with memory of them, during construction. The current attic level, from whence ghostliness emanated, equated to the old 19th century second floor.

Walking home, arm in loving arm with girlfriend Martie, Caitlyn spotted their incorporeal flatmates through the small attic window. Two shades, kissing.

'Sneaky devils.'

The profiles, faintly detailed silhouettes, were immediately identifiable: the slender build and hawklike nose of one; the broad shoulders and moustache of the other. Combined with the address, the deduction was obvious.

'They're still together,' said Martie happily.

GHOSTLY HAND IN HAND, Sherlock and John kissed in their old room, a shadow overlaying the new attic, grateful for this almost insubstantial yet comforting touch.

They only impinged on the world with poltergeisted sound and shade. Through force of will, they made the air rush and wrenched objects from places of rest.

What would John give to wield a pen again? What would Sherlock sacrifice to speak directly to the living?

Anything but each other. It's why their spirits lingered. They refused to be parted. Not even death could break their bond.

WHAT SILENT LOVE HATH WRIT

CALAIS RENO

The police station was quiet, just the clatter of a typewriter, the shuffling of papers and feet, and an occasional cough. Someone had brought me a cup of coffee and a biscuit, set them in my hands without a word. No one spoke to me; the quiet was a blessed relief.

In my ears, the falls still roared, a terrible voice that numbed all my other senses. I'd walked up and down the path with the policemen who came to investigate, showing them the footprints that did not turn back towards Meiringen, the walking stick left there, the silver cigarette case, the note.

There was nothing more to see, nothing to say. I'd failed. Using Holmes's own methods, I'd understood what had happened; the error was mine— not an error of deduction, but a failure to observe.

The Swiss lad who came, begging me to attend the dying English woman, was in traditional garb, like a postcard. I noted this at the time, and it ought to have triggered something in my brain: *a costume.* Holmes often used costumes in his investigations; I'd more than once failed to recognise him dressed as a priest or a plumber's apprentice. The Swiss lad was Moriarty's agent. I saw, but did not observe. My error, another lesson I'd not learned.

Holmes had encouraged me to return to London. What that meant, I could not bear to think.

In the quiet station, thinking was all I could do. *He's dead, fallen into that dreadful cataract. He won't appear later tonight and tell me how he escaped, how he bested Moriarty. He is truly gone, and I'll never see him again.*

Freeing society of that master criminal was his last wish, he said in his note. He wrote while Moriarty waited, already knowing he would not survive.

... my career had in any case reached its crisis ... no possible conclusion to it could be more congenial to me than this.

'May I get you anything, Doctor?' Kahler, the police sergeant, leaned over me, his face filled with concern. 'Perhaps you will return to your hotel?'

I nodded. Sitting in the station was a kind of limbo, a place where I could still hope I was wrong, that any moment he would come through the door, dripping wet, laughing that he'd given me such a scare.

I am a soldier. I will not stay in limbo when hell is where I must go.

Back in my hotel room, I sat looking at the bed where he'd slept last night. Perhaps he hadn't slept; when his mind was engaged in a problem, he often sat up, turning possibilities over and weighing them.

I'm an old campaigner; it was only after I returned from war, broken and weak, that I ever had trouble sleeping. It wasn't long after I moved in with Holmes that my nightmares ceased.

That night at the hotel, I had gone to sleep, confident our enemies were far away.

We'd argued when the telegram arrived. He insisted that with Moriarty still at large, I should go home. I refused, equally insisting that I would never leave him in danger of his life.

You do not know me, Holmes, I said, *if you think I would ever leave you.*

He looked sad then, but smiled. *No, I do know my Watson.*

My deficiencies he knew as well. When he saw the Swiss boy and knew his errand, he used that excuse to send me away. I am a doctor; he knew I could not refuse the summons. I would see the lad, hear his tale, and believe him.

This hurt more than anything he could have said. He had kept me close for my loyalty, my steady marksman's hand, my doctor's skill. After ten years as his partner and friend, I ought to have learned his methods, but I had not. As I examined the scene of that final, fateful conflict, I had imagined him hovering at my shoulder, exasperated at the inefficiency and inaccuracy of my observations.

I had missed something, and before leaving Meiringen, I had to discover what it was.

I did not sleep. When it was morning, I had a cup of coffee in the dining room, tried to eat a piece of buttered bread, and returned to the police station.

'Have you found him ... his ... the body?' I asked. 'I would like to bring it back to England with me.'

Kahler shook his head. 'Doctor, you must understand. We've had a heavy snowfall this winter. Now it is spring, and the melt is at its peak. The water descends from the falls at some thousand cubic feet a second. No one can survive in such a deluge. Very dangerous. In the summer, the flood will slow, and by early autumn, perhaps an experienced diver can search the basin, if the body has not surfaced by then.'

The picture this put into my mind made my vision grey out for a moment. I held onto the desk and took a deep breath. 'I understand. But I must be notified. His family will wish to bury him.'

'Of course,' he said, nodding. 'I myself will write to you.'

The journey home was a blur. My mind kept returning to how we'd left London in fear of our lives, trying to outsmart Moriarty by changing trains; then the hotel in Brussels, the dreamlike days wandering through Alpine villages and lonely mountain passes. I'd relaxed my guard under the influence of the peaceful scenery; he had not.

I went first to Baker Street, bringing Holmes's bag. His brother would deal with his possessions, I assumed.

Mrs Hudson was there, and already knew. She wept, and I comforted her, repeated what he'd told me, that it was his finest moment, that he had gladly sacrificed himself to bring down the most dangerous criminal in Europe.

'He always took such risks,' she said, dabbing her eyes with a hand-kerchief. 'I'm glad you were with him, Doctor.'

Climbing those stairs was hard. I carried his bag up and set it inside. I hadn't lived in these rooms for years, but they were as they always had been. Holmes was not known for tidying up, so there were papers on every surface, books lying open, empty teacups, plates with toast crumbs. The smell of tobacco and old books hung in the air. For a moment, I closed my eyes and imagined myself standing in the doorway for the first time.

It was no good. The ghost of Sherlock Holmes would always inhabit these rooms.

I returned to my own house. Mary greeted me at the door. She looked pale, I thought, and thinner than before I'd left, but I attributed that to her sympathetic nature. It was to her that our neighbours and friends came for solace and advice. That sensitivity had drawn me to her when we met. She knew how much Holmes meant to me and grieved for what I'd lost.

The crape band on my hat was the only outward display that I mourned. When, after a month, I did not remove it, Mary said nothing.

I called on Mycroft Holmes to offer my condolences. We'd met twice before; I was not surprised at his reserve. The body had not yet been found, I told him, and shared my conversation with Kahler.

He waved this off. 'I received police reports from Meiringen and have seen to the death notice. Dr Watson, my brother never expected to live a long life. It was often a dangerous life, as you can attest. He knew the odds when he went up against Moriarty and considered his own life the price of victory. He would not wish to see you mourn.' He sighed and shifted his bulk in the chair. 'There will be no funeral, in any case. Nor a memorial.'

'No memorial?'

'It was his wish. He did not believe in an afterlife, and thought mourning customs pointless, the unnecessary lengthening of grief over a natural event.'

This shocked me. I knew that my friend's understanding of all things emotional differed from my own, but I'd never heard him say a word against funerals and memorials. I recalled how gentle he was with Mary, who became my wife, questioning her about the disappearance and probable death of her father.

I had no reason to challenge his decision, though.

Several of Moriarty's champions wrote to the newspaper, making attacks against Holmes, suggesting that he'd invented Moriarty's crimes and lured him to his death. Calling my account 'The Final Problem,' I set forth the events as clearly as I could. Once that was done, I took the band off my hat and went back to practicing medicine.

My life resumed, though changed, and I realised how great a part of my thoughts had been filled by my friend, even after I married. My affection for him was the reason for our separation. People speculate about bachelors sharing quarters, and I did not want his reputation besmirched by any imputation that we were more than friends. In all honesty, I'd never had such a close friend before, even dearer to me than a brother. This worried me; it's one thing to have friends, to join a club for masculine company, quite another to ... well, our friendship was intimate, but no more than what was proper between men. He was not a man who wanted such things, believing they would bias his judgement. I accompanied him on cases, and often we would spend an evening talking and smoking, reviewing the details of an investigation. This was how we'd lived for years before I met Mary.

When I realised how our friendship might be viewed, I began to consider marriage. Holmes was a solitary man; I believe he never cared what people might think of us. He was unhappy when I left; I made the decision for both of us, to protect him.

I was a bit old to be considered an eligible bachelor, but Mary was older as well, beyond the age when a woman might expect to find a husband. For this reason, we never expected children and were astonished to discover that she was pregnant. In the dark months after Holmes's death, we looked forward to the birth.

In October I received the first letter. I opened it, thinking it might be from an old schoolmate or an army chum. When I saw what it was, I laid it on my desk and thought about Sherlock Holmes. He could deduce much from an envelope and a letter, much more than I ever could. But before me lay a small mystery; I considered what my friend would see.

Both the envelope and stationery were foreign. Even if the postmark had not contained characters of some oriental language, the paper felt foreign made. Holmes would have looked for a watermark; I found none. He would have known from the weight and dimensions of the items where they came from.

There was no greeting or signature. The letter was a poem, one I recognised:

> *No longer mourn for me when I am dead*
> *Then you shall hear the surly sullen bell*
> *Give warning to the world that I am fled*
> *From this vile world with vilest worms to dwell;*
> *Nay, if you read this line, remember not*
> *The hand that writ it; for I love you so,*
> *That I in your sweet thoughts would be forgot,*
> *If thinking on me then should make you woe.*
> *O, if (I say) you look upon this verse,*
> *When I (perhaps) compounded am with clay,*
> *Do not so much as my poor name rehearse,*
> *But let your love even with my life decay,*
> *Lest the wise world should look into your moan,*
> *And mock you with me after I am gone.*

It was written in small, neat letters. The ink was black, the paper cream-coloured. The words of the poem bid the reader not to mourn, lest the world mock their love.

I sat, silent; tears stood in my eyes. My mourning had continued, even months after his death. Though the world saw me going to and from my surgery, carrying out the business of living, my grief had not lightened at all.

... for I love you so ...

Who would send me such a message? The death of a friend is sad, but not momentous for a man with a wife and a child on the way.

But what if someone had known what I felt? I had not loved Holmes improperly, though I loved him dearly. With Oscar Wilde in the news, however, our relationship might be suspect.

The postmark scratched that theory. I knew of no one in the Far East at this time. And I had no acquaintance who would send me a sonnet.

It was then that I noticed that some of the letters were slanted, while the rest were straight up and down. The poem was meticulously written, as if it had been typed, except for these several words, which were italicised:

... dead ... I am ... not ... I ... am ... not ... gone ...

There are no coincidences, Holmes had often said. *The universe is rarely so lazy.*

If these words were written in a different hand, they were meant to be read as a message.

My heart pounded in my throat. Again, I heard the roar of the falls, saw the carefully propped Alpine stock, the note placed under the silver box.

I am not a greedy man; I do not ask for the impossible, only the improbable.

Please. Come back to me.

Perhaps my hope would be disappointed, but I carried on hoping, cautiously.

Two months after the letter, another hope was disappointed. Mary was in pain and began to bleed, and we both feared that she was about to miscarry.

It was after midnight, of course, the hour when all such emergencies occur. I called Anstruther, a colleague, and he came at once.

Alas, the tiny spark of life that had given me the heart to carry on, the child I hadn't asked for but had been given—that miracle had never existed. Not merely a false pregnancy; it was cancer, Anstruther said. It had given her all the symptoms; we'd wasted weeks thinking that all was well. As a doctor, I reproached myself for missing the signs.

'I'd have thought the same,' Anstruther told me. 'You did nothing wrong.'

She succumbed quickly, within a month. One year after losing Holmes, I was alone.

The second letter arrived six weeks later, in the dregs of a long, bitter winter. I'd poured my energy into visiting my elderly patients, many of whom were ill with influenza. Carrying on, I held faint hope close to my heart.

When I arrived home that night, the house was dark and cold. The woman who cooked for me was ill and I had told her to stay in bed. Once a fire was started in the grate, I sat down to look at the envelope.

Perhaps someone with a knowledge of Chinese could tell me what the postmark said, but I was sure that information would not answer my doubts.

It was another sonnet, hand-written like the first. Again, Shakespeare:

> *When to the sessions of sweet silent thought*
> *I summon up remembrance of things past ...*

There were no italicised words, just a note at the bottom, in the same hand:

Work is the best antidote to sorrow.

I had not heard from the Swiss police. The story of Holmes's death was no longer news.

DURING THE YEAR THAT FOLLOWED, nothing of note happened. To all appearances, I was alive, walking the streets of London with my bag, tending patients, receiving at my surgery those who were not bedridden.

My practice was failing, though. I barely managed my expenses, and lacked the ambition to acquire patients who could pay my fees. I treated them regardless, moved into a flat above the surgery, and made do with what I had.

Days were all the same. Mornings I made hospital and house calls, and afternoons I waited at the surgery for patients. Each evening, I locked the door, went upstairs, and ate my poor supper alone, contemplating what my life had become.

Though I'd mourned Mary and the child we'd never had, that sorrow had softened into a fond memory. I did not think of remarrying.

For Holmes, my feelings were complex. There are men who love one another; I knew several. These were not licentious men; some were in committed (if illegal) relationships. The ancients believed this is the best and purest of loves. I'd never applied this to myself, but now realised what I thought of as an intimate friendship with Holmes was in fact love. I loved him.

This revelation shook me. I had truly loved Mary, but she was not my lodestar; it was Holmes I'd always orbited, just as a planet travels around its star. I saw it now: I'd been cowardly, calling my love something else. I hadn't married to defend his reputation, but to avoid the rejection I feared.

Over the months, two more letters arrived. *Love letters.* My sight now clear, I recognised it:

> *... O! learn to read what silent love hath writ:*
> *To hear with eyes belongs to love's fine wit.*

Reluctant to say, he couched his feelings in borrowed verse.

> *For thee watch I, whilst thou dost wake elsewhere,*
> *From me far off, with others all too near.*

Just as I lay awake, thinking about him, he was missing me.

When the third year began, I had heard nothing from my poetic correspondent for months. I hoped this meant he was travelling, on his way home.

I felt unmoored, able neither to believe that he would return, or to get on with my life. A foolish fancy, I told myself, to think that these poems came from his hand. But I could think of no other explanation.

Even so, there was no reason to believe Holmes would return. He'd left because of danger and feared to return until danger was gone. There was no return address, leaving our conversation one-sided. What could I have said?

What made my heart sink was the fear that he'd been found, that one of Moriarty's lieutenants had survived, and had cornered his quarry. The thought of Holmes dying in a foreign land, unknown and unmourned, made many of my nights sleepless.

I returned from work one day to find a letter waiting for me, though not the one I'd hoped for. The return address was a town on the Mediterranean coast, Montpelier. Curious, I tore it open at once.

The writer was Hector Michaud, who described himself as a scientist. He sought a consultation for some condition he did not describe. Having read all my stories, he knew I was a medical doctor. In one of my stories, he said, I had described his symptoms perfectly. From this, he believed I could help him, and begged that I come to Montpelier. He would pay all my expenses, of course, and I might stay at his villa.

I laughed out loud. That John Watson, who ate beans on toast and reused his teabags in order to pay his bills, could be sought as an international expert, invited to enjoy a Mediterranean seaside holiday, was beyond belief.

Sceptical, I did some research, using Holmes's scrapbooks. Hector Michaud was real, I found, a renowned researcher in coal-tar derivatives who resided in Montpelier.

Even if I could not help the man, it was a chance to escape the gloom of London and my never-ending grief.

Three years earlier, I'd sailed from New Haven with Holmes, landing at Dieppe. This time I took a train from that same port to Paris, and from there south, to Montpelier. At the station a carriage waited for me. My French is passable; the driver said the house was remote.

I wondered if it had been a good idea to come so far, knowing so little about my patient. I'd wracked my brain, going over the many stories I'd written that involved diseases, but could not place which might have inspired him to write his letter. Perhaps he was an eccentric, or even a criminal of some kind.

He came out of the house to greet me himself, and my impression was of an elderly man in the peak of good health. He moved easily and with energy, welcomed me graciously.

'You are no doubt puzzled, Doctor,' he said. 'A man you do not know summons you urgently, giving no details of his *maladie*. Yet here you are. It speaks to your great devotion to your patients, I think, that you have come and wish to help.'

I accepted his firm handshake, thinking of the last time I'd put devotion to a patient over my own sense of caution. I would forever regret leaving Holmes at the falls to attend the English woman. Perhaps I'd been fooled once again.

We sat in a parlour; tea was brought, and small sandwiches.

'I know Englishmen love their tea, but surely you are tired from your long journey,' he said. 'Please ask whatever you wish, and I will see that you have it.'

'If you are willing, I would like to examine you so that I can begin my diagnosis.'

'Soon,' he replied. 'No hurry, doctor. Your stories are all delightful, but sometimes the details escape me. You knew the great Sherlock Holmes intimately, *bien sûr*. What was it he called you? Conductor of Light?'

I smiled stiffly. 'He meant it with irony, I think. Sometimes my deductions were so far off the mark, it helped him see the solution. If you think I am a detective, you will be disappointed. Whatever problem troubles you, I will do my best to diagnose, but I cannot pull an answer out of thin air. Neither could Holmes, to be honest. He worked diligently to reach solutions. I fear I've made his process seem much simpler in my stories. He often rebuked me for that.' I shifted uncomfortably. 'Readers like a bit of magic better than science.'

His eyes lit up. 'Ah, yes! I am a scientist. I do not expect magic from you, Doctor. I have confidence in your medicine.'

Other people were in the house; I heard them moving around. It was a large mansion, with a staff of servants, silently appearing and withdrawing. Nevertheless, I felt as if someone were watching me.

'Can you describe your condition?'

He smiled ruefully. 'I must be honest, Doctor. Not for myself have I summoned you.' His eyes focused over my shoulder.

I did not turn immediately. To do so would invite disappointment.

'I have a friend who requires your skill, and your compassion.'

When I heard someone take a step into the room, I finally stood and turned toward the door, prepared to greet my host's *friend*.

In confusion, I gasped and took a step forward, then back. He looked thin, but healthy. He had always been lean, but now he looked weary as well. I'd imagined him undercover, hiding in boltholes, sleeping in barns and basements, fearing for his life.

Michaud had slipped out of the room. I heard him talking to the servant in the kitchen, asking about dinner.

I felt tears on my cheeks.

Holmes watched me, his face uncertain now.

I was angry, without understanding why. Here was the thing I'd wished for, dreamed of for three years. He'd sent me letters so I would know he was alive. He'd had Michaud send for me now.

What reason did I have for anger? Or was it self-blame?

'Watson.' He looked down. 'I owe you a thousand apologies.'

'No,' I said. 'It's I who am sorry.'

He fixed me with a look of bewilderment. 'Why are you apologising to me?'

'I shouldn't have left you. I was too dull to see it was a ruse.'

'No, no!' Distraught, he waved his hands. 'I deliberately misled you. Had I not reassured you that it was the right thing to do, you would not have left.'

'But why?' Understanding hit me then, like a blow to the solar plexus. My knees nearly buckled. 'I see. You had already made your plan to leave. I would have been an encumbrance.'

He strode towards me, his arms raised, then hesitated, let them fall to his sides, his eyes avoiding mine. 'I hadn't made my plan. The boy's story told me that Moriarty was close, and I was afraid to have you present for that confrontation. You would have tried to protect me, and he would have killed you. I couldn't let that happen. I encouraged you to go because I was afraid.'

At these words I began to feel light-headed. Holmes caught me as I collapsed, calling for brandy. In a moment Michaud was there with the bottle, and Holmes held a glass to my lips.

'I'm all right,' I said, sitting up. 'Please, don't trouble yourself.'

He helped me to the sofa and sat beside me. Michaud retreated again.

'You received my letters?' he asked. At my nod, he sighed. 'So many times I wanted to explain myself, but feared I would put you in danger. You were being watched, at least at first. I headed east, to Tibet, where I stayed for two years. It was there that I finally conceived the idea of writing you an anonymous letter, giving a clue that you might find.'

'I did,' I said. 'The letter itself was a mystery, and right away I thought of the many cases you'd solved with coded messages. Still, I dismissed it because ... I feared I might be disappointed.'

He took my hand in his. 'When I heard of your bereavement, I sent again, and after that I kept on, until I had to leave and begin making my way back. You see, I always intended to return. And I hoped ...' He looked away, his eyes sad. 'Forgive me, Watson. I have offended you.'

'Offended?'

'I am not a sentimental man, but when I was alone and wishing I were home, I thought of you, and ...'

'You hoped I would hear what *silent love hath writ*.'

'Yes.' He smiled through his tears. 'You see, Watson, I am not purely a cold, unemotional reasoner, as I pretend to be. When it comes to love, I am just as foolish as other people. Concerning you, my judgement was completely biased. I should have had you at my side from the beginning, but I *couldn't*, Watson. Do you understand? I could *not* let you die defending me, as I knew you would. My love for you ... But set aside your concern, dear friend. I am what I am, and I only hope you can overlook what my nature is and forget what I said when I was far away, missing you.' Looking away, he let go of my hand.

'*Cold* and *unemotional* are the very last words I'd use to describe you,' I said, grasping his hand. His fingers *were* cold, but it was excess emotion that did that. 'You have a heart, Holmes, and if you're offering it to me—'

I felt his hand begin to tremble. He turned his head as if he could not bear to look at me. 'You need not comfort me, Watson. I will remain here a bit longer before returning to England, and when I do, I have no expectation—'

There was nothing for it. I took his face in my hands and kissed him.

I pulled back then and looked into his eyes. 'You have deduced incorrectly, Sherlock. Yes, I will call you that now—because I love you.'

'You have a heart, Holmes, and if you're offering it to me—'

He froze, my words only gradually making sense to him. He gave a soft gasp, and then began to kiss me back, making little sounds of joy and disbelief.

'John,' he breathed. 'I have never been so happy to be wrong.'

The Adventure of the Empty House is not the full story of how Sherlock Holmes returned to London. That journey, with a week's stay in Paris, will never be published in *The Strand*. It is true that there had been a murder, and the one who'd fired the bullet that killed Ronald Adair was none other than Sebastian Moran, who'd kept Holmes from returning sooner. It is also true that Holmes lured Moran to that house with the hope that he might also put a bullet into Holmes. There we finally saw Moran arrested. He went to prison for murder, though there are many other crimes which might be attributed to him. That night, we put an end to a dark chapter for England, and for ourselves.

But even the thrill of standing beside Holmes in that darkened house, watching his prey caught in the trap, even the relief of seeing Moran taken away in darbies—no, none of the events of that night can surpass the joy of coming home again, walking through the door of 221B, being greeted by Mrs Hudson, and seeing our old rooms just as they had been.

Old habits were resumed, but new routines became part of our shared life as well. We are sentimental, but I trust that our judgment has survived the ordeal. Our days continue to be full of adventures— chasing criminals down alleys, searching for missing treasures, solving murders—but there are many quiet evenings when we sit together in companionable silence.

Then Holmes will rise from his chair, hold out his hand to me, and offer me quite another kind of adventure. 1895 is not a year when such adventures can be described, dear reader, so I will leave them to your imagination.

ONE DAY WE WILL BE

LARC ENCIEL

Holmes was different when he 'came back from the dead'. He was the same curious and intelligent man I had known. But something ... had changed in him.

It was around that time that he became more affectionate, let's say. I often caught him staring at my face as I explained my views, and if I ever failed to comprehend something from a case we took, he would explain it patiently. He always wore a soft look on his face when I expressed my gratitude.

Then there were the subtle touches. From my elbow to my arm. To the hem of my sleeve whenever we walked, and the small of my back with no one around. It made me yearn for his affection more.

Then one night, the both of us shivering from the rain—him with a knife wound in his side and me with a broken wrist—he confessed his love.

Now we are retired in Sussex, our hearts overflowing with love. Sherlock tending to his bees while I work on the first book of our past adventures. Though we couldn't be seen together outside as I truly wanted, I hope that this book I am writing will one day resonate with our readers. A book full of adventures and love.

Free of prejudice, as one day, we will be.

A LOVE ELEMENTARY

LINDA M. CRATE

i always knew
that i loved you,
i never liked your wife
because in my mind
it was always supposed
to be you and i;

every bit as elementary
as the case coming together at the
end, dear watson—

i suppose perhaps my love
was too subtle for you to
understand,
but no one likes being too
obvious;

i am just glad that today it is

you and i
solving crimes and finding time
to love each other the way i always
hoped that we might.

HONEY
BOOKER WEGNER

Back when we took up residence with dearest Ms Hudson, she was the cook and Watson, the breadwinner. I, with few to no kitchen skills of my own—aside from more fundamental chemistry—and cases too infrequent or, shall we say, financially complicated (Watson would call *me* soft-hearted instead, the hypocrite) for full and tangible payment, found myself often between these two responsible adults providing food, shelter, pocket money, and company. I often felt as though I gave little but entertainment in return.

Upon learning of my thoughts on the matter, Watson was quick to reassure me of my place in the life we shared. In our halcyon days of retirement, I do not doubt him. We may require the odd falsehood about where he lives now and with whom, but everyone of import knows the truth. And after all our time in the public streets and papers of London, there are some small things meant for us alone. His wind-watered eyes after a walk by the seaside; his dancing hands as he plays with the stray cat we have taken in; his face flushed and warm from the fire at night.

He is still the breadwinner. He is also, now, the cook.

'Holmes,' he calls to me from the kitchen one caramel evening.

'Yes?' Though I have finished the latest book I'd bought from a quaint little store in town, the cat is comfortably paying no rent whatsoever in my lap (her name is Mary Shelley, she is entirely black save for half her muzzle, and she is a queen among felines), and I am loathe to move her. 'What is it, dear boy?'

There is a knowing laugh from around the corner, as if he is humouring me somehow. He usually is. 'Shelley's with you, is she?'

'She is her own cat and can do as she pleases,' I retort. Watson chuckles again, softer, socked feet on the wooden floor.

He turns a corner and reveals to me a silver tray, lifted high so I cannot see what he has put upon it. This is a game of mine. His glasses reflect a dandelion glow, yellower than the cheerful fire, and the minute slide of porcelain on metal signifies two plates alongside the more obvious teapot. The tray smells of honey.

Watson is a good cook. Not phenomenal, but his fare is certainly hearty and filling; he'd been sick of army food, he explained to me once. And since he had no landlady or wife to look after him during his first few months home, and only a veteran pension to keep him afloat, he'd taken to making his own food. This was one of the few things I did not learn about him until recently, a rarity for me who thought he knew all there was to know of John Watson. Now I know he loves windy days and cats and cornflowers, and he cooks a hearty lamb pie.

But better than even dear Ms Hudson, my Watson can *bake*.

'They're honeycakes,' he says, setting down the tray on the coffee table and relaxing into the loveseat. 'No need to deduce it, as they're right here, and are not about to commit a crime.'

'Not even the crime of remorseless indulgence?' I murmur. The cakes are golden and soaked in dark, glittering honey from my own beehive, with the spongy consistency of furled peonies. They're probably fresh from the oven. 'These smell heavenly, my dear.'

Shelley, sensing my excitement, turns into a rare darling and slips off of my lap so that I might reach for one. Watson, however, bats my hand away. 'They're still too hot, silly man. Wait a minute.'

To placate me he offers a cup of Earl Grey, palm-warm, and smiles when I take it with my eyes scrunched up in faux-grudging. His grey moustache curls up at the edges of his mouth. Shelley stretches herself over the carpet, obviously enjoying the fireplace's heat as much as we do. Watson leans over to stroke her coat.

Slowly, as though hurrying might disturb the crystal moment, I exhale. The trees outside rustle their sunset dresses. Owls begin to philosophise. Distantly, I hear the ocean riling up for a night on the town. The taste of dinner—local fish, grilled in rustic form with crackling salt and spice—dissolves under quiet waves of tea.

My love might describe it better, poet that he is, but I am content with the evening as we behold it together.

'They're cool enough now,' he says, voice low. I take my piece and begin a new game of guessing the ingredients within. Honey, of course. Almond extract. Baking powder. Watson knows exactly what I'm doing. He rolls his eyes as I finish with the treat, wipe my hands on a napkin Shelley has gnawed the edge of, and recite to him the recipe as though I'd written it myself.

'Show-off,' he laughs, warm and kind. 'Genius. But you forgot one.'

'I couldn't have,' I say primly, abandoning my seat on the couch only to relocate on his lap as if I am the cat. 'I even heard each ingredient as you pulled it out.' I lean into him. Due to the peculiarities of normal force, we do not become one entity, and despite his firm arguments that I am a complete human being, I find myself still believing that I am the brain and he is the body—eyes, hands, heart —through which I view the world. I feel his heat and his skin. On him I smell sweat and cinnamon. At the risk of becoming maudlin in my old age, my world is this cottage and this cat and these cakes— and him, gentle blue eyes, skilled hands, fire-touched heart.

'What is it then, John?' I ask, pressing my cheek to his hair.

He whispers into my neck, *'Love,'* and I don't know if he's answering the question or calling my name. It doesn't matter.

'You are incurably sappy,' I tell him, 'but I confess I am no better.'

BEE AFRAID

BERTIE M.

T he morning was greyer than it ought to be when I awoke, for I never rose this early without cause. But that cause soon became apparent—a knock at the door, loud and long.

'Who on Earth is disturbing us at this hour?' I muttered resentfully, rubbing old sleep out of older eyes.

'Only the foulest dregs of society, my dear boy,' Holmes declared, sitting up beside me in a flash. *'Capitalists.'*

At first, I marvelled fondly at his observational prowess—until I realised he might perhaps have drawn his conclusion from the irritating bout of sales chatter sounding from the doorway.

'Good Lord,' I groaned. 'Again?'

I had attempted to negotiate with them the afternoon prior, but it seemed the single-minded marketers were prepared to hound us until the day we died.

'Indeed. I fear there is only one remaining recourse.'

Holmes sprang to his feet like a rabbit, with an eternal vigour that defied his age.

'Watson?' My dear companion looked at me with an intensity that hadn't graced his features in years. *'Release the bees'*

I stared back at him in complete and utter silence.

'Not the honeybees, of course. They shan't give their lives for such an ignoble cause. The bumblebees, however, have been suitably trained for combat—'

'For the last time, Holmes, I am *not* releasing the bees!'

REMINISCENCE
N. HOLMES

I was awoken by a light chuckle in my ear. Slowly, as I regained consciousness, I became aware of the warmth of the man who lay behind me, with his arm around my waist. I turned to find Holmes staring at me with affectionate eyes and a gentle smile gracing his lips.

'What's so amusing?' I said in half a whisper, my voice heavy with sleep, turning back to my previous position. Holmes's arms tightened around me, and I felt him smile even more broadly against my neck.

'It seems I have grown more sentimental with age,' he said against my skin. 'The result of prolonged exposure to a contaminating agent, no doubt.' In spite of the ironic remark, there was a tenderness in his voice which even now was rare. His fingers brushed through my now almost completely grey hair, and I couldn't help but feel that tenderness multiply tenfold inside my chest, my heart momentarily in pain from the strong emotion. I turned again to look at Holmes's face and his arms quickly circled around my back.

'And what prompted such a fit of *sentimentalism* on your part?'

'Why,' he said, a hand moving to caress my cheek, his eyes fixed on mine. 'You, of course.' His hands moved along my face, slow and precise, almost calculating. My eyes fluttered shut, and a slight sigh escaped my lips. I could feel his fingers mapping my skin, tracing the shell of my ears, moving softly down the bridge of my nose and upon my parted mouth. Suddenly I was reminded of the first time he had touched me like this. A long time had passed since then, and yet he continued to do it with the same fascination and awe he had expressed then.

'I see,' I said, my eyes still closed and my voice only the barest of whispers. 'You were reminiscing.'

I felt him nod against my neck, his lips continuing the pattern his fingers had begun. I knew *what* he was thinking, and yet I couldn't think of any particular reason *why* he had begun reminiscing about our first time sleeping together. I told him as much—with some effort, since his mouth had moved upon my stomach in the meantime, and all coherence I had possessed merely moments ago had disappeared. Holmes obviously knew this, and much to my despair, his attentions to my body promptly ceased. In an instant, his face was next to mine again. His eyes shone the same way they did every morning since our retirement: full of contentment and an inner peace that, thirty years earlier, I would not have thought possible. Not this far from London, at any rate.

'You really don't know why?' he asked me, a beat later, manoeuvring both of us into a sitting position, as if to look at me more closely, surprise evident in his eyes and even a hint of amusement colouring his voice.

I felt myself blush with some embarrassment and even more annoyance when Holmes threw his head back and began laughing heartily, letting me go. It was then that I set my foggy, lust-filled brain to work out what it was that I was supposed to know. It took only ten seconds of reflection. Holmes was still laughing when I threw my pillow square on his face.

'Happy anniversary,' I said, with mock bitterness, a smile breaking through my wavering scowl. 'You know I am terrible with dates.'

Holmes wiped his eyes, which had overflown with unshed tears, sighed and looked at me again, his lips pressed in a tight line that kept wavering with the threat of yet another fit of laughter at my expense.

'The great John "Trail of broken hearts on three continents" Watson forgot an anniversary!' exclaimed Holmes, his tone one of absolute delight. 'Anyone who heard you now would think *I* was the hopeless romantic, not you.'

Instead of answering the way any other man would in my position, I did the most sensible thing one could do to shut Sherlock Holmes up: I kissed him. Immediately, the smirk that curved his lips disappeared as I softly grabbed his bottom lip between my teeth, drawing a growl from the back of his throat. His hands pressed insistently against my back once more, drawing us closer. Our mouths opened and I pushed my tongue against his, this time swallowing the moan that escaped between Holmes's lips. A moment later, in very much the same abrupt manner he had employed earlier, I broke the kiss.

It was my turn to laugh at his betrayed expression.

'You little devil,' he mumbled, crossing his arms over his chest, and turning his face away from me, with the utter theatricality only he could muster. His voice was cold, but the small smile upon his face turned his performance into none other than that of annoyed fondness, one we were both exceedingly familiar with.

'All yours,' I whispered, moving to caress his upper arm. For an instant I was mesmerised by the sight of Holmes in our bed, much as

I had been the first time I was granted the opportunity to witness it. And yet, this moment could not compare in the slightest.

We had been young then—for being forty-three and forty years old respectively was *not* being old. Not considering the life we led. We had been young, and we had suffered, and we had lost—I had lost the two people I had loved the most. I had been ripped apart by grief; the best parts of me had been stolen away by the unwavering hand of Death. To this day, I cannot say what it was that stopped me from grabbing its hand too. Perhaps, a part of me had known I was meant to wait a little longer. Nevertheless, nothing could have prepared me for the gift I received three years later. The public is already familiar with those events, but there is much that they don't know. That they can never know.

They could never know how I had been put back together almost as painfully as I had been torn apart.

During the day—and indeed, part of the night—of Holmes's return it had been easy. I felt whole again. I had Holmes by my side, all in one piece! It had been hard to believe then, but the fact that both Lestrade and Mrs Hudson had acknowledged his presence as well had comforted me enough to put any doubts about my sanity to rest. That night, I had gone to bed in my old room in Baker Street feeling a new man. I was certain I would have the best night of rest I had had in years, and many days of happiness would follow.

Instead, I woke in the middle of the night, with Holmes' name stuck in my throat. I was suddenly convinced that all the events of the day before had been a delusion. A deep anguish overcame me, and I sobbed and begged God to at least spare me the madness, since I was already destined to die alone. I begged for mercy and for forgiveness for what felt like an eternity stuck in front of paradise, the entrance to which I was being denied. My throat had gone sore, and every sob had felt like a part of me being newly ripped away. I could not see anything beyond my tears. I could not hear anything beyond my screams. At some point I became aware of a pair of painfully thin yet strong arms that had circled around me; I became aware that foreign tears had joined my own. I could hear only a broken whisper, repeated like a sacred chant, although I could not understand it at the time.

I'm sorry, I'm sorry. God, John, I'm sorry.

I cannot say how long we remained in that position, for the exertion of the previous day caught up with me yet again, and I fell into a deep sleep, surrounded by the heat of the body that held me in its arms like a child.

I blinked into the present, and found Holmes looking at me, his eyes full of worry. One of his hands had moved upon my face, which, I distantly noticed, had become wet with tears. 'What's wrong?' he asked, in the same broken whisper from our past. I smiled and covered his hand with mine, delighted at the simple feeling of his own aged skin against my own. I took it away from my face and held it between my own hands for a moment. My mind was still seeing the Holmes he had been then, the one who had welcomed me into consciousness after that terrible night. His face had been stricken with the very same grief I had experienced the night before. I had touched his face too, then—I couldn't help myself—marvelled at the trace of tears, marvelled at the sight of naked emotion that his eyes could barely contain, feeling for the first time the undeniable reality of the touch of his flesh under mine, of the blood rushing through his veins. Of the heart that beat inside his chest. Young, alive.

His hands had held mine, exactly as I did now. Our bodies were older, but the feeling was the same.

I let go of his hands to grab his face. I kissed his forehead, feeling Holmes's lips doing the same on my own skin thirty years earlier. I kissed his brow, and his nose, and his cheekbones, retracing the path

Holmes had traced upon my face that morning in Baker Street. 'I love you.' I whispered to his lips, as he had then.

'My John ...' Holmes whispered in return, a sweet smile curving his lips. And then, as if this too was a sacred chant: 'I love you.'

At some point I became aware of a pair of painfully thin yet strong arms that had circled around me.

He closed the remaining gap between our mouths with delicacy, his lips brushing mine almost cautiously. He too, was remembering. But we were no longer in Baker Street, the sun was not barely rising upon our windows. We were no longer fearful of Mrs Hudson waking up to start her day and discovering our secret (although she had known, bless her). And this was not the first kiss we had shared. I pulled Holmes closer, forcing my tongue inside his mouth, and tried to precisely convey that. I pressed my hands up and down his back, mentally cataloguing every scar, knowing the exact location of each mole without needing to see them.

The first time we had touched like this he had had fewer scars and fewer moles. His skin had been pale as the snow, and still taut with youth, although already showing signs of the passing of time. His hands had wandered over my skin, slowly, fearfully. He had said nothing but my name, over and over, like a wretched man's prayer, his heart too heavy with repentance to love me freely. But I had loved him for the both of us. My hands wandered over his now slightly darker skin—a gift from his morning swims—instinctively, knowingly. I heard his breathless laugh in my ears, the gentle teasing, the infinite adoration, freely given and freely returned.

'John,' he said, and it was nothing at all like the first time he had said it—except for one thing: the adoration was the same, even stronger. 'Oh, John,' he sighed. 'I'm—' A loud growl interrupted him, and I couldn't help but smile when his face turned pink, and he stared at his stomach with bewilderment, as if he had forgotten about his own humanity. (And knowing him as I did, he probably had).

'Hungry?' I finished for him, placing a final kiss on his cheek. 'Come, let's have breakfast,' I said, pulling him out of bed with me. 'There will be plenty of time to reminisce later.'

DO YOU REMEMBER
KYNDALL POTTS

'Do you remember?' said Holmes as we stared into the fire. 'Do you remember how we outsmarted England's most nefarious villains? Like Milverton?'

'We didn't outsmart Milverton. The lady killed him.' I pulled the blanket closer around us.

'Minor detail,' he scoffed.

'Amberley?' he continued.

'Put away for life,' said I as I curled my fingers around his. 'You were brilliant.'

'Ah, what times those were,' said he. 'We made a good team.'

'Do you miss it?' I asked, resting my head against his shoulder.

He didn't answer.

'Holmes?'

'I do. Sometimes. The thrill. The danger. The glory. Don't you?'

I considered the question. It had been a year since we'd moved to Sussex. The twelve months had been blissful. Getting up when we felt like it. No responsibilities other than the bees. Making love at any hour of the day. Or not at all. Long walks and long naps. Reading by the fire.

Retirement had mellowed Holmes. I hadn't expected this. I had expected him to rebel against the march of time. But he'd accepted it with grace. He was different now. Reflective. Serene.

'Yes,' said I, honestly. 'But growing old with you is more than I could have hoped for. I love our life.'

'Dear Watson.' He smiled and leaned down to whisper in my ear, 'Take me to bed.'

ENCORE

WITH CHARITY FOR ALL
EC BOSS

Papers from the estate of Sherlock Holmes
Last will and testament, with enclosures: letter and key

To our own dear girl,

You reading these words means I am not there to comfort you, as you have comforted me since your father left us both. It has been a colder world from the loss of his smile, the grace of his laugh. I hope that living secure in the knowledge that he, and we both, loved you from the moment you took your first breath until the moment we took our last, will help to make the roads you walk a little clearer and your steps more sure.

The solicitor will have informed you of the portion allotted to you from our estates. The key entrusted to you will open a box of treasures of greater or lesser value. I wonder what you will make of what you find there: a photo of a long forgotten South American opera singer, a ring once worn upon a noble hand. Souvenirs of cases solved, others bitterly never to be forgotten. You may keep them, or sell them, or toss them in the Thames as your wisdom bids.

With these things is a much greater treasure by far: writings of your father which have waited long years to see the light of day. Of his published works, many a case was withheld until those involved had passed beyond the reach of the law or the glimpse of the public eye. How much more did we ourselves keep back? Details about our lives, our hearts, and, of course, you, my dear, your very existence.

They now fall to your keeping: the daughter of John H. Watson. My goddaughter, Charity Marie Holmes Watson.

And the choice as to their future is also in your hands.

Shall they join our small mementos in a watery grave? Or may they be shared with the public who loved us, but who with full knowledge of our lives would have cast judgments upon us both and likely taken you from your father's care? Or consigned that kind, brave soul to prison for the crime of love? Much less my cold, cynical person—close enough to the criminal class to be part of it—proven at last.

You, too, would be affected by the publication of the truth of our lives. Damning your family's name to ignominy or infamy. So, the final choice is yours.

I offer my small contribution to help guide you in your deliberations. An account of my return from 'death.' A time when truths were revealed between us. The time when I met you.

Read on and choose. But whatever the choice, live your life in peace and prosperity. Your happiness is the greatest tribute we could ask. Know me always to be:

Your father's lifelong companion and

Your loving guardian,

Sherlock Holmes

. . .

MY ESTEEMED FRIEND AND COMPANION, Doctor John Watson made it part of his life's work to publish romanticised versions of our adventures together. He provided the reading public with a properly heartrending account of my final hours and supposed demise at the hands of Professor Moriarty, master criminal.

Scarce a soul could have lived up to the eulogy he wrote for me. But those lines inspired me to try.

It gave me hope. It made me wonder: could a man write those words for another and not feel something? Something beyond friendship alone?

For inside me I carried a secret. One that had arisen in me unbidden: its seeds sown in that laboratory at Barts, watered by the Work we shared, and bloomed bright in the noonday of conducted light, and simple, unadorned companionship. Never spoken, never acknowledged.

That love I carried inside urged me to return to him when the time was right.

After I was redeemed from death, my homecoming was unheralded and unremarked by any—save the stern words of caution from my brother Mycroft and the sneaking suspicions of survival held by that final remaining confederate of Professor Moriarty: Colonel Moran.

Returning home to 221B Baker Street, I found it was not the sanctuary I'd dreamed of during my travels. Dust sat heavy on the mantel. Our chairs had a dispirited air, long having given up waiting for their owners to return.

On my entrance, I missed my mark. Rather than meeting Mrs Hudson after she had received a carefully worded note from my brother warning of my return, instead I startled the good woman into a shrieking fit when carelessly I rid myself of whiskers and cane.

I should have learned my lesson and given my Watson due notice. But instead, I surprised the man and had him fainting in my arms for punishment.

I was loath to let him go.

His face when he saw me! How pale he became. How he trembled. And I realised what a thoughtless wretch I had been, springing this spectre on my dear Watson.

I ministered to him as I could. Soon his eyes were fluttering. He was waking, and intelligence came back to those serious brown eyes once more. I could not resist the urge to touch him, to lend comfort and to take my own.

He spoke my name once more, in tones of disbelief.

'A thousand pardons, my dear Watson!' I cried.

'But how is this possible?'

Putting a hand to his brow, his cheek, I said, 'My dear fellow, I am so sorry. I had no idea you would be so affected.'

'Holmes,' he said, reaching out a hand to touch my arm. His eyes told me he did not believe it. Of course he didn't. What a fool I was.

'Yes, Watson,' I said, clutching his arm firmly in turn. 'I have returned.'

And I told him why I had fled. I told him how I had longed to inform him—of all people—that I had survived, but confessed that his belief in and writing of my demise should convince those whom I most needed to deceive.

'Surely, Holmes, you could have trusted me to hold this secret for you as I have so many others?'

'I am sorry, Watson, that I did not. Let us hope that there will be no future such test of either of us.'

We sat thus, until word came of a patient waiting. I resumed my disguise and assured Watson I would be in attendance upon him that evening, to discuss how the case he assisted Lestrade upon coincided with my own pursuit of Colonel Moran.

He gave me his address (which I was already in possession of) and clasped my hand warmly.

'If this was just a dream, I shall still be glad of it. For the few moments more that it has let me spend in your presence.' His face was most affected.

'Have no fear Watson, I shall be with you again soon and whisk you off for adventure.'

∽

As WATSON HAD REQUESTED, I arrived at his abode sharply at 6 pm. No more delays!

'Watson,' I said, taking him in.

His hair was newly clipped, his chin shaved. He wore a crisp shirt and a green coat I had always admired. The clothes fit well but were tailored for a body more lean than I remembered. His eyes were shadowed; his face was lined. His hair was now streaked with grey where it had been glossy black before.

He took my hand warmly into both of his own. He bid me join him by the fire.

On his mantel, I saw a picture with his Mary. Taken at the time of their wedding, it sat in a place of honour.

In the photo, I saw happiness shining in both their faces. And now in the flesh, I saw traces of sorrow that my friend had endured. His parents, his brother, then myself—or so he thought—and his dear Mary, gone. Let alone other friends and comrades throughout the war. Patients whose lives he had fought unsuccessfully to save. Even enemies he may have struggled with and brought to their end.

So much death on the register of this man's life. So much loss.

'Watson,' I said, my voice thick with emotion, surprising myself. 'I am so grieved at your misfortune.' I indicated the photo. 'Her absence must be felt by many, she was an ornament to the lives of all who knew her. But it is your heart which will be most burdened.'

Watson looked at me with wonder, not expecting me to acknowledge her in this way. Or, perhaps, at all.

How arrogant I had been, disdaining sentiment. My time away, alone and separated from all I held dear, had changed my views. There was no time to be wasted. Love was a truth undeniable.

'Holmes, I now wish to introduce you to the woman in my life.'

My heart stopped when Watson said those words. I realised that I had only begun to understand the depths of my self-deception.

When Watson had married, I had told myself that the sadness I felt was unhappiness at his misguided choices. My aloofness protected me from the hurt he invited in. My lack of bias allowed the cold, clear light of reason to reign supreme.

Of course, my Watson had never wanted any of those things.

I had seen from the start that his heart was large, that his keen eye saw the world with humour and interest, and that his compassion was quick to follow. He had a talent for empathy which allowed him to make others feel at home.

He had no desire for invulnerability. No hope to live a life free of the influence of others. He gave to me his friendship and loyalty, freely and willingly. Just as he gave his care to all those in need around him.

My talk of objectivity, my boasts of living above it all were all just that: mere boasts. With no weight and no strength to them in the face of what I truly desired.

My John, returned to me, solely mine alone.

All that passed through my mind. But as of old, I suppressed my feelings. Giving merely a small smile, I said to him, 'And who is she, dear fellow, this lucky creature? May I make her acquaintance?'

'I had hoped you would say that, old man.'

And to my confusion, Watson rose. Would he conjure her out of some cupboard to turn the joke on me, as I had dramatically revealed myself to him?

He sent for a Miss Taylor. I girded myself.

A woman of moderate years entered the room. She was wearing dark clothing, neat but of no great elegance. Her hand showed the mark of writing, some inkblots around her fingers and colour on her cuff.

Perhaps Watson had found someone practical yet educated. Looking at Miss Taylor's face I saw lines which showed she had suffered in life but also a look of kindness, evidence that it had not spoiled her spirit.

My first thought was to congratulate Watson on finding a new help-meet who could match him for intellect and be a partner in the difficulties of being a practicing doctor.

However, there were traces which made me hold my tongue and observe further.

Miss Taylor waited for word from my Watson. The man himself continued to stand beside me. Rather than looking at his beloved, his eyes were on me. I even thought I saw a small smile curl his lip.

I looked more closely at her.

Her hair was a dark colour, chestnut and glossy, full of health. Though her face was even and respectable, her hair was perhaps her best feature. This gave me pause.

My friend Watson had a ready appreciation for the comportment and spirit of an individual. But I knew his biases.

His Mary had been what might veraciously be claimed as 'among the fairest of women.' And though my Watson might be swayed to admire a person for their dignity or character, it would take a person of exceptional beauty for them to claim his heart, and for him to feel the pull of attraction.

So, she was plain. And I was surprised that my Watson would woo her. But also, there was clearly a child in her life. A very young child. Babe in arms, said the stains of milk upon her arm, and not able to walk for itself said the repeated imprint of a pram on her laced leather boot. And doted upon, said the scrap of fabric tucked away in her sleeve.

The hypothesis at play here was that my Watson had engaged the finer feelings of a homely working-class woman who had a child.

I looked to him, waiting for him to introduce us. He saw my unspoken query and complied.

'It is a pleasure to make your acquaintance, Miss Taylor, and I hope we may be able to meet the child who will someday be the recipient of that.' I gestured to the garment for a doll which peeped out from where she had stowed it.

'Excellent, Holmes,' said Watson warmly. 'Miss Taylor, would you please do me the kindness of bringing her down?'

I looked askance at my friend. Still Miss Taylor? Not much of a warm welcome for a companion for life.

And then realisation broke upon me. This was not a beloved companion. This was a governess for a small child. Some small child as should be in the care of my friend. A light began to dawn, but I had not yet fully seen the truth by its illumination.

I could have asked at any time. But pride, it goeth, as they say.

She looked at Watson with concern. 'It is much too late for that. She is resting and I dare not disturb her.'

'Then, perhaps we shall steal in upon her,' said Watson.

I was arrested by the sight of him as he spoke. His eyes were bright. His features animated. He looked at me with such a warmth in him, as if this was of great moment.

I nodded my agreement, though entering a child's nursery at night was very close to the last thing I would volunteer to do, unless urged there to avert a crime.

But, as ever, I could refuse my Watson nothing.

So, there we were, in stocking'd feet, tiptoeing silently into a spacious chamber dedicated to this enigmatic child.

I examined my friend's hands as we walked together. But there was no ring. How could he have his fiancée here, with a room dedicated to her child already, if they were not married? Where could she be if the child was not with her? I consulted my memory, but there had been no hint of it in the papers, nor word from my homeless network. I would have known if Watson had remarried. What had been missed?

The mystery was resolved when we reached the bedside. A small child, approximately the age I had envisioned from the evidence of the caretaker.

'Holmes, how I have longed to see this day,' whispered Watson. 'Meet my daughter, Charity.' Risking the governess's wrath, he lifted her from the cot.

I looked down at this dark-haired cherub, lying swaddled in my dear friends' arms before me. Perhaps it was fancy, but I could see it now: the fine turn to that tiny nose, much like my dear friend. And the curl of that lip, perhaps I could see the faintest hint of his lost Mary.

'Meet my daughter, Charity.'

'She is beautiful, Watson,' I said.

'Thank you, Holmes,' said Watson, setting her down. After she was settled once more, he grasped my wrist. 'I never hoped you could meet her, as you were gone, along with my Mary. I thought at best we could all be reunited at Heaven's door.' A sad look crossed his brow. 'But in my heart I wished this could be.'

'You do miss her still,' I said softly.

'Of course,' he said, but he gazed at me, now with such wonder in his eyes. 'However, I will not ask for more than one miracle, not today.'

I put my hand on his where he held me, and we stood a while looking down at the sleeping child in awe.

THE DAYS when my Watson and I had gone together into the den of the lion were with us once more.

His investigation with Lestrade was hopelessly off track, of course, and I soon caught him up on the truth of the case. But when I vouchsafed the particulars of my plan to him, Watson was afire with disagreement.

'No, Holmes,' he said, his brilliant eyes flashing. His shapely cheeks flushed admirably with his passion. 'There must be another way. We cannot have regained you only to lose you once more to the very threat that drove you away from—from all of us, from your life.'

'Watson,' I said, making light of his fear. 'There is no danger. The man's efforts will be directed through trickery. The marksman will think he has me in his sights, but it is he that is the prey.'

'You will let me make my own judgements as to the degree of danger to you? Will you let me know the shape of this trap then? So often you race off on your own and only bring me in after the fact. I can endure that no more.'

'Of course, my dear fellow.' I softened my tone, seeing real grief in his face. 'Let us go down to Baker Street together and I will show you the means by which he will be defeated.'

We went together, arm in arm. I felt a warmth in my stomach, feeling his strong arm in mine, and his side brushing against me as we crossed the pavement. I glanced at him, my desire awakening once more in his presence. Magnified, indeed, by seeing him again after so long.

Watson met my eyes and a feeling of complicity spread through me. My perfect and intimate companion. I could need no other. If only my John could feel the same.

But he had left me for Mary. Our partnership had continued after his marriage, but our intimacy had been compromised. No more the simple happiness of our bachelor quarters together.

With his child now, I could only expect that he would be on the alert for a mother to care for her and his household at the soonest opportunity. His love of the work could not keep him by my side, where he belonged, forever.

We crept together into the empty house. Stationed ourselves in a room across from 221b. Peering out we could see 'my' silhouette in its window. As we looked, 'I' moved, as if to look out in a different direction down the great causeway of life that is Baker Street.

We saw no sign of Mrs Hudson's shadow as she moved the wax effigy. The illusion was complete.

Watson and I settled in, as we had done together so many times. We waited in suspense for some action by the culprit, to show his hand. The comfort of long familiarity fell upon me. I wished only for my pipe to complete the picture.

'Holmes ...' Watson's voice came out of the darkness. For a moment I was transported back to times in exile with these self-same long vigils when I had sorely missed my trusty companion.

Now though, he was here. I could reach out if I wished and prove his reality. I resisted the temptation to do so.

'Yes, Watson?'

'I ...' his voice was uncertain. Something troubled that brave heart. My own went out to him, thinking again of all the loss he had so recently endured.

So often in the past, I had deferred matters of emotion to Watson. To comfort a grieving widow or child, to dispel the unease a witness might be experiencing. He had been my right hand in danger and my eyes to the soul. So often this was so out of pure laziness, for of course I could see the needs and the wants of others. I had a care for them at moments, too.

But for Watson, caring was more than just a duty. Compassion for him was an effortless springing of the heart. It is, I believe, what impelled him to become a surgeon. In the ranks of the military—a man of war—his true place and role was to provide succour and aid to those in need. His was a heart full of love and charity for all.

But when we found each other, that day in Barts lab, it was he that was in need. As was I, though I had not the slightest notion of my true poverty until I found my Watson.

And then, when I lost him once more, the gaping hole in my world was starkly apparent. My helper, my friend, my companion.

And I had left him behind. With the warmth and support of a beloved and loving wife, true. But the world in its callous wisdom had robbed my friend of the greatest love of his life. Finding him again, willing to rejoin me despite my cruel deception and desertion, was more than I deserved.

Now in this moment, standing beside him in that dark house, I vowed to never leave him alone to carry the burdens of the heart. Of others, or of his own.

'What is it, Watson?' and I reached out my hand to him in the dark. Upon feeling it, he grasped mine with his own.

I gave his hand a squeeze of encouragement. Then another. How right it felt. How warm his fingers, enclosed in mine. How I longed to never let him go.

After a moment, before the comfort I offered should slip from the decency of brotherhood and friendship into the unrestrained chaos of something more, I loosened my grip.

But my Watson's fingers tightened. Even as I pulled my hand away, his followed mine and renewed that connection.

I heard his voice again. Stronger in tone now, more sure.

'Holmes, when I thought you were gone, thought you were dead …'

I waited in suspense. Greatly daring, I skimmed my thumb across the back of his hand, in encouragement and comfort. This seemed once again to invigorate him.

'There were many things I wished I had said. That I wished I had told you.'

'Watson,' I said, all the care and admiration I felt for him finding their way into my tone, not able to be muted. Freed by the darkness that hid the look of—surely—adoration that must be on my face. 'No words are ever wasted between us. You have been all to me that any friend could ever be.'

'Yes,' he said, breaking in upon my words even before I had finished. 'That is just what I would say to you, Holmes. You are my all.'

And he fell still. His words echoing in the darkness of the night between us. Warming in the hold of our two hands. A spark struck in my heart as I reflected on them, the fervour of his tone.

What could they possibly mean?

What?

But feeling his hand move once more, to intertwine his fingers with my own—I could have no doubt of their meaning: that my Watson's heart was as lost to me as was my own to him.

It was then that we heard a footstep upon a stair below. My Watson was in place beside the door in a moment, stepping lightly to avoid making the floor creak. I took position where the intruder might see me and be distracted in his surprise.

Barely could I have hoped that Moran would find us there. That we ourselves could be the ones to capture this creature and take him in.

Of course, my Watson was ready to bring him down when he did enter. That brave soldier was upon him before the Colonel realised. I have my own strength and powers, but it had never escaped me how dashing Watson appeared when in the full use of his own.

He had Moran on the floor, was upon him, holding him immobile in moments. He looked at me with a wide grin of triumph. It was all I could do to resist taking his face in my hands and kissing him then and there.

'MY DEAR HOLMES,' said Watson, 'You know that it is my deepest wish to work with you in your investigations. My time is doubly taken now, my responsibilities greater than they were even when I was married.'

We sat together in the sitting room at Baker Street. Watson had joined me for a celebratory pipe and glass.

We had congratulated Mrs Hudson, together with Lestrade, for her key contributions to this happy conclusion. Not only the case but also to the legacy of evildoing left by Professor Moriarty. Ending too, the long lapse in my life.

I was ready to resume occupation of Baker Street, but there was just one thing missing. Something I had no possible expectation of being returned there. Watson's words confirmed this certitude.

'I understand, Watson,' I said, wishing to interrupt him, not able, I was sure, to face the rejection which I saw presaged in his words. 'You are the best of companions and I have taken as much of your time as you could have given.'

Watson gave a look to me, an arch raise of his eyebrows. One I have received many a time when I had spoken too soon or said something he could not believe.

So often in the past, I had made good my word, my observations having found their way to the truth which eluded him. But I hoped that this time, this deduction about his life could be wrong. His words in that dark room gave me cause for hope. To which I clung despite evidence to the contrary.

'Yes,' he continued. 'Which is exactly why I am seeking to sell my practice and hope to find a situation for me and my household to raise Charity, with economy and means that will suit a family.'

'Does that mean,' I said, willing the excitement I was feeling in my heart to not show itself in my face or voice, 'that you are considering resuming your old occupation?'

'Yes, precisely. I would go into business with you, if you'll have me.'

'My dear fellow!' I cried, unable to hide any of the glee which filled my heart. 'Have you?! I am yours, do with me as you will.'

'My dear Holmes,' he said, clasping the hand which I had offered to him, as I had leapt up from the chair. Those words, spoken to me many a time before, held a new richness, a deeper meaning with the look then in his eyes. 'I should most certainly only do as you would will it.'

'Then move back in, with me, you and your daughter are always welcome wherever I am.'

'But how?' he asked, apparently wanting the same thing as I but not knowing how it could be accomplished. 'What room is there for a nursery here?'

'All things are possible, Watson,' and I took him down to speak with Mrs Hudson about arrangements at Baker Street which could be made to accommodate us all.

All my efforts were bent now on one purpose: to afford Watson the ability to sell his practice and take up again full time with me. I had some funds, and could apply to Mycroft for more, sufficient to the purpose. But we could not buy the practice out, what would we do with it?

The answer came in the form of a distant relation which Mycroft had been in recent contact with. One fellow named Varner who, desiring to relocate to London from Leeds, was in want of a position.

He was a doctor.

'Holmes!' Watson cried, flying up the steps to tell me the news.

'Watson?' I asked, cool as butter.

'You,' he said, stepping close to me. 'Thank you.'

'My dear fellow, what for?'

He said nothing but turned to the window to close the curtains. And then closing the door to the hall, he came back to me. Putting his hand to my cheek, he gave me what I had long wished for but never dreamed would be mine: his lips on my own.

'You know, of course.'

My eyelids were fluttering, I was taking in all the sensations about him: texture, sound, scent. I would memorise this moment to remember it a hundred years hence.

'Mycroft,' I was able to utter.

'My thanks to him as well, then.' He pulled me up from my chair and brought me to the settee, where seating me beside him, he began to strip me of my tie, jacket, waistcoat.

I had not the strength in me to resist him. I may have helped in his endeavours. I know not what I did in that moment, my senses had flown.

'There is but one more condition I ask, before Charity and I make this our new home,' he said, bringing himself also to shirt sleeves.

'Name it,' I said, meaning that with my very soul.

'Never again will this place,' he said with a meaningful look, 'or your person, be the target for any schemes to catch a criminal.'

'I swear it,' I said.

'Say my name,' he breathed.

'John.'

Letter to the publisher:

Dear sir,

It has been many years since the writings of my father, Doctor John H. Watson, made famous the adventures of the singular Sherlock Holmes. Their circulation in your periodicals made them household names and brought great prosperity to your company. My family thanks you for your remembrances at the time of their deaths. And I send you, as well, the fond memories of a small child who learned her letters with the inky blocks of your letterpress.

Along with these wishes, I send another gift, and a directive.

With our great friend's death, a number of additional writings have come into my possession: my father's work, and some by Mr Holmes. Previously unseen by any outside eyes, not even my own.

You may only guess at my excitement when I opened them! You may recognize the feelings, as they will mirror your own. But there may also be trepidation in your breast when the reason for their suppression until this date becomes apparent to you.

So, it is this that I say: England owes Sherlock Holmes the truth.

As well does it owe my father to recognize and honour his true nature—who made sacrifices, large and small for the Kingdom, and took his wounds in a misguided war. Who served humanity in every way he knew how. But my father would not expect this favour, and although he wrote the words to be read, I know him well enough to believe that their being seen by myself, my future children, and those who call our family friends, would be enough.

And Mr Holmes ... He who turned down a knighthood, dismissed kings in favour of a clever, feminine mind, and took the part of paupers over princes. He would not care who read about the true richness of his heart and inner life, the portrait that his intimate friend and companion of so many decades painted for informed eyes.

But I do care. As should you. As should every man, woman and child of this sovereign nation—including that head upon which the jewelled crown rests.

And not because Mr. Holmes delivered our nation and others from mischief on many occasions. Rescued innocents from destitution when he could. And admitted fault when he could not. Not even for all the services that my dear—I shall say it—fathers, delivered to so many, so willingly, and with glad hearts.

But because they, like so many others, deserve the dignity of being seen. They, like so many others victimised by our Empire, had the right to freedoms which they did not enjoy. And they, like all those wronged—many of whom these two championed during their life-times—instead led lives overshadowed by fear and threatened daily with loss.

You ~~will~~ shall publish these papers because it is the just thing. I enclose them for your review, for immediate publication. You cannot fail to see their quality or their value.

And if your heart should quail, I hope you will welcome a visit by me to provide the needed encouragement. For you will remember, along with my letters, I learned my god-father's methods very well.

Your sincere friend,

Charity Marie Vincent (née Holmes Watson)

A GUIDE TO FLOWER LANGUAGE

Flowers Holmes brings in chronological order.

Snowdrop: hope
Olive: peace
Rosemary: remembrance
Rue: regret
Yarrow: cure for a broken heart

Jasmine: amiability
Oak: bravery
Hyacinth: asking for forgiveness
Nile lily: beauty, purity

Lilac: reminiscence
Orange blossom: eternal love
Violet: modesty
Edelweiss: courage, daring
Mint: consolation
Evening primrose: silent love

Pansy: recipient occupies giver's thoughts
Larkspur: levity
Eucalyptus: protection
Azalea: fragility, temperance
Sweet William: gallantry
Elderflower: compassion, humility, zeal

∾

Flowers Watson brings in chronological order.

Amaryllis: pride
Lily of the valley: return of happiness
Wheat: abundance
Apple blossom: preference
Yarrow: cure for a broken heart
Snowdrop: hope

NOTES

THE PLOT THICKENS

1. Patricia Gherovici, *Please Select Your Gender: From the Invention of Hysteria to the Democratizing of Transgenderism* (New York: Routledge, 2010).
2. Vaneet Mehta, *Bisexual Men Exist: A Handbook for Bisexual, Pansexual and M-Spec Men* (Jessica Kingsley, 2023).

A CORRESPONDENCE

1. *The Bible*, Mark 4:31-32

HOLMES ON HOLIDAY

1. H. G . Wells, *The First Men in the Moon* (Strand Magazine and The Cosmopolitan, 1900).

BUT SWEETER STILL

1. Jessica Roux, *Floriography: An Illustrated Guide to the Victorian Language of Flowers* (Andrews McMeel, 2020).

CONTRIBUTORS

AUTHORS & POETS

ARTISTS

EDITORS

Alexandra Fox (she/her) runs on caffeine and executive dysfunction. An American author and frequent expat, she loves travel and sweater weather, and has been enamored of Sherlock Holmes since stumbling upon him in a library thirty years ago. When not writing queer romance or searching for misplaced coffee mugs, she can be found editing under her legal name, Tiana M. Reynolds.

EC Boss (she/her) is a lifelong reader and believer in the power of art and story. She is a game designer, environmentalist and writer from the United States. She grew up reading all kinds of adventure fiction and has long admired the observational powers of Sherlock Holmes and the companionship he found with his loyal Doctor Watson. When not nudging centuries-old sleuths into the present day, she loves to sing, bake and mess around with the yo-yo.

S.J. Lock (she/her) is an avid reader and writer, fueled by the need for adventure and the smell of books. She grew up loving mysteries and fell for Sherlock Holmes along the way. Aside from writing, she enjoys riding her motorcycle, traveling and spending time with friends and family.

Rita Smith (she/her) is a storyteller by nature and a librarian by coincidence. She doesn't remember a time when there hasn't been a story occupying most of her brain space. She does, however, remember the time her mother had to stop reading The Adventure of the Speckled Band to her because of the SPOILERS. When she's not concocting a story or sharing others' stories with small people, she practices the martial arts and treads the boards in local theatre.

SM Lawson (she/her) rediscovered the joy of writing later in life, supported by fandom and fanfic authors. Since starting writing in 2013, she has created almost one hundred transformative works. In addition to writing "On Stage Please" for this anthology, she contributed the poem "Dancing by the Red Sea" for the anthology Anna Karenina Isn't Dead from Improbable Press (to be released early 2024). She believes strongly in happy endings, and for her writing to be a source of entertainment, comfort, and joy for readers. She lives in Toronto, Canada with her husband, daughter, cat, and several dust bunnies under the bed.

CONTACT US

EC BOSS (EDITOR)
   www.shieldcrescentpress.com | AO3 @emilycare | Tumblr @keirgreeneyes
CHAINED-TO-THE-MIRROR (ARTIST)
   Instagram @chainedtothemirror | Tumblr @chained-to-the-mirror
LINDA M. CRATE
   Facebook @Linda-M-Crate | Instagram @authorlindamcrate| X @thysilverdoe
ANNA GRAHAM DOE
   AO3 @spacemutineer | Tumblr @spacemutineer
LARC ENCIEL
   AO3 @allsovacant | Instagram @allsovacant_writes
ANKE EISSMANN / KHORAZIR (ARTIST)
   https://khorazirart.wordpress.com/ | Tumblr @khorazir
ALEXANDRA FOX / TIANA M. REYNOLDS (EDITOR)
   becomingafox@gmail.com | Instagram @becomingafox | Tumblr @becoming-a-fox
   lefttowriteedits@gmail.com | lefttowriteedits.com | Instagram @lefttowriteedits
S.C. FRASER
   AO3 @S_C_Fraser
GOOOLABATOOO (ARTIST)
   Instagram @gooolabatooo | Tumblr @gooolabatooo
NARRELLE M. HARRIS
   narrellemharris.iwriter.com.au | AO3 @221b_hound
N. HOLMES
   caprice-of-light.neocities.org | Tumblr @radix-pedis-diaboli
LF HOWARD
   AO3 @littlefluffyclouds
LILITH INKWELL
   Tumblr @inkonice-main
LISBETH KING
   AO3 @Lock_John_Silver | Instagram @l_kingk | Tumblr @lisbeth-kk
SM LAWSON (EDITOR)
   AO3 @standbygo | Instagram @sm_lawson | Threads @sm_lawson |
   Tumblr @blogstandbygo
S.J. LOCK (EDITOR)
   AO3 @bluebuell33 | Tumblr @bluebuell33
BERTIE M.
   AO3 @aceredshirt13 | Tumblr @aceredshirt13

ATLIN MERRICK
https://improbablepress.com/pages/atlin-merrick | AO3 @atlinmerrick |
Tumblr @atlinmerrick
JACO MISMEANDER
AO3 @mismeander
N.J. MOWRY
AO3 @notjustmom
ELEANOR NEWELL
AO3 @Silvergirl
HOLLAND PARKER
Instagram @hollandparker81 | Tumblr @mybestfriendmademe
SHAI PORTER
Tumblr @Iwantthatbelstaffanditsoccupant | X @Iwantthatcoat
KYNDALL POTTS
AO3 @CumberCurlyGirl | Twitter @CumberCurlyGirl | Tumblr @CumberCurlyGirl
CALAIS RENO
AO3 @Calais_Reno | Tumblr @calaisreno
EM ROWENE
www.emrowene.com
RONIT SILVERSEEKER
AO3 @TheSilverSeeker
RITA SMITH (EDITOR)
AO3 @mom2boys | Tumblr @momma2boys
SC TAYLOR
AO3 @simplyclockwork | Tumblr @simplyclockwork | X @clockworkfic
CARISSA WING
AO3 @hardboiledbaby | Tumblr @shewalksinthenoir

Afterword

Thank you for reading our offerings in celebration of the freeing of the Sherlock Holmes canon. To borrow freely from William Shakespeare, on behalf of the artists and writers gathered on this stage, we say:

> *Thus far, with rough and all-unable pen,*
> *Our bending author(s) hath pursued the story,*
> *In little room confining mighty men,*
> *Mangling by starts the full course of their glory.*
> *Small time, but in that small most greatly lived*
> *This star of England*

> — *Henry V, Epilogue*

As you have seen, the Victorian era cannot contain the great detective and his Boswell in our imaginations; within these pages, you have travelled from a twenty-first–century theatre to Surrey in the late 1960s, with a stop in a contemporary bookstore, and then back to the familiar days of 1895.

What is it about Sherlock Holmes that so captures the imagination that, as his brother Mycroft quips, *[We] hear of Sherlock everywhere?*

In preparation for writing this epilogue, I searched my memory for my first encounter with Holmes. It is likely that I watched Sherlock Hemlock solve The Case of the Chicken Salad Sandwich on *Sesame Street* in 1970 or giggled at the antics of Sherlock the Squirrel on *The Magic Garden*. The silhouettes of his deerstalker, Inverness cape, calabash pipe, and magnifying glass were already as familiar to me as Red Riding Hood's cape or Rapunzel's tower-length braid.

What I remember best, however, is lying snuggled next to my mother as she read me a bedtime story. The great detective and his doctor were investigating a death on a country estate where a cheetah and a baboon roamed the grounds. Things were going along swimmingly until my mother paused, flipped ahead a couple of pages, and declared it was time to go to sleep.

I wouldn't discover the ending of *The Adventure of the Speckled Band* until it showed up in my seventh-grade literature anthology five years later. (And I realised that my mother, with her intense fear of snakes, could not bring herself to finish reading that particular story to me.)

Neither my mother nor I could have explained the enduring popularity of Conan Doyle's creation. The Index of Sherlock Holmes Pastiche Characters (www.schoolandholmes.com) lists 487 novels and 208 children's books based on Conan Doyle's famous detective. From J. M. Barrie and Mark Twain to Neil Gaiman and Kareem Abdul-Jabbar—we mustn't overlook Dorothy L. Sayers and Nancy Springer—the world's only consulting detective is ubiquitous.

You can kit yourself out in everything from the official Sherlock Holmes tartan to the 'Detectives [sic] Desire' costume that includes high-cut panties and a vinyl cape to go with the omnipresent deerstalker (currently available on Etsy). One might join the John H.

Watson Society or a scion society of the Baker Street Irregulars, attend 221b Con or Holmes in the Heartland. Tumblr and Twitter—I mean X—are full of Sherlock and Johnlock fans.

Johnlock is what drew us to prepare this book for you. It began with Alexandra Fox's dream of an anthology celebrating the love that was not free to speak its name. We are a motley crew, worthy of following Wiggins through the streets of London in the employ of Baker Street's most famous resident. Some of us were already published in the real world, others were new even to the fan fiction world, having published fewer than twenty fics on Archive of Our Own. We are artists and project managers, researchers and editors, social media experts and Discord newbies. What drew us together is our love of those Baker Street boys and a conviction that they are, and have always been, queer.

Graham Robb in *Strangers: Homosexual Love in the 19th Century* writes: 'Everyone already knows, instinctively, that Holmes is homosexual. Screen adaptations are a good test. The least convincing are always those that provide him with a girlfriend. The most convincing, like Billy Wilder's *The Private Life of Sherlock Holmes* (1970)—promoted as "a love story between two men"—are those that exaggerate his camp behaviour.' Sherlock Holmes is a singular individual—both brilliantly calculating and unabashedly unconcerned with social convention.

A great observer of humankind, he can don an impenetrable disguise with little more than a few articles of clothing to embellish his changes in posture, voice, and dialect. Like many queer people, he is an expert at hiding in plain sight. John Watson, soldier and doctor, is both chronicler and audience stand-in. But he is no wallflower; he is always ready to grab his trusty revolver and abandon his patients or reading to follow Holmes into danger. Like us, Watson is enamoured of Holmes's deductive skills. But that is not all he loves. He sees the Holmes beneath the surface, the great heart that fuels the great mind, the knight errant championing the downtrodden and the unprotected. These are the stories we wanted to bring to you, our readers: tales of two men united by their love of justice and each other.

So we lit a lamp in the window of 221b, sending the signal to our favourite authors and those with whom we are less familiar. We asked them to write the story they've always wanted to see published, long or short, funny or poignant, prose or verse. And here they are—hand-picked with loving care and illustrated by three talented artists. The love that did not, could not, dared not speak its name has blossomed into the rose you hold in your hand. We hope it will be a treasured bloom in your garden for years to come.

Rita Smith
2024

FURTHER READING

BOOKS AND ANTHOLOGIES

DeMarco, Joseph R. G., ed., *A Study in Lavender: Queering Sherlock Holmes* (2011).

Derleth, August, *In Re: Sherlock Holmes: The Adventures of Solar Pons*, Solar Pons (1945).

Douglas, Kameo Llyn, *Rare and Wonderfully Made* (2022).

Fries, Wendy C, *Sherlock Holmes and John Watson: The Day They Met* (2015).

Gray, Elinor, *Compound a Felony: A Queer Affair of Sherlock Holmes* (2015).

Hall, Alexis, *The Affair of the Mysterious Letter* (2019).

Harris, Narrelle M., *A Dream to Build a Kiss On* (2018).

Harris, Narrelle M., and Atlin Merrick, eds., *Sherlock is a Girl's Name* (2024).

Horowitz, Anthony, *House of Silk* (2011).

Marcum, David, Sonia Fetherston, and Derrick Belanger, eds., *Sherlock Holmes is Everywhere* (2019).

Merrick, Atlin, ed., *A Murmuring of Bees* (2016).

Merrick, Atlin, ed., *Spark: How Fanfiction and Fandom Can Set Your Creativity On Fire* (2023).

Meyer, Nicholas, *The Seven-Percent Solution* (1974).

O'Dell, Claire, *A Study in Honor*, The Janet Watson Chronicles (2018).

Patterson, James, and Brian Sitts, *Holmes, Marple & Poe: The Greatest Crime-Solving Team of the Twenty-First Century*, Holmes, Margaret & Poe (2024).

Piercy, Rohase, *My Dearest Holmes* (1988).

Springer, Nancy, *Enola Holmes: The Case of the Missing Marquess*, Enola Holmes (2006).

SHORT STORIES

Gaiman, Neil, 'The Case of Death and Honey', in Laurie R. King and Leslie S. Klinger, eds., *A Study in Sherlock: Stories Inspired by the Holmes Canon* (2011)

King, Stephen., 'The Doctor's Case', in *Nightmares & Dreamscapes* (1987).

WEBSITES AND ONLINE JOURNALS

Organization For Transformative Works, *Archive of Our Own AO3* (2012) [web archive] https://archiveofourown.org/.

Sherlockian: The Portal for the Great Detective (22 November 1994), https://www.sherlockian.net/.

So Far Down Queer Street (July 2022), https://downqueerstreet.com/.

The John H Watson Society, *The Watsonian: The Journal of the John H Watson Society* (2013), https://www.johnhwatsonsociety.com/the-watsonian/.

FILM AND VIDEO

Sherlock Holmes and the Case of the Silk Stocking, Masterpiece (26 December 2004).

The Private Life of Sherlock Holmes, The Mirisch Production Company/Sir Nigel Films (29 October 1970).

Sherlock Holmes and the Adventure of the Furtive Festivity (3 August 2019) https://www.youtube.com/watch?v=TQaoCdh7q6I.

Sherlock Holmes in the 22nd Century (6 May 1999).

RADIO PLAYS AND PODCASTS

Bert Coules, *Sherlock Holmes* [radio play], BBC Radio 4 (November 1989), https://www.bbc.co.uk/programmes/b01j9gzs/episodes/player.

Ian Geers and Lauren Grace Thompson, *Fawx and Stallion* [podcast], 224bbaker (11 September 2024), https://www.224bbaker.com/.

Sherlock & Co [podcast], Goalhanger Podcasts (10 October 2023). https://open.spotify.com/show/5yfvdowYlnFCyXRTD5ITqb?si=0f8c9749e5024af1

ABOUT AKT

akt supports LGBTQ+ people aged 16–25 in the UK who are experiencing homelessness or living in a hostile environment. They support young people in finding safe homes and employment, education, or training, in a welcoming and open environment that celebrates their queer identities.

Coming out, or being outed, can lead to young people becoming homeless—24% of homeless youth identify as LGBTQ+. Once homeless, queer youth are more likely to face violence and discrimination than young people who aren't LGBTQ+. They're also more likely to develop substance misuse issues and experience sexual exploitation. This can take a huge toll on their physical and mental health.

Being supported in an inclusive environment that celebrates their identities is vital to improving their life outcomes.

Proceeds from sales of *When the Rose Speaks Its Name: A Sherlock Holmes Anthology,* minus printing and distribution costs, will be contributed to akt. To learn more about akt or make an additional donation, please find them online at: https://www.akt.org.uk/

www.ingramcontent.com/pod-product-compliance
Lightning Source LLC
Chambersburg PA
CBHW031153050726
47495CB00019B/1660